A WOLF'S BANE

Luna Wolf Series Book 1

D.M.Barton

DMBbooks

Copyright © 2024 DMBbooks

Cover created by GetCovers.com

I've been taking my writing seriously for a number of years now. And to say that it gets easier would be a huge lie. It's still as hard as the first time I sat down to write out a manuscript. I still hit writer's block. My motivation still goes for walks and doesn't return for days on end.

So I will dedicate this novel to anyone out there thinking about becoming an author. Who is struggling to get their manuscript finished. You can do anything you set your mind to. So don't give up and keep working hard. One day you'll be in the position to see your books in the hands of readers.

CONTENTS

Title Page
Copyright
Dedication
Chapter 1 — 1
Chapter 2 — 13
Chapter 3 — 42
Chapter 4 — 78
Chapter 5 — 97
Chapter 6 — 119
Chapter 7 — 144
Chapter 8 — 178
Chapter 9 — 209
Chapter 10 — 247
Chapter 11 — 277
Books By This Author — 285

CHAPTER 1

The night was coming to a close in Baldur City. The clubs and pubs were kicking out patrons in the liveliest part of the city. It wasn't even a weekend night and it was busy as hell. Pushing my way through the crowd. Pulling my leather jacket tight around my body. Eyes looking at the faces as I passed by.

Big eyes showing my vulnerability. Getting a few drunken smiles from groups but nothing more than that. Pushing past a couple of women throwing up inside a bin. Carrying on with my journey towards the quieter end of the strip.

This was the fourth trip past the businesses of entertainment tonight. I wasn't out for a good time. This was business. A young lady had come to me for some help retrieving something she had lost.

She was mugged and not only was her money taken. So was a ring that had been in her family for decades. The police told her that there were so many muggings in this city. It would be near impossible for them to find the exact mugger. Even if they did. The likelihood they would get her stuff back was beyond impossible.

So she had come to me. Hiring a private

investigator was an interesting move for a mugging. I didn't have the same resources that the police had. But unlike them, I didn't have rules to follow. Not to mention I had abilities that I could call on to aid my investigations.

I had inherited my father's werewolf abilities of strength and speed. My sense of hearing and smell was off the charts. But I also gained weaknesses like silver and my inability to control my anger. It had landed me in trouble on multiple occasions. Hence why I was a private investigator.

Running my own business so I didn't have a boss to answer to. Making my own hours and picking my own cases. However when I hadn't had any clients for a while. I ended up out in the city at three in the morning hoping to get mugged.

I passed by a small group of men. Eyes picking out the shape of them in the dark corner. My werewolf sight able to make out facial features. Logging them in my brain but forgetting them when I didn't hear footsteps following me.

My arm clung to my bag which was slung over my shoulder. Not something I would normally wear but it was for the case. I had sprayed it with one of my uglier perfumes. Giving off a strong sense of flowers that smelt like they had long since died. Another weakness my werewolf smell gave me was the ability to smell every single note of perfume. Making it much harder to find one I truly liked. But for tracking this one will work perfectly.

My ears picked up footsteps coming towards

the corner ahead. My arm loosening from my bag. Open hands. Knowing what was about to come and ordering myself not to react. I could take a guy apart in seconds but that wasn't the plan tonight.

The steps came louder until a shape came around the corner. I yelped out in a high-pitched voice but to my surprise so did another lady. Bumping into her and having to catch an arm before she snapped a heel and fell on her arse. "Are you okay?" As I asked my eyes shot past her. Seeing no one I looked into her eyes.

"Oh yeah. I'm so sorry. I was in a rush." She looked over her shoulder like someone was right behind her. Turning back to me with wide eyes. "I thought someone was following me."

"I don't see anyone. You're okay." Blowing out a frustrated breath. About to turn and make another pass down the street when I caught a whiff of aftershave. Smelling it on the lady. Not like she was wearing it. It was a hint, second-hand scent coming from her coat. She had recently been hugged by a man. "Where are you coming from?"

"I'm on my way home from work."

"Where do you work?"

"Huh?"

"Where do you work?" Seeing the way her eyes shifted around me. Avoiding eye contact. So I moved a step closer. "Alright, tell me who you work for."

"The bar, just down the street."

"No. Who you truly work for. The game is up. I know what you're really doing out at this time of the morning."

"I don't know what you're on about."

I could be wrong but I noticed that she wasn't moving on. Standing in front of me like I hadn't just accused her of lying. Taking another sniff of the air. Catching that same aftershave smell but coming from further down where she had come from. "Where are you heading?"

"Home."

"Why don't I walk with you?" Giving her a nice innocent face. "I could do with the company. I hate walking home alone after a night at the strip club." Leaning and whispering, "I feel everyone can tell I've got a wad of cash in my purse. Makes me uneasy."

"I'm really sorry but I have to get moving. I'm sure you'll be fine."

"I hope so. Last time I got mugged I just threw them my bag and ran off."

"Sorry." The lady gave me a smile before trotting off in her heels. Watching as she rummaged around in her pocket before pulling out a phone. Giving someone a text judging by how fast her thumbs tapped over the screen.

Blowing out a sigh as I made my way down the street. Heading towards that smell of aftershave. As I grew closer to where the man was hiding I could hear his breathing getting faster. Taking a deep breath myself and putting on my damsel in distress face as he leapt out.

Seeing the flash of metal as a knife was pulled. The guy wearing a balaclava. A deep voice, completely put on, came out of the hole. "Give me the bag."

My voice coming out higher than normal. "Oh please, don't hurt me. Here, take it. There's plenty in there for you to have." Letting the bag slip down my arm and chucking it towards him. Putting my hands up in defence and backing away. "Just don't hurt me, please. I'm so scared."

"There's a good girl." Biting the side of my cheek as I was called that. Feeling the beast inside my head wanting to smack the smirk from his face. "Give me your phone."

"It's in the bag." Lying since I wasn't going to be carrying my phone with me when I planned on getting mugged. There wasn't even any money in the handbag for him to enjoy. "Just let me go, please."

"Alright. Tell anyone about this and I'll find you and make you pay."

"I won't. I promise. I'll stay quiet." Keeping my hands up. The man looked around before he ran off. I delayed my pursuit for a few minutes before following him. My nose picking up the trail of that terrible perfume easily.

The man hadn't come far from his home base. A few streets over I came up to a small building. It would have been a nice place to raise a family if it hadn't been for the total neglect. The whole street down here were the homes for crack heads and criminals. Able to smell the remnants of drug making coming from one of the terraced buildings.

So close to entertainment street since the businesses had such low rent thanks to the nearby threat of low-lives. Following the perfume up to the fifth door on the left. The windows had been boarded up. The door covered in peeling paint.

I gave it a gentle push and it slowly slid up with a creak. Getting the stench of waste and gone off food as the air escaped like it was running away. Making my nose wrinkle as I tried to pick out the people inside. Nothing could get past that horrible smell. Fighting the urge to gag.

I chucked that thought deep down, taking short breaths from my mouth. Swearing I can taste what had gone off. Poking my head through the gap. Seeing a long hallway leading off. One door to the right that must lead into a front living area.

The next one could be the bathroom since the smell was worse there. The hallway headed to an archway that led into the kitchen. The counters covered in mugs, glasses and dirty plates. Wondering if they even washed anything before using it again.

The stairs to the left led up the next floor. My ears picking up movement from up there. Possibly some kind of sleep talk. Pushing through and shutting the door softly. Hearing someone going through something from the lounge. Looking around the corner and seeing the man who had held me at knife point.

Seeing the contents of my bag on the floor. My purse being turned out. The annoyance on his face that there was nothing inside for him to have brought a smile to my lips. The handbag was chucked across the room. "Did you not find what you were looking for?"

The man jumped. His hand going for his knife so I chucked myself at him. Hands grabbing a wrist each. Easily lifting him from his feet to slam him into the wall. The whole building feeling like it shook under the impact.

My fingers gripping him tight. The knife being dropped as he cried out in pain. His face filled with fear. Those eyes almost completely blacked out by his pupils. "What have you been taking?"

"Get out of my house."

"I doubt you own this place and I don't agree with squatters rights." Pulling him back and slamming his body into the wall. "What have you been taking?"

"Up yours."

Feeling the wet splat of his saliva as he spat in my face. Bringing a hand to wipe it from myself. Rolling my head as I thought about subsiding my anger but then I shot my forehead into the bridge of his nose.

The man going dazed as he fought to stay conscious. Giving him a moment before giving his face another crack. Letting him drop as he succumbed to that sleepy feeling. Leaving him on the floor as I surveyed the room.

Using my sleeve to make sure I had cleaned my face thoroughly enough. Moving from the body and over to the fire place. Flipping open little jewellery chests and boxes. Things that had been nicked from people's homes. Most of them holding stolen jewellery and cards. Finding two that held all kinds of drugs.

Picking up those two boxes and heading to the kitchen. Having to put my sleeve over my nose to stop that horrid stench from invading my nostrils. Clearing as much of the sink I could before turning on the taps. Brown water kicking out in spurts.

Dumping all the drugs I could find down the drain. Ruining them for consumption. Once the boxes were empty I decided to head up stairs. The ring I was on the search for hadn't been in the lounge.

The stairs creaked under my small weight. The bannister not safe to hold onto as I made my up. Away from one smell and into another. This bathroom was worse than the one downstairs. Clearly not been cleaned in years. Maybe decades.

Finding the soft speech coming from a bedroom above the living room. Inside was a double bed with a duvet that had more stains than clean fabric. The woman laying there had hear arm sticking out. A needle still stuck inside her limb.

Moving in to take a closer look when a body hit into my side. I hadn't even heard the footsteps coming from behind me. My shoulder hit into a chest of drawers that looked newer than anything else around her.

Things being sent to the floor including me. Managing to twist around to land on my back. The man that had tackled me fell on top. I shot out my palm into his face. Then slammed it into his neck.

The man pulled his hands up to defend himself but it meant he fell forwards. Wrapping my arms and legs around his body. Holding him there and squeezing. Hearing his breathing getting shallow as I felt his ribs against my thighs.

Shifting around to get an arm over his shoulder. Bringing it around his neck and squeezing. Angling my arm down to put a strain on his spine. Helping my forearm close off his windpipe. Pulling and twisting my body until I heard a slight snap. The body went limp so I shoved him aside. Getting up on my knees next to the bed. The lady hadn't woken during the commotion. My hand touching to hers. Slowly pulling that needle from her arm.

As I placed it to the floor the lady scratched that bleeding spot. Fingers nail grating some of her skin off. Her eyes drifted open. She looked like she was fighting the need to close them again. Seeing me sitting there. "Who are you?"

"I'm nobody."

"Am I dreaming still?" Ignoring her question as I saw a ring sitting on her wedding ring finger. Nice and big like you would find in an antique store. The large green jewel looking dull like it had been infected by its surroundings.

"That ring. Where did you get?"

She quickly pulled her hands away. "It was a gift."

"From one of your friends?"

"My fiance, actually. He proposed."

"That wasn't his ring to give you. Someone needs it back." I reached forward but she pulled back again. "Look, I'm leaving with that ring."

"No, it's mine. It was given to me."

My hand shot out and wrapped around her wrists. Gripping tight which made her whimper. Pulling her hand towards me. "You either hand over that ring or I'll cause you pain."

"You can't come into our home and bully us around."

"Your home?" Letting out a short growl as I brought her hand closer. Going to grab that ring when she pulled her fingers into a fist. "Give me the ring or I'll snap your fingers." My touch trying to pry her hand open.

"No, get off. That's mine."

"It belongs to the woman your friends mugged. She's had it in her family for ages and you lot just took it from her. Last chance. Give me the ring."

Her eyes locked onto mine. She pulled a vile face and spat her words. "Get lost, bitch!"

Blowing out a sigh as the anger boiled up in my thoughts. My beast rolling around in it, growling to be released. I yanked her arm so she flopped onto her front. Grabbed one of her fingers and snapped it sharply. The woman screamed. Her body trying to writhe around in pain but I pinned her down until I slipped the ring from her finger.

The lady balled up into a ball. Holding her injured digit to her chest. Her screams filling the room. "Maybe next time you'll do as you're asked." Breathing out. Cooling my thoughts. I had retrieved the ring. That was my goal.

I took a step towards the door but I couldn't

go any further. Peering back at the woman as she laid there crying. Seeing the drugs sitting on the bedside cabinet. The horrible sight of the room. Blowing out an annoyed breath as I walked back and picked her up.

Cradling her easily in my arms and carrying her down the stairs. Out into the night air and carried her all the way to the nearest hospital which took me twenty-five minutes. Walking through A&E to the lady behind the desk. "This woman has taken drugs and she's got a broken finger."

The nurse tried to tell us to sit down when the woman I carried screamed out. Waving that oddly angled digit in her face. A couple of men were called through and the lady was carted away on a stretcher.

I went to leave when the nurse called to me. "We'll need some details about your friend."

"She isn't my friend. I found her on the side of the street. I know nothing about her." Turning and leaving before she could ask me any more questions. On the way back to my apartment I called the police on a pay phone. One of the few relics still operational in this city.

Telling them about some suspicious activity at the house I had visited. The response didn't give me much hope they would actually send someone down there to check it out. I hung up and walked the rest of the way home.

Once there I climbed the stairs. Me and my room mates lived on the top floor. Two out of the three apartments were rented by us. We had turned one side into living quarters which was mainly used for sleeping and washing. Maybe small snacks.

The other side was where we spent the day when we were home. The kitchen was fully utilised as well as the living area. This was also where I had my office. Instead of having one on the street where scorned ex-lovers and husbands and wives could find me. I kept myself safe here.

I turned left and entered. Heading into my room down the hallway and climbing into bed. Chucking my jacket off with the ring still in the pocket. Kicking off my jeans and flinging my top to the corner where my laundry basket was over-flowing.

My foot reached out and I flicked on the fan that would keep my werewolf body from over-heating. With my alarm set for the morning I laid back and drifted off. Getting a night void of nightmares which was a pleasant and rare time.

CHAPTER 2

After a quick shower and finding some clothes that didn't smell bad I headed out before everyone else got up. Moving down the street on foot to the cafe I loved to frequent. I met all my clients here. The coffee was great and it was familiar ground. Knowing the exit out the back would lead me to an alleyway that came out on the other side of the block. Handy in case I needed to escape.

I pushed open the door as Sally flipped over the open sign. Giving her a soft smile as I entered and walked over to the table near the back. The smell of the grills being heated up filled the air.

I sat and she came over with her little pad. The lady owned this place for the last eight years. You could see the weight it had on her shoulders. Crows feet showed the wear when she smiled. "Are you having a coffee today?"

"Yes, please." She headed off without asking about the extras I wanted in my mug. I had been coming here long enough for her to know I always took my decaf with a drizzle of caramel. Out came my phone and I quickly listened to the messages left on my voice mail.

Most of them were silly cases that wouldn't be worth my time. I wasn't the cheapest investigator around which meant when someone wanted something simple solved, they weren't going to fork out for my price. So setting up a meet would be a waste of time.

One did pique my interest though. A woman left a simple message. She didn't explain what kind of help she was looking for but I could hear the sadness in her voice. The thing that caught my attention was the mention of my payment. Half up front. The second half when I completed the case.

For someone to be bringing that up first had to be someone to take seriously. Giving her a ring. Surprised she actually picked up since it was just after half seven. "Hello? Who is this?"

"Hi, you left a message on my voice mail. My name is Megan with Luna Wolf Investigations."

"Oh, wow you start the day early."

"I'll take that as a compliment. Are you free today for a discussion?"

"Sure. I've got some spare time before lunch."

"Alright. Half eleven okay?"

"Yes."

"Do you know Sally's Cafe? The one on Canary Street?"

"Yes, I do. See you then."

"Will do." Putting my phone away as my coffee was brought over. As I looked over Sally's shoulder I saw my client come walking in. She was young, like me. The same long brunette hair. Mine was pulled back in a ponytail but hers was dangling in thick curls. She was clearly pampered with the amount of money she had at her disposal.

She spotted me and came walking over. Dismissing Sally with a wave that seemed a little arrogant. The lady took the seat opposite me. The look of excitement written across her face. "I'm hoping your phone call means you've retrieved what I asked?"

"Yes." The ring was pulled from my pocket and placed on the table. She snatched it up in her hand. Lifting it to her eye, a huge smile appearing on her face. "You seem very happy to see it."

"It's been in my family for ages. It was my turn to have it."

"Clearly." Watching as she marvelled at the piece of jewellery. Something telling me she wasn't missing the ring as such. More like the value it held at auction. "Do you have my payment?"

"Of course." She pulled out her purse. Seeing the wad of cash wedged inside. Some of it staying behind as she pulled out my grand worth of payment. Giving it a quick flick through. My brain estimating that it was all there before folding it up into my back pocket. "Pleasure doing business with you."

"Likewise." The lady stood and left the coffee shop, not taking her eyes off the ring the whole time. For the next few hours I kept listening to my messages. Looking on the internet. Passing the time.

I had gone through three mugs of decaf and a slice of chocolate cake. Sitting there with my hands wrapped around the warm porcelain. Feeling the heat against my palms. I took the last bite of my cake. When Sally came by to take the plate I said no to a refill.

My eyes peered over to a group of elderly ladies who seemed to be here every time I was. Always explaining what their children have been up to or gossiping about their neighbours. Smiling to myself as I peered over at the heated discussion about someone called Margaret who has been using the wrong soil in her flower beds. Chuckling to myself. Wishing I had problems that small to worry about.

Hearing the ding of the bell hanging over the front door. A quick intake of air brought the smell of strong perfume. The smell of freshly done nails making my nose crinkle as I pushed the smell away. Clearly putting on too much if it was still lingering that bad at lunch time.

Under it all was the scent of freshly laundered clothes. Getting an image in my head of a lady well dressed. Turning to see a woman in a fancy looking jacket that hid everything apart from her expensive looking heels.

Big curls bounced every time she shifted her head. Bright red earrings matching her nails and lipstick. Those lips pursed, blowing air over those sharp nails. Smiling at my guess. My fingers wrapped around my mug when the ding came again. Another woman had entered but she was the complete opposite. Hair could have done with a quick brush. Her clothes were very casual like it was the first ones she had come to.

The woman's look was filled with worry. Her eyes landed on me and I gave her a soft smile. Sally saw the look between us so didn't bother asking if she would be taking a table or not. Whilst the visitor slowly dodged in and out of tables I breathed in the air.

Not with my werewolf senses. Using my other heritage to sift through the air. The leecher ancestry from my mother allowed me to sniff out any supernaturals around me. Whilst other leechers could suck on scents they found, gaining strengths and weaknesses. I couldn't. Something had gone wrong when my mother was pregnant. I could only sense them. It made me an outsider to my own kind.

So I never really used it unless I needed to. Which made my talent below average but I could tell this woman was human. Which fit my life perfect. Since I never really fit in anywhere with them. I steered clear of anything supernatural.

Giving the lady a smile as I stood. Taking her hand in mine. Her voice coming out soft, her eyes red like she had been crying just before walking in. "Mrs. Clark?"

Seeing how she looked at me cautiously, "I'm guessing you're, Megan Fiske?"

Nodding, "Yes, please sit down. Would you like a coffee?"

"Sure." She slung her bag off her shoulder and sat opposite. I gave Sally a wave and made a drinking motion. Over came the large pot of black liquid, filling up an empty mug.

The conversation stopped until the owner had

walked off to tend to someone else. "Thank you for meeting me." Her eyes looking over my face. Seeing there was a question lingering on the tip of her tongue.

"Yes?"

"You seem a little too young to be running your own business."

"I'll take that as a compliment." Giving off a soft laugh. "Mrs Clark. You rang me. I assume because you've tried the normal avenues."

"I see your point."

"So how about you tell me why you're here and we can go from there."

"Okay." Still getting the unsure smile as a photo was pulled from her handbag. Looking down as it was slid over the table. My eyes looking at the young face smiling at the camera as she played with a football. "This is my daughter. Melanie."

"She's beautiful."

"Thank you." I picked up the photo to study her features as the mother spoke. "A few days ago she went missing. She went to a club with this boy she met." Making mental notes about the boy but not wanting to interrupt her. "She never came home. I left it till the next night and I hadn't heard anything from her, not a text or a call."

"Unusual for her?"

"Yes." The lady took a sip of her coffee before pouring in some of the sugar sachets. "When I went to the police..." There was a pause, making me study her expression. Sadness seeping through even more.

"They said…"

I wasn't one for soothing my client's feelings. But I reached over and gripped her hand. "It's okay. Just take a deep breath. Take a moment then carry on."

"Thanks." I got a smile, giving her eyes a brief sparkle through that sadness. "They had found a body. A Jane Doe until I was brought down to the morgue to identify her. It was my little girl." Suddenly she burst into tears.

Quickly pulling a tissue out of her sleeve and covering her face. I bit my lip as I sat there, taking the moment to look at the photo and think. Mrs Clark wasn't here because she wanted me to find her daughter. The body was already found. So what was she expecting me to do?

Looking up as Mrs Clark blew her nose. The tissue being balled up in her hands. "Sorry about that."

"No need to say sorry. It must be hard."

Her nose was quickly wiped. "My baby overdosed. I didn't even have a clue that she did drugs."

"So you would say this was strange behaviour?"

"I guess. But maybe I just didn't know what she was into. This guy, the drugs."

"Mrs. Clark. Is this the daughter you knew?"

"No. She was sweet, kind to everyone. Great results in school."

"Then hang on to that memory. You have no idea what happened."

"That's why I'm here." Out came an envelope. My eyes seeing the notes sticking out the corner. "I want you to find out what happened. Why she was killed."

"That's all you need to know?"

"Yes. For my peace of mind."

My hand reached out for the envelope but I didn't pick it up. "What about the police? Aren't they on the case? Bringing in the people responsible?"

"Honestly, the detective in charge doesn't seem all that interested in finding out who did it. She isn't the first. He said there are so many drug dealers and clubs. It would take the whole force a year to shut them all down."

"Seems like a jack-ass to me."

A soft laugh caught her by surprise. "That's exactly what I thought. So I'm not holding out hope."

"So you've come to me." Finally picking up the money. Giving it a quick look, not insulting her by counting it right there at the table. Slipping it under my leather jacket sitting next to me. "I can't go around threatening drug operations and gangs. I'm not suicidal. What I can do is track down this guy you mentioned. Perhaps I can get you some answers through him."

"Thank you."

"Did she ever mention his name?"

"I have no idea who it is. Will you be able to find him?"

"Find the first clue then follow them like breadcrumbs until he pops up. I've been doing this for a couple of years now. I'm getting pretty good at it. I'll let you know when I have what you're asking for."

"You really are my last hope."

"Your daughter's body. Which morgue is she in?"

"Great Arthur Hospital."

I knew the morgue assistant there. "I'll get to work straight away. I know it's not going to make you feel better. But try the apple pie here. It's truly amazing. My treat." I grabbed my jacket and slipped it on, sliding the money into the inside pocket.

Turning and passing by the counter where Sally stood. Slipping over a couple of notes to cover what I had plus an extra coffee and a slice of the pie. The ding signified my departure from the cafe.

Looking left and right as people wandered past me. Most had scarves wrapped around their necks. Thick coats keeping them warm as the wind blew down the street of shops. I was happy in my leather jacket and jeans.

Making my way down to the small lay-by I had parked my bike in. Climbing on board and slipping my head into my helmet. Turning the key and feeling the thing come to life. The loud thick roar growling as I set off down the road.

Following traffic towards Great Arthur Hospital. It was the largest hospital in the city and the only one with it's own morgue. Lucky for me, the assistant there has helped me out many times in the past. A gift for getting her out of trouble with her family.

I pulled into the large car park out the front of the hospital. Moving down the side to where the morgue sat. A staff entrance sitting between two plants made out white stone. I parked right at the front in the motorcycle spot.

Going through the entrance and finding a young girl sitting behind the desk. A pencil spinning around in her fingers. Another stuck behind her ear.

"Hey, Leanne."

"Megan. What are you doing here?" The girl shut the massive thick book on the desk with a thud.

"I decided to pop by. See how the studying is going?"

"Have you not seen how thick this thing is? There's stuff in here I doubt the historians knew. Just sounds made up." Laughing as she tapped her pencil against the book cover.

"I'm sure you'll do fine. You've aced every exam so far."

"They're getting harder." She pushed the book away like it would make her feel better.

"You'll be fine. I'm going to nip in and see how the doc is doing."

"Wait, you can't."

Making my way through the double doors before she could protest again. The air already getting cooler as I walked down the hallway. Passing the records room, a storage cupboard, through another pair of doors and into the coldest room.

Three large metal tables sat in the middle. Seeing the drains underneath where the blood would pour away. A large sink over to the right where utensils were sat all clean and fresh. Ready to be used for the next autopsy.

"Julie?" Looking around but not able to see anyone down here. Moving deeper into the room. Noticing a couple of files sitting on the side. Shifting through them but not finding the one I needed.

Heading to the small desk in the corner. The computer coming to life when I nudge the mouse. About to start clicking through files when footsteps brought a voice into the room. "Can I help you?"

Turning with a smile but that quickly changed. The woman wasn't my friend. This person looked like she had swallowed a wasps nest. An apple in one hand and her phone in the other. Shooting back, "Who the hell are you?"

"Excuse me? That's my desk you're nosing about." She came closer. I gave out a yelp as she grabbed my elbow and yanked me away from her desk. Looking at her with a dark stare as she checked the computer. "Now, what are you doing down here? Are you some kind of reporter?"

"No, I'm a PI."

"That's even worse." She turned around. Looking pissed off enough to throw a punch. "You need to leave."

"I just need to have a quick look at a file. That's not too much to ask, is it?"

"You must be joking. You're not even supposed to be in here." She placed her apple down and came at me. Fingers grabbing at my elbow.

Quickly yanking my arm free. "You're going to have to stop touching me if you want to keep eating without a straw."

"You threaten me again and you'll find yourself in jail." The lady gave my shoulder a push, nudging me towards the exit.

My anger started to boil to life as I stared at her. Having to bite my cheek so I didn't say anything. This was my only chance to get a look at the autopsy report. "I would really appreciate it, if you would let me have a look." Reaching inside my jacket pocket and pulling some notes from the envelope. Waving them between my fingers. "It'll be beneficial for us both."

Realising my mistake as soon as she saw the notes. Her face twisting in disgust. "You honestly expect me to take a bribe so you can poke your nose in my files?"

"Well.."

"No!" My body jumping at her sudden volume. "You will march your arse out of here before I get security to chuck you out."

Mumbling under my breath, "I'd like to see them try."

"What was that?"

"Alright." Shoving my money back in my pocket. "You don't have to keep yelling. I'm going."

"Good and I don't want to see you around here again."

Biting my lip, stopping myself from antagonising her more. Staying silent and turning to leave. Hearing her footsteps carrying her off towards the metal tables. Looking over my shoulder. With her back turned to me I quickly stepped to her desk.

Fingers picked up the pen and pencil sitting there and snapped them in two.

Dropping them into the bin as I left. Blowing out a frustrated sigh knowing the beast in me wanted to snap her little neck for being so obnoxious. Giving Leanne a smile on the way out. Keeping my mouth shut so I didn't take my anger out on her.

Instead of getting on my bike I paced back and forth. Knowing when I ride angry it dangerous for everyone nearby. Annoyed that the beast wasn't getting easier to control when someone pissed me off. Leaning my back to the wall. Smacking my heel against the brick work which made the whole thing shake.

Digging my nails into my palms, blowing out growls until my heart started to slow. Feeling that anger slipping away. "Why the hell did she have to be so arrogant about it?" Pulling out my phone and dialling the number of the previous morgue technician. The line picking up. Spitting out my words before she could greet me. "When the hell did you change jobs?"

She laughed despite my clear anger. "She pissed you off, didn't she?"

"And you don't seem surprised."

"That's because she's been pissing me off for years." The doctor laughed down the line.

"I don't see why she needs to aim it at me."

Another laugh came which had me smiling. "I wish I could have been there to see your face."

"No you don't. You know how angry I can get."

"Oh yes." She giggled again. "I remember." Rolling my eyes as she kept laughing. Waiting for her to calm herself. "I assume you came to the hospital for some help?"

"So you're still here?"

"Yes, I've only moved departments. A nice promotion and a wage hike as well."

"Good for you. Does your new position allow you to access files from the morgue?" My eyes watching a doctor walking by with a paper cup of coffee.

"Not with you it doesn't."

"Damn. So you can't get my eyes on an autopsy report?"

"No."

"Damn. That was my only lead unless I want to visit every club in the city with a picture."

"What are you investigating today?" Sounds of food being munched coming through the phone.

"Melanie Clark. She over-dosed in a club. I was hoping to get a hold of the report and see if you guys had figured out what kind of drug it was. That would narrow my possible clubs down a lot."

"Hold on." The sounds of keys being tapped came in the background. Watching that coffee drinking doctor taking a seat on a bench. My eyes studying his cute face. Giving him a soft smile when he looked over and saw me. The man looked straight back down like I was wearing a sign telling him to piss off.

Chewing at the corner of my mouth as I waited.

"You better not be stuffing your face."

"I'm helping, I'm helping." A few more keys were punched before she spoke again. "Now, I can't get you access to that information. But I might be able to get you to someone who has it. Detective Dawson."

"And who is that supposed to be?"

"The man in charge of the investigation."

"You mean the chump who doesn't seem interested in solving it?"

"That sounds like him. We sent over the reports as part of his investigation."

"And why the hell can't you just send them my way as well?"

"Yeah. That would be a great way to get fired. Sending autopsy reports to an unregistered email. Such a brill idea."

"You don't have to be so sarcastic."

The doctor laughed which annoyed me this time. "You know me. If I'm not laughing or joking around. It's going to be sarcastic."

"Perhaps you should grow up."

There was a slight pause before she replied. "You broke her pencil didn't you."

"It was her stationary or her neck." The doctor burst out again. The laugh just going on and on until I cut in. "Which precinct is this detective stationed at?"

"I can do you one better. Give me an hour or two and I'll send over his address."

"You're going to give out a detective's home address?"

"It's not like I'm giving it out in phone booths.

You're a friend."

"If I'm your friend then why do you laugh at me constantly?"

"Because you take life serious enough for us both."

"Alright, thanks for the help. My signal is cutting out."

"Bye, Doofus. And next time you ring it better be about a girl's night out with shots and men dancing on stage half-naked."

"I'm going to pretend I didn't hear that."

"Fun. Get some of it."

"Get on with some work." Cutting the call off before she could hit me with another remark. Putting my phone away and climbing onto my bike. Pausing for a moment as I thought what to do next.

I could do a little investigating but without the detective there wasn't a clear route to take right now. So I kick-started my bike and headed back home. Knowing I could relax there whilst thinking of my next move.

Parking out the front of my building I wedged my bike between two cars pretty much outside the steps. One of the reasons I loved riding in this city. Taking my helmet up to the top floor. As I passed the first door I head footsteps coming from behind it. Blowing out a long sigh as it opened quickly. "Oi."

Turning slowly, "Yes?" Looking at that bald head. Wrinkles covering that and his face. Looking even worse when he had his face twisted in annoyance. "How can I help you today?"

"Don't give me that nice girl routine. I heard you coming home this morning. Woke me up and I couldn't get back to sleep."

"That's the problem with living in an apartment building. It's not all about you."

"You could have the good manners to not stomp your way up the stairs."

"I didn't stop." Giving him a stern look. "Why don't you go back inside and get on with your day. I'll try and forget your face and do the same." He opened his mouth to talk. "Good day!"

Leaving him there and entering the apartment to the right. Shutting the door and leaning against it. Blowing out breaths. "He is such an old fart." Pushing off to the long table we had just inside the door.

Each person had their section and their own little bowl. I placed my helmet under mine. Hung up my leather jacket and placed my bike keys and the two lots of money in the bowl. That would cover my side of the rent for the next month and then some.

Moving past the hallway toilet and into the largest room of the apartment. The living area to the left where our massive television sat surrounded by shelves of movies and weird trinkets. Including a sword prop from my favourite movie running across the very top. It's been brought down on many occasions when no one else is home to witness my antics.

Coming to the right, one of my room mates was sitting at the dining table munching on some cereal. His blonde, floppy hair almost touching the milk when he lowered his mouth to his spoon. Plopping myself down opposite him when I noticed no one else around. "What's up, kid?"

The twelve year-old looked up with milk dribbling down his chin. "Hey." Giggling as his food almost dropped back into his bowl. Connor quickly finished off his mouthful before he spoke in his surprisingly deep voice. "Hey, Megan. How was your day?"

"Not bad. A little hiccup but I got a new client which is the main thing. How about you?"

"School was school. Still going easy."

"That's good but be warned. At some point that'll change and it'll hit you hard. Make sure you're keeping your head down and studying."

"I know, you tell me that at least once a week."

"Just in case you forget."

"Yeah." A spoonful disappeared into his mouth.

"Where's your father?"

Connor shook his head until that cereal was eaten. "Not home."

"Work?"

"Out."

Feeling confusion rising up in my thoughts. "How did you get home from school?"

His eyes slowly lifted to mine. "I'm not a kid any more."

"Connor, you're twelve." My eyes dropping to his meal. "And you're eating cereal at four in the afternoon."

"Milk is good for my bones."

Reaching my hand into the cereal box and grabbing a handful, munching on those little pieces. "No more walking home from school, please. None of us want to be hearing about something happening on the news."

"It won't."

"Connor." His big eyes locked onto mine. "For us."

"Okay. No more walking home. I'll just stand outside the school on the street waiting for someone to come get me."

Smirking as he smiled right back. "Fair point. If your father isn't there to pick you up again, get the school to ring home. You know Ivy is home ninety percent of the time. She can come grab you if need be."

"I didn't want to be a burden. It's only a short walk."

"A lot can happen in a short amount of time." Watching as he lifted his bowl up to finish off the milk. "You want me to cook you something?"

"Is it going to be edible?" Flicking a piece of cereal at his head. "Oi. No wasting my cereal."

Laughing as I grabbed the box and put it back in the cupboard. "You got any homework to do for tomorrow?"

"Ivy got me to do it as soon as I walked in."

"Good. Go zombie out in front of the television then like a normal kid."

"Cool."

"No eighteen rated movies though. Your father never let's me forget that."

Connor giggled as he put on an animated superhero show which I have been sucked into watching far too many times. The bowl got rinsed out and left in the sink.

As I made my way down to my office I heard the soft buzzing of a tattoo gun. Making a right instead of a left. Moving through the half wood, half glass door to Ivy's studio. Her name in stickers across the pane of glass, Magickal Tattoos. A little on the nose since she was a light witch.

We had taken the larger of the two bedrooms and transformed it completely. Inside was a chair sat in the middle of the room. Shelves held her inks and other items of the tattooing business. Ivy was sitting on her rolling stool.

A black sleeveless dress showed off her smooth arms. Not a single tattoo in sight. Some of her clients had mentioned how strange it was but they just didn't know the amount Ivy had hidden.

Sitting in the chair was a young man getting his arm tattooed. Letting out a soft laugh as I saw his face screwed up in pain. "How's it going in here?"

The guy shooting his eyes open. That pain suddenly vanishing as he locked eyes on me. "Wow, you are beautiful."

"Hitting on me whilst you're getting a tattoo done? That's ballsy." Moving closer and peering over Ivy's shoulder. Seeing the tribal pattern scurrying up his arm in thick black patterns. Something typical you saw everywhere. "How's your day been?"

"Almost packed solid. Skinny boy here is my

last one."

"Skinny boy?" The kid's words coming out like a whimper as the pain scorched his skin again. "Do you talk like that to all your clients?"

"Only ones who can't take the pain." Ivy smiled as she dipped the gun into the black ink and went back for another pass. Questioning me without looking up, "How about yours? How did it go with the client?"

My eyes looked at that tattoo as we spoke. "Good. She got her ring back and I got a nice wad of cash. Also got another client."

"That was fast."

"You know I like to keep myself busy." Taking a pause to enjoy the look of pain on the guy's face. "She wants me to find out who's responsible for her daughter overdosing."

"She does realise the city has a police force."

"A bunch of donut eating morons." Both of us giving the customer a quick look which shut him up.

"They don't seem all that interested in the case but I'll be meeting up with the detective tomorrow morning. Hoping he'll be a little willing to help me out with some information."

"And if he's not?"

"I'll charm him."

"You?" Ivy finally broke concentration and looked over her shoulder. Her long black hair fell down her back in thin braids as she sat up. "You have charm?"

"Don't you think?"

Skinny boy scoffed. "I can already tell you don't

have any charm whatsoever." I quickly flicked his tattoo which made him jump and yelp like a little puppy.

Ivy bit back laughter before adding. "Oh yeah, real charming."

"Okay, maybe I'll kick his arse until he tells me."

"You never know, he might enjoy it."

I laughed as I walked to the door. Stopped to look over my shoulder. "Leon wasn't there to pick up Connor again?"

"Nope. And when he gets home I hope he's got enough space up his arse for my foot."

The customer looking between us. "You two are a little scary."

"Thank you." The tattooist smiled wide because she genuinely took it as a compliment. "I'm almost done then you can run away."

I giggled as my eyes ran over the shelves full of ink. Noticing the little treasure chest I had gotten her a few birthdays ago. Inside were all the ingredients that were too magical to have on display. She wasn't allowed to use any of them on humans. One of the reasons she was tattooing in our apartment and not her own shop.

She was forbidden from running her own place when the government found out she was using magick to help humans. To help heal the tattoo or perhaps bring better luck. Small charms but none the less, illegal for a witch.

It was also the reason why she couldn't conjure spells with the aid of ingredients. She hadn't finished her training when all this happened. And her teacher refused to give her any more lessons as punishment.

The final thing my eyes ran over was a picture frame hanging on the wall next to some of her art pieces. A happy couple holding a baby with jet black hair like Ivy. When she was still very young they had disappeared.

Ivy was taken in by a witch family who were close with her parents. Taught her their light magick. It came from the goodness inside each caster. And despite her snarky comments, she was a good character and a very close friend. One of the few supernatural things in my life that I actually welcomed.

Leaving the studio I crossed the hall to my little office. Not as fancy as her work place. It consisted of one desk that I found in a dumpster a few streets over. Shelves that looked like they could fall down at any moment.

One valuable thing in here was a picture of my father with me on his shoulders as a toddler. It wasn't long before his pack ejected him from their ranks. The wolf was the alpha of alphas. He was in charge until they had had enough of his split interest.

When you're in a pack, they are your family. I didn't fit in because I couldn't shift. Even on a full moon when there was no choice. That beast side of me never came out. I never transitioned and I swear that's the reason my anger is so volatile. That beast is itching to get out and it's getting angrier and angrier.

I picked up the photo and placed my butt on

my squeaky chair. For a person who barely wrote anything down. There were piles of papers sitting atop my desk. Most of them were hand-written receipts for jobs. Waiting to be filed properly. But they sat there like little reminders of how disorganised I was.

I placed the picture frame down and dug out my laptop from it's charging drawer. Opening it up I started hitting the newspaper sites. Searching for overdoses in the city over the last few months. My client's daughter wasn't the first.

The plan was to use my hand drawn map of the city behind me to pin-point each one. See if there was a pattern or a home base for these drugs. Only after the first twenty I gave up. And that was only for the first week of November. Let alone for December and January. There were a lot more than I realised which goes to show the capabilities of the BCPD.

Next, I searched for news on drug busts. Seeing a few of them here and there but they were few and far between. Nothing major, they were all small fish. Plus, this was only the human news. There was a whole world out there that wouldn't be reported in the papers.

The government had files and files of information only I didn't have access. I knew someone who did but I wasn't about to start calling her. Whenever we spoke we argued. Sometimes small things but most of the time they were big. Yelling and screaming. The last was fourteen months ago on my twenty-first birthday.

A loud bang came from the front door. I jumped up and rushed out. Followed closely by Ivy. Both of us stopping when we saw Leon stumbling over towards the kitchen counter. The man could barely stand up straight. Holding onto the counter for dear life. He was a skinny guy and not too much taller than myself.

My eyes shifted over to Connor who caught my look. No doubt he could see the anger in my eyes because he quickly plugged in his headphones and slipped them on. As Ivy moved over to check on Leon I moved to the man standing in our doorway.

Looking him over he wasn't a big man. Delicate features. Thin but it was clear from his muscles that he worked out. Very lean, standing confident with a big smile that seemed to be alcohol induced. "Who are you?"

"Wallis. You could say I'm a friend of Leon's."

"A friend?" Looking over my shoulder to see Ivy getting our room mate to drink down some water. "It's not evening yet. How long have you two been drinking?" Crossing my arms over my chest to hide that I'm digging my nails into my palms. Feeling the leak of blood running over my fingers. Trying hard not to lose it. Mainly so Connor wouldn't witness the violence.

"We started at eleven. A good six hour session. I don't think Leon should drink cocktails. They go straight to his head."

"Is that so? Where did you two meet each other?"

"Bumped into each other at the supermarket.

I invited him out for a lunch and one thing led to another." The man smiled the whole time. His teeth so white they almost looked fake. The fact he seemed to find this all so funny grated on my nerves. "I didn't realise we would be getting so drunk. My mistake."

"It sure is. Did you know he had to pick up his son?"

"Connor, sure. I told him that a twelve year old would be fine walking home. He needs to start growing up and looking after himself after all."

Chewing on the corner of my mouth, fighting that urge to launch a tirade of words at him. "That's not for you to decide."

"Neither is it yours. Leon is the father. It's his responsibility."

"Excuse me?" I reached out and grabbed his wrist. Squeezing it hard enough to make him wince and back away. Letting go of him and slamming the door in his face. Blowing out long slow breaths. Cooling my thoughts but it was no good.

I spun on the spot and stomped towards Leon. But a few steps is where I stopped. Seeing that goofy smile of his. The man was out of it but he was clearly having fun. Wanting to let my anger wash over him but I couldn't.

It had been a long time since he had smiled because of a guy. His past relationship had ended a while ago but it had left a lasting effect that he carried with him every single moment of his life. My eyes looked down from his face. Seeing the scars criss-crossing his left wrist. Anyone who spotted them always called him out for trying to commit suicide. Only the truth was much worse.

Ivy looked up at me. "He'll be fine."

Nodding as I rubbed my fingers over my palms. Feeling the small cuts healing up quickly. "Apart from the hangover in the morning which he definitely deserves."

"That we definitely agree on."

"You're not going to heal me?" Leon's speech was slurred. The words barely recognisable. A finger was lifted and he playfully flicked her nose ring.

"No, I'm not." The witch looked over to Connor who still wore his headphones. "You left that boy to walk home. A hangover is you getting off lightly."

"Let's take him to bed." Moving closer and slinging one of his arms over my shoulders. Leon was a skinny guy and I could have easily carried him by myself but the three of us hobbled across the hallway.

As Ivy dug her keys out of her pocket I heard the door at the other end opening. Looking over to see the bald head poking out once again. The wrinkles so clear even from down the hallway. Blowing out a frustrated breath. He wasn't someone I wanted to deal with when my anger was already so high. "Sorry for the noise. We'll keep it down."

"You make sure you do." His voice hoarse. The man coughing like he chain-smoked all day long. "I've had enough of you three banging about."

Ivy swung the door open and grabbed Leon's other arm. "We know, you tell us at least twice a week."

"And at least once a week you threaten to tell the board about our behaviour." Chucking in my comment.

The man grumbled then shut the door loudly. We deposited Leon onto his bed in the lounge. Pulling the curtain across after placing a bowl by the side of his bed. Ivy headed for the door. "I'm going to send my client home."

"I'm going to head to bed, you okay with Connor?"

"You know I am. He's no trouble."

"I know."

Her eyes locked onto mine. "You okay?"

"Yeah." Taking a deep breath. "Just the anger."

"It's still getting worse?"

"Only slightly."

"I'll have another look into it but I don't think I can help much."

"I appreciate it all the same." Ivy gave a little wave with the jangle of her bands. Then I headed to my room. Pushing the door open. Stepping over the dirty clothes that covered the floor.

I exchanged my clothes for some fluffy pyjama shorts and a vest top. Pulling my long hair back into a neat ponytail. Using the lighter on the drawers to set off some incense. Filling the space with that thick aroma.

I parked myself at the centre of my bed cross-legged. Letting that scent waft up my nose as I took some deep breaths. Concentrating on how they filled my lungs. The outside world slipping away as I focused.

With each breath through my lips I thought about it taking specks of my anger with it. Emptying myself of that rage that boiled at the surface of my thoughts. Cooling off slowly. Smiling as I felt it leave my mind. My heart rate dropping even more.

Getting to that centre of peace. Lulling the beast into a deep sleep that would hopefully last a bit longer than last time. About to open my eyes when I felt something in the room. A gentle touch to my right arm.

There wasn't a presence in the room but I felt it again like fingertips gliding over my skin. A shiver ran down my spine as cold spread up my arm. Not just over my skin but inside as well. Like ice crystals were starting to form through the centre of my bones. Aching as it reached my shoulder. I shifted my body, pulling my arm away.

Gasping as that icy grip grabbed my throat. Taking away my breath. My eyes shot open but they quickly rolled into the back of my skull. My body dropped back lifeless but my mind was still alive. That icy grip not letting go as it pulled me from the land of the living. Tossing me into the darkness of death where I no longer breathed. No longer swallowed. My body left behind. The only thing that I brought with me was my soul and that wasn't safe in a place like this.

CHAPTER 3

Feeling a tear trickle down my cheek. Lifting my fingers to brush it away but it had already turned to ice. The brittle drop crushed under my fingertip and turned to dust. Rubbing my hand over my eyes I opened them.

Seeing my room covered in ice. Icicles dangling from the bottom of my curtains. As I shifted to the edge of the bed ice cracked and snapped underneath me. Standing up I could feel the cold air washing over my bare skin.

Reaching out and running my touch across the top of my drawers. Ice dust kicking up into the air. Then I saw my bedroom door. Just like the last few times I've been pulled into this world. The entrance to the room I'm currently occupying was there only now it was a single pane of ice. A perfect reflection of my environment except for one change.

Standing there, mirroring my actions, wasn't me. It was the girl from that photo my client gave me. To be more exact. It was her soul, her ghost. I moved forwards. Each step bringing us closer until I could reach out and touch the door. Seeing the snowflake symbols at the sides.

My fingers touching tip to tip with Melanie's. Pausing for a moment because I knew what was coming next. My lips moving and this is where the reflection disobeyed my actions. "What do you want to show me?"

"My death." Watching her fingers start to sink through the ice. Coming over my hand, sending a shiver running down my spine. Fingers gripped my wrist and I was yanked into that world on the other side.

The cold running over my body as I fell forwards. Thumping coming to my ears, shaking my body. Feeling so solid in this figure. Then those feelings came. Like I couldn't catch my breath. Every intake just made me cough up chunks from my stomach. Retching it out and feeling whatever was inside coming out over my chin. Splatting over my bare arm.

Then my eyes opened. Seeing faces looking down at me but what caught my eye was the ceiling. The blue and green colours washing across my vision. Dark clouds moving with it like a storming ocean in the sky.

The movement making my stomach twist even more and I chucked up again. My head flopping, eyes rolling back. The sensation of my body shaking and fitting. Foam coming out over my lips.

Sinking deeper into that mind, losing touch and smell and sound. The music a far away thud until it cut off completely. Pain coursing through my entire body. Like a big red ball growing to encompass my whole world before that ice came back like a blizzard crashing against my body.

Knocking me back into my crystallised bedroom with a stumble. Leaning against the wall as Melanie stared at me. Seeing the sick and the foam marking her skin. The lifeless eyes staring through me. Mumbling under my breath. "That didn't really help."

"Why did this happen to me? Why do you get to live."

"I didn't choose this for you. All I can do is say I'll try my best to find the people who are responsible."

"Trevor. Find Trevor."

"Trevor? Is that the guy you were with?"

"Trevor. Find him." Her voice losing it's power as she started to fade. My brighter hair colour showing through. Skin tone changing from dead to living and there I was wearing my pyjamas.

Pressing my palm to the mirror and rubbing away the condensation. Smearing it to my palm with bent fingers. "Why the hell can't they take this crap with them?" Turning around to my bed. Seeing the cold dust covering my bed spread.

Grabbing the corner I gave it a shake which filled the air. Blowing out a breath and scooting my fan back with my foot. At least I wouldn't need that on to keep me cool. I slipped under the cover, feeling the coldness covering my body. Giving me a bit of a shiver but it was only seconds before I was settled.

The cold allowed me to drift into an undisturbed sleep. Getting me to the morning for a good nights sleep. As soon as I was up I stripped my bed of that wet sheeting and dumped it into the washing machine in the kitchen.

Footsteps brought Ivy down the hallway. Giving her a soft smile as she let her thin braids down. "Another one?"

"Yeah. This time it was my client's daughter."

"An overdose. I bet that was fun." I let out a soft laugh but it was shortened by the memory of choking on my own sick. "Did she give you anything helpful?"

"Trevor. Whoever the hell that is."

"Keep your chin up. You're meeting the detective today aren't you?"

"Yeah. Hopefully he'll allow me to follow him around. Maybe a Trevor will pop up somewhere."

"You never know." Her tall figure came closer and wrapped me up in a tight hug. Enjoying the comfort before she pulled back. "I'll stick your sheets in the tumble dryer when they're done."

"Thanks." Turning and grabbing a glass of water. "You busy today?"

"I got some bookings and a few messages about possible walk-ins if I have the time. Might even get a lunch break today."

I sipped my water. "Leon has work, right?"

"Yes. So perhaps he'll act like a father today."

"I can hear you." Turning to see Leon come walking out of his curtained off room. "You two should learn to whisper when you're talking about someone."

"Whispering would mean we're trying to keep

our feelings hidden." Seeing him rub his forehead. I was still angry with him but I offered him my glass of water which he took with a smile. "Headache?"

"Check."

"How's your stomach?"

"All I'll say is thanks for the bowl."

Ivy rubbed her hand over his forehead. "Maybe next time you won't go drinking at lunch and who was that guy?"

"I don't know. He just appeared and I just, lost myself with him. I've never had that happen before."

"That doesn't give you an excuse to forget about Connor."

"I know, I know. I can't believe I did that. At the time it just slipped my mind."

Taking my glass back and finishing it off before rinsing it out. "Make sure it doesn't happen again."

"Of course."

Giving Ivy a smile before heading back to my room to get changed. Grabbing a pair of jeans and a white t-shirt from the last concert I went to. Finishing it off with my leather jacket. Filling my pockets with my keys and my phone. Taking some notes from my payment yesterday for when I got hungry.

Using the address my friend had sent me last night I headed over to where the detective lived. Parking up outside his apartment building. Up to the fourth floor which was near the top and knocking on his door.

Someone grumbled from inside before the door was pulled open. Getting an eyeful of toned muscles. A pair of tight black boxers. The only thing they covered was his modesty and not doing a great job at that. Eyes lifting over the massive tattoo that covered his chest and abs, seeming to disappear around the sides.

Then I saw Dawson's grin. White teeth bright compared to his tanned skin. A trimmed beard covering his cheeks and chin. The detective neatened his black hair by running his hands through it from front to back.

Clamping down sharply on the thoughts of how hot he looked right now. This was business, not pleasure. "Detective Dawson?"

"And who might you be?" The man leant against the door frame. One arm reaching up high, stretching out that impressive body.

"My name is Megan. I'm a private investigator."

"That's a shame. I don't talk to your kind. Pleasure to meet you and if you ever want to have some fun. Please feel free to drop by another time."

He went to close the door but I quickly shoved my foot in the way. "My client has lost her daughter. She's asked me to investigate because the police aren't doing their job."

"Oh?" His eyes looked down at my foot before opening the door all the way. "Since you're on my doorstep. I'm assuming that means I'm in charge of this case."

"Yes."

"So you come here to what, have a go at me?"

"No, I've come to ask for your help." The man turned and walked back into his apartment. The fact he didn't close the door had me following him. Closing it behind me I ventured towards his kitchen. My eyes running over the unfinished tattoo that covered his back. "All I need is access to the autopsy report."

"Is that all?"

"Yes. I've been told you were sent it along with the others that fall under this case."

He paused with a bottle of whiskey in his hand almost about to fill up a glass with it. "Where did you hear that from?"

"I have my sources. A PI should never give those up."

"I can respect that. Don't want to get your friend into trouble." I watched as he filled the glass almost up to the rim. "But I'm still trying to understand why I would let you have that information."

"It would help me. That means it would help my client. The one who's upset with you guys for not taking this seriously."

Dawson turned taking a few gulps of his drink. "What makes you think I'm not taking this seriously?"

Taking in the image of him standing there in his underwear. Having whiskey for breakfast. "You really want me to point out what's wrong with this image?"

"How about we skip that part and you just head on your way."

"I'm not leaving here until I get what I came for." Crossing my arms over my chest. Giving him the sternest look I could.

A smile teasing his lips. "What's your name again?"

"Megan. I run Luna Wolf Investigations."

"Wow, that's quite a name. Luna Wolf?" I nodded. "So you're by yourself? You don't have any help?"

"That's right." A little surprised that he knew what the name stood for.

"But you're here. Asking for my help. Not very lone wolf, is it?"

"I do what is needed to help my clients."

The glass was emptied into his mouth. Surprised he didn't refill it. Instead he placed it next to the sink. My eyes running over the place. Some of the stuff here was nice. Maybe a little beyond a detective's wages.

Seeing some photos stuck on the fridge. Him and a group of friends dressed up for paintballing. Many of them snapshots from night outs. Seeing a card for the local butchers as well as a tattoo place.

Bringing my eyes back to him as he turned. "I've got some bad news. Even if I wanted to help you. I couldn't. Those reports have already been forwarded on to my superior. I don't have them any more."

Biting my cheek to stop myself from swearing at him. Breathing in and out slowly. "You can still help. We can go visit the morgue. Get the report from them personally."

"That would involve getting dressed and driving all the way down to the hospital."

"And?"

"My plan for the day was to hang out here." My ears picking up someone moving down the hallway to my left. Water running in the bathroom. "You can find the door by yourself, right?" His finger waving in the air. "Back the way you came."

Before he could walk off I picked up an apple from the bowl on the counter and chucked it at him. Hitting him on the back of the head. "You seriously don't give a crap do you?" Dawson turned with an angry stare but I was already falling down through my own anger to care. "When Mrs Clark told me she didn't think the police were taking it seriously I thought it was the typical slow working you guys do."

"We don't…"

"But it's not like that at all. You really are going to go back to bed and sleep with your friend in the shower. Not bothered that people are out there dying. Losing their lives because you can't be bothered to leave your apartment long enough to stop the bad guys."

"Look, Megan."

"No, you look." Stomping over to him. Poking his chest with my finger. Becoming more annoyed by how hard his pecks felt. So I poked it harder which brought a wince out of him. "People rely on you guys. Protect and serve. You should do your damn job."

Dawson opened his mouth to speak but stopped himself. Pulling a soft expression with those bright blue eyes. "Can I at least get dressed first?"

"Huh?"

"I can't go out like this."

Eyes moving over him as he opened his arms. "You've got five minutes."

"And five minutes to get my friend ready to leave as well."

"Whatever." Spinning around and heading out. Blowing breath after breath as I made my way down the stairs. The cool air hitting my face as I stepped outside. Sucking it into my lungs. By the time the detective came walking out of his building I was fully calmed.

Sitting on my bike I watched him kiss the skinny blonde who was dressed like she was heading out clubbing. Clearing my throat when there didn't seem to be an end to them necking each other. She walked off and Dawson came over to me with a huge grin. Annoyingly, he looked good in the black jeans and shirt he was now wearing. "Very nice bike."

"Thanks."

"But I'm not getting on that thing."

"I'll meet you there then."

"Fine by me." The detective walked off whistling. Chucking his keys into the air and catching them. A flatbed truck sat by the curb. Flashing lights shone as he unlocked the vehicle. The bodywork shining like it had been cleaned this morning. The engine roared and he pulled out but stopped next to my bike. His face appearing out of the window. "Last one there buys breakfast."

Shaking my head and preparing a sarcastic remark but he had already driven off. Laughing like a small child. I didn't want to be giving in to his games but I couldn't have him winning either. Kicking my engine into life and swerving into traffic.

Managing to make my way past him thanks to my small size. His massive truck getting stuck more than once. Arriving at the hospital by the morgue entrance and parking in the same spot as before. Waiting more than twenty minutes before the truck came into view.

He parked in one of the staff spots but put a print out of his badge and his information with it on the dash. Then he emerged with his hands full. A carry case containing two drinks in one hand. Two bags with grease spots leaking through the paper in the other. "Breakfast is served."

Rolling my eyes but taking one of the bags from him all the same. The smell of meat wafting out of the bag made me salivate. Pulling out the wrap and taking out half of it with one massive bite. Groaning softly at the amazing taste. The sauce giving it a nice spicy kick.

"Looks like I picked right."

"Lucky guess." Finishing off my wrap in two more mouthfuls. Grabbing one of the drinks Dawson had placed on my bike seat. Taking a sip but spitting it out. "Bad guess."

"That's my one. You don't like black coffee?"

"That's vile. How can you drink that?" Picking up the second cup and sipping it cautiously. Happy that this one was sweeter. "That's better."

"I put in quite a few sugar packets in that one.

Figured you could sweeten up a little."

"I sweeten up for my friends. Not idiot detectives."

"Keep drinking. I'm hoping it'll kick in soon."

"Don't hold your breath." Taking a few more sips before placing it back in the cup holder. "Come on. We've got an autopsy file to get."

"You don't do thanks. Do you?"

"You want a thank you for getting me breakfast? You lost the bet, you placed."

"No, no. I agreed to help you. You don't seem very appreciative of that?"

Laughing at his comment. "I had to yell at you to change your mind. Once I get this report you can go back to banging blonde chicks and day drinking."

"I don't just bang blondes. Brunettes are pretty cute as well."

Stepping to him, "Let's get one thing clear. You will never get me into bed."

"Doesn't have to be a bed."

"And one more comment about me sexually, I'll bust your head open."

Dawson smiled but he nodded all the same. "You're feisty. I'll behave."

"Good. Let's go." Taking a final chug of my coffee and then chucking the rest in the bin. Pushing through the doors.

The reception chick looked surprised it was me walking through. "Megan, I can't let you in there again. The doctor was so angry. She threatened to fire me."

The detective came walking up behind me. "She's working with me, cutie. No need to worry."

"Oh."

"We'll see ourselves in."

"Okay."

"I know the way." Rolling my eyes as Leanne seemed to have forgotten I was even there. So starry eyed at the hunk she's come face to face with.

Not making a comment since I was getting access because of him. Moving down the hallway I could hear the doctor's voice before I even walked through the doors. "I don't care if you're a detective, you can't come walking into my morgue demanding files."

"It's not a case of me barging in here whilst you have a body open on the table."

"I don't care. You need to ring beforehand and book a time. Not just drop by when it suits you." Then I walked in and her face grew even redder. "I should have known you were behind this. You think you can push me about to get what you want?"

"How am I pushing you about?" Already feeling my blood pressure rocketing.

Dawson stopped all arguments with his loud voice. "Here's the thing. You work for the hospital. I work for the police. You want more of these bodies being dumped on your tables? As much of a bitch you are, I doubt you would want more people to overdose. So you will give us a copy of the autopsy report of the last girl in here. And I really do hope you comply or I'll have to go over your head."

Watching him use his position was actually quite fun. His sudden change from being his jokey self to this serious man at work. Putting the doctor in her place which I enjoyed immensely. The lady pulled a pissed off look but she still walked over to the filing cabinet.

Digging around for this file gave me a chance to nudge Dawson's ribs. "That was impressive."

"Almost as impressive as my abs?"

Groaning as he looked down at me, giving me a wink. "I was impressed. Now, not so much."

"Very short lived but I'll take it."

The doctor came back and I wanted my piece of the pie. Snatching the file as she offered it to the detective. "Thanks for your help." Grinning at her which made her even more pissed off. We left the morgue. The detective getting checked out by Leanne whilst I didn't even get a goodbye.

I sat sideways on my bike and scanned through as Dawson finished off his black coffee. The report pretty standard for an overdose. Knowing it wouldn't hold information about where she was found or anything like that. But what was interesting was the toxicology test.

"It's got the usual aspects of drugs but this thing, I've never heard of it."

He took the file from my hands, "Done a lot of research in drugs? Perhaps you had a wild upbringing."

"The internet is full of information if you're willing to look for it. Makes a great distraction."

Snatching the file right back. "Anyway, you've done your part. You can take my appreciation however small it may be and be on your way."

"You don't want more help?"

"From you? How much more help do you think you could offer?"

The detective grinned as he placed his finger into the file. "This compound of drugs are very unique. I happen to know someone who could point us in the right direction."

"Us?"

"Yeah." He smiled but I simply stared back. "I could give you a speech about how your words changed my perspective. Or that I'm secretly a good guy at heart. But honestly, I just want to spend as much time with you until I get you into bed."

Shaking my head. "That's never going to happen. And honestly, I can handle this by myself."

"What if I can prove to you, that you need me."

"Go on then, thirty seconds and counting."

"I've got a snitch and I also know all the clubs that deal drugs."

"Most of them do."

"I know dealer's names and I might even be a little friendly with a couple."

"Do a lot of drugs do we?"

"Occupationally, I meant."

"I'll be fine. Thanks for breakfast and the file." I folded up the papers and slotted it inside my jacket. Swinging my leg over my bike.

Dawson placing his foot behind my kickstand.

"How about a bet then?"

"I'm not interested."

"Wait until you hear the stakes." Looking up at his grin. Raising my eyebrow in question. "If you win the bet. I will not only leave you to do your investigations without any interruptions from me."

"I could have that any way. All I have to do is ride away."

"True but I will also throw in a thousand quid."

"Really?"

"Sure. I'm that confident."

"I don't have a thousand pounds."

"No, no. If I win, all you have to do is go on a date with me."

"Right." Rolling my eyes. "Even if you win a bet, I'm still not sleeping with you."

"Who said anything about us sleeping together? I simply said a date. That's all. Get your mind out of the gutter." He walked off towards his truck.

Calling over to him. "So what's the bet?"

"Before this case is over, you'll admit that you needed me."

Contemplating it for a moment. Knowing that a thousand pounds would be great for a nice holiday. "Prepare to lose."

"I'll be preparing for our date." Dawson threw me a wink which I couldn't help but smile at. "Follow me. We'll go see my snitch."

"Lead the way you muppet." We left the hospital. Moving through the streets until we pulled up underneath a part of the monorail that ran around the entire city. Climbing off as Dawson got out of his truck.

As he led the way I noticed we were heading towards one of the homeless villages that have popped up around the city. People made these places their homes. Building a little complex of metal huts for them all to live in.

With the cool air they had drums dotted around. Burning wood and anything they could get their hands on to stay warm. Huddled around them in groups. Looks we sent our way as we entered the complex. A little worried about my bike sitting there. Keeping my helmet with me.

Dawson picked up the pace when he spotted someone sitting by the wall munching on something that was clearly found inside a bin. "That's him."

"Let's make this quick."

"Don't like hanging around the homeless?"

"Trying to make me feel bad about that?"

"No. It was simple a question."

"Uh-huh." Giving his shoulder a nudge before we arrived at his snitch.

The man looked up at us with a piece of chicken hanging from his mouth. Dawson crouched down next to him, leaving me standing to watch. "Dawson. Haven't seen you around these parts in a while."

"You promised you were going to stop. You didn't. So I stopped coming." The detective looked around before pulling out his wallet. Offering the man a note which he took quickly and hid inside a pocket.

"What do you want to know?"

"Drugs. Something you're well versed in."

"You're paying me to give me a lecture?"

"We're looking for someone who's selling something new. Making kids overdose. Heard anything along those lines?"

"Yeah, I've heard of some people working on something new. They're calling it V-Dux."

"That's a stupid name." Both of them looked up, making me go quiet as they carried on their conversation.

"Where would we find some?"

"There are a couple of places. But you didn't give me enough money for that information."

I went to chew my lip but it wasn't going to work. Lunging forwards and grabbing a hold of his tatty clothes. Picking him up and slamming him against the wall. Dawson jumped up and grabbed hold of my arm. "What the hell are you doing?"

"My job." Looking this guy in the eyes. Letting my anger shine through in my greens. "Here's the deal. You tell us everything we want to know. And I won't snap your neck right here."

"Okay, alright." His hands tried to pull mine off of him. "I'll tell you, just let me go."

"Information first." Pushing harder. My fist digging into his chest.

"There are two clubs. RDJs and In The Ruff. They're the most popular for the dealers you're looking for."

"Thank you." Letting him drop to the floor.

Turning and walking off. Telling my mind to cool down. I got the information I needed and that was that. Getting back to my bike and swinging my leg over.

The detective came walking over slowly. His eyes holding a cautious nature. "What was that?"

"Your way wasn't working."

"Doesn't give you the right to rough someone up like that."

"It worked."

"I don't care if it worked. That man has helped me close cases. Just because he's homeless doesn't mean you can do that."

Looking up with a smile. "You think I did that just because he's homeless? I wouldn't care if he was a CEO or the mayor. I would have done the same."

"You have anger issues."

"Tell me something I don't know." Watching his reaction to what happened written all over his face. A part of me didn't care. It was how I was, I couldn't change that. But a bigger part of me felt annoyed at myself.

His change in attitude towards me was so drastic all because of my anger. I hated that part of me more than others could. Blowing out a sigh. "Look. I do have anger issues. What I did wasn't right. I apologise."

"It's not me you should be apologising to."

Looking past him to the man still crumpled by the wall. "If I walked over there right now. He would run away screaming." I looked up into Dawson's eyes, seeing the smile he was trying to hide. "Besides, you're the one who seems to be annoyed about it."

"Since when do you care what I think? You've been trying to get rid of me, remember?"

"I remember. But that face you pulled. I've seen it too many times to count."

"Ex-boyfriends?"

"Yes but mostly friends. Don't let it go to your head though."

"We wouldn't want that." He pulled a massive smile. "So is there a safe word I can use when you're getting out of control."

I couldn't stop my laugh. "Only if you want to get punched."

"Got it. Stay out of your way."

"Pretty much." Enjoying the less flirty side of the detective. "I will try my best to keep it in check though. If that helps."

"That will have to do. Especially since we're going dancing tonight."

"Still trying to get me on a date?"

"For the case. But that doesn't mean we can't enjoy ourselves as well."

I rolled my eyes but found myself not getting as annoyed by him. "Which club?"

"We should start with In The Ruff."

"The smaller of the two?"

"Yes. It should have less drug traffic. Keep us far enough away from the gang making this stuff. But close enough to try and turn one of their peddlers."

"That's a good idea. You're not as dumb as you

look."

"Keep giving me sweet compliments like that and I'll think you're sweet on me."

"Keep dreaming." Even his flirty nature seemed more light hearted now. Shaking my head as I slipped my helmet on. "I'll see you there at nine."

"You don't want me to pick you up?"

"With flowers?" Giving him a wink before slipping my visor down. Shouting through the plastic. "Nine, see you there." Then I rode off from the homeless scene. Taking a more leisurely ride since I wasn't on a clock or racing. On my way home I stopped off at one of the many parks in the city.

Taking up a spot near the entrance and making my way in. Grabbing a hot dog from one of the carts situated around the place. I didn't need to eat as much as humans but when I smelt meat I couldn't help myself.

Munching as I kept walking. Seeing the scene in front of me. People walking dogs. Kids messing around by the trees. It was nice to slow down once in a while to enjoy the world.

But then I noticed someone watching me off in the distance where I had entered. Keeping my eye on him as I veered off the path to make my way through some of the oak trees. The branches bare, the floor littered with those gorgeous orange leaves.

Peering over my shoulder every now and again to make sure the guy was still following me. He was so I pushed deeper where the forestry got thicker. Bringing my stalker to where there were few eyes to watch what I had planned for him.

I passed behind one of the larger trees and pressed my back to it. Bringing my hearing up, catching the man's footsteps crunching over the leaves. Breathing in slowly. Pulling on my leeching abilities. Pressing my ability hard which formed a headache behind my eyes. Shutting them to keep my vision from shaking.

Blowing out a shaky breath as I didn't catch anything. This man was human which meant he wasn't about to know what hit him. Waiting for when he came close enough and I spun out of my hiding place.

My hand grabbed his wrist. Pulling him closer then shoving him back against the tree. Straining his elbow against the bark. Bending his arm the wrong way slightly. My other hand coming up around his throat. Cutting off his ability to scream. "Why are you following me?"

"We saw what you did. What you asked him."

"We?" Keeping the pressure on him as I leant out from behind the tree. "There isn't anybody else out there."

His voice starting to wheeze through his lips. "They're waiting by your bike."

"You thought you could handle me all by yourself?"

"I know I can."

"Your current position begs to differ." Keeping my eyes on the park trying to pick out any of his buddies. Distracted so I didn't see his hand move.

Feeling the sudden plunge of silver into my gut.

My hands releasing him as I fell back. The sting of that metal burning the inside of my gut. Blowing out grunts of pain as I pulled it free. That stinging still there like acid dripped into my wound.

The guy stepped forwards over me. "Looks like you're not so tough after all." My eyes focusing on him as he picked up that blade. Kneeling over me. The sting of that silver pressing to my neck. My eyes going wide as I felt it slip against my skin. A dribble of my blood leaking out. Burning against the knife. His face screwing up at the reaction. "What the hell is that?"

"You're not so bright." Digging deep to the beast inside my brain. Feeling the roar of rage coursing through my thoughts. My fingernails grew and I felt my teeth become more lethal. Knocking his hand from my neck and lunging up. Digging my teeth into his neck. Shaking left and right.

Ripping through that flesh. Feeling blood pouring into my mouth. Drinking it down in victory as I pulled back. Ripping a chunk out of his neck. Kicking him away as he started to bleed profusely.

The man tried to gain his balance but he hit the tree and slumped into the dirt. He tried to crawl and shuffle but he was getting weaker by the second. His life bleeding from his wound. I rolled over. Licking my lips. The beast revelling in that metallic taste.

Then I pushed up to my feet. My anger still pulsing right at the surface. The animal inside wasn't done with him yet. I sliced my claws through his neck and yanked as hard as I could. The skin ripped then his spine snapped at the base of his skull.

Breathing out growls as I chucked the head to the floor. Kicking the body over into a bundle of limbs. My eyes snapping up to the park scene. No one heard a thing. No one noticed what had happened.

Grabbing the body by the feet and dragging it deeper into the forest with the head balanced on top. Finding a nice bush then kicking a bunch of leaves over him. No doubt someone would find the body sooner or later. But I would be long gone by then.

Pulling out my phone I switched the front camera on and cleaned up my mouth and chin as best as I could using a ripped off piece of the guys t-shirt. I checked the knife wound in my stomach. Happy to see it had stopped bleeding. If that had been a blade made of silver my injury wouldn't have closed. Luckily it was just coated in it.

I zipped up my jacket to hide my blood stained top. Then I left. Heading back to my bike I noticed there wasn't a single person here that didn't belong. Taking my time to check each person in the area before I was happy the guy had been lying. Climbing on and heading back to the apartment to have a very long shower.

The whole ride I felt the beast had been sated just a touch. Allowing it to settle deep into the back of my mind. Getting home I headed up and straight into the bedroom side of our apartments. Jumping in the shower and standing there for what seemed like an hour just letting the water wash over my body.

I ran my fingers across my belly. By the time

I had gotten home it had sealed up. Leaving a slight indent in my skin that would be gone in a couple of hours. Leaving no clue of what had happened.

Finally washing and getting out I wrapped myself in a towel. Giving my face a look in the mirror. Making sure every drop of blood had been cleaned. Looking at my vest top on the floor. My investigations never brought me this close to blood. Usually it was missing people who had run away or someone thinking their other halves were cheating.

Once inside my room I chucked the top into my washing basket. Raiding my wardrobe I ended up pulling out a few dresses for tonight. Even though it wasn't a date it was still a night out at a club. Working but still. I liked to look my best.

The only problem was I couldn't pick one out. I wanted to look good but judging by how things went today. There could be more action. Putting one of them back since it would be way too tight to run let alone fight in.

Grabbing the other two I made my way across the landing with my hair still wet. Pushing through and seeing Leon, Connor and Ivy sitting at the table by the far wall playing a board game.

Eyes lifted from the game as I walked over. The tattooist cheering with a clap. "Looks like someone is getting ready for a night out."

"It's for work."

Leon laughed as he moved his piece around the board. "You're going to look amazing in that towel either way."

Connor turned in his chair. Seeing his eyes going wide. I gave his ear a little flick. "It's rude to stare, little man." He apologised and turned back around to pay attention to what was happening with the game. I held up my dresses. "I need opinions. I need something I'll look good in but something I can possibly defend myself in."

"That kind of investigation?"

Nodding to Ivy. "It seems like it could be."

"You can take care of yourself. I feel sorry for the other people."

My memory flashing to what I did to that guy in the park. "Me too." Wiggling the dresses. "What do you think?"

Leon pointed with a wad of fake money at the one in my left hand. "That's the one you wore for new years a couple of years ago, right?"

"So this one?"

"God no. Your arse looked flumpy in it."

My jaw dropped. "Flumpy? And you didn't think I needed to know that at the time?" Dropping my left arm. "What about this one? Does it make me look like a hippo?"

"I was just being honest."

"Be less honest when a girl asks for your opinion."

Ivy giggled as she leant over to him. "Why the hell are you poking the bear? Are you crazy?"

I was tempted to throw a coat hanger at her. "I heard that."

"I know." She gave me a big grin. "Forget him,

you looked great in that black dress."

"So you think I should wear it?" My room mate paused, eyes dropping to the board game. "You know what, don't even say anything. I'll wear the red dress tonight."

Turning just as Connor spoke up with his sweet voice. "I thought you looked great."

Looking over my shoulder. "Now that is how a gentleman gives his opinion. Don't grow up to be like your father." Giving him a wink before heading back to my bedroom. Getting into the red dress which fit a little better since the last time I wore it.

Turning left and right in the mirror. Checking my behind a little more than usual thanks to Leon's comment. Using my curling iron on my hair for the next half hour before it was all done. Pulling back most of it into a messy ponytail. The rest hanging down either side of my face just the way I liked it.

I stood in front of the mirror and checked myself out. The flowing bottom half of the dress would allow me to kick out my legs if need be. The top clung perfect to my toned figure. One of the pros of having werewolf genes.

Matching a pair of red flats with it before heading back across. Getting wolf whistles and cheers from my mates. Grabbing a glass of water before grabbing all my bits and bobs into a small purse that I borrowed from Ivy.

Once my booked taxi arrived I headed out. Getting dropped off just down the road from the nightclub. Seeing the large sign lit up in purple neons.

Seeing how people were dressed a little more reserved than myself. Seeing a seventies theme amongst the queue. Cursing under my breath.

Moving along the path towards the back of the queue. Then spotting Dawson waiting up by the entrance. Chatting to the bouncer like they were best friends. When he spotted me I could see the wide eyed look I got thanks to my red dress. Moving past the queue as he waved me over.

I nodded to the rest of the people waiting. "Clearly there's a theme tonight." My eyes running over the black jeans and black shirt he wore. Liking how the top clung to his arms. The material looking like it could rip if he tensed too much.

"Hey, my eyes are up here." Punching him in the ribs which made him giggle. "Francis here is going to let us in."

"Oh really? And how have you managed that?"

"By using my charm." The detective grinned wide then pressed his hand to the small of my back. Shifting a little but it was a simple touch. If his grip moved lower then he'd have a broken arm to speak of.

Entering the tall entrance. Moving past the coat checker and up some more steps. Into the massive dance floor that dominated the area. The seventies theme affecting the music as well as the decorations.

Laughing as I spot some of the patrons have missed the mark by a decade or two. Turning to Dawson who was standing there shaking his hips to the music. Unable to stop the smile that curled my lips. "You're an idiot, you know that, right?"

"What!" He leant in after shouting.

"Where do you want to start?"

"How about a drink?"

Pulling back to look into his eyes. Then rolling mine. "Fine but nothing too extreme."

"One blowjob coming right up."

"Oh, see a guy you like." Laughing as he playfully nudged me on his way up to the bar. I moved myself to the very edge of the dance floor. Looking over my shoulders to check the booths by the walls first.

Seeing people having a good time. Some of them maybe having a little more fun than they should in public. But nothing to do with drugs. Turning my attention back to the dancers. The crowd made it hard to spot anything going on.

With such a big dance floor I decided to slip in between the moving bodies. Starting to shake my hips to the music. My hands grabbing hold of people as I moved through. Getting close to the centre where it was just heat and sweat.

Finding myself getting squashed up against a tall gentleman. Looking up he flashed a huge grin like he had trapped a spider in his web. I shook my head and turned to walk away but he grabbed my hand.

Getting spun back in surprise. Two arms coming around my waist. Feeling his fingers tapping at the top of my arse. I gritted my teeth, not wanting to make a scene. Grabbing his wrists and going to pull them from me but they wouldn't budge.

Putting a little more effort but he still didn't

let go. Looking up a little worried. Letting down my leecher guard and allowing the air around me to slip up my nose. His closeness made his scent waft up my nostrils. Getting that ashy smell and realising that he was a vampire.

I wasn't defenceless but being this close to something so dangerous wasn't my idea of fun. Tiptoeing up and leaning into his ear. "I'm not prey. Let go and we won't have a problem."

"You haven't even given me a try. Just one dance." Leaning back and looking up into his eyes. "You know you want to."

Staring as his pupils seem to pulse with power. Feeling myself being swayed but then my control came snapping back. Happy that it was one of those strengths of being part leecher. Shaking my head slowly as I reached back and grabbed his finger.

Giving it a sudden snap which made him grunt in pain, covered up by the music. "Compelling doesn't work on me. So back off or I'll snap something that's a little more precious to you." My other hand coming forward and grabbing his crotch harshly. Digging fingers into that package. The vampire bent forwards to try and pull it away but my grip was too tight. Leaning into his ear. "Let go of me."

A nod in confirmation before his arms slipped from my waist. Watching as he snapped his finger back into place to heal. Flashing a soft smile before turning and leaving. As I moved I decided to leave my leeching ability open. Not pushing it. Letting the air pass across my nose as I moved. By the time I exited the dance floor my brain felt like it was going to explode.

It wasn't just groups of humans here. The place was filled with all kinds of supernaturals. Unfortunately it was mostly vampires. Happy that they weren't outnumbering the humans but it had me wondering why such a high number in one club.

Pressing my back to the wall and watching until Dawson came back. Grabbing the drink, not even asking what it was before taking big gulps. Needing it after that encounter with the vampire. The ashy smell still lingering in the air around me as a reminder. "What took you so long?"

"When was the last time you went clubbing? If you don't have cleavage, you don't get served."

"Should have got your pecks out then." Blowing out a sigh as the alcohol hit my stomach. Hoping it would shift those nerves quickly. "Spot anything drug related?"

"The bartender was very friendly with information. Told me I'm looking for a little dude wearing too much jewellery. Usually hanging out by the staff door upstairs."

Clinging my drink to his. "Let's go see what he has to say."

"Lead the way, gorgeous."

"You first, I don't need you checking out my arse the whole time."

"Then why wear such a dress?" Dawson's comment was joined by a huge smile. Something about it was so soft and friendly. Like this was his natural default setting and I shouldn't take it to heart.

Letting him go first as we found the stairs to climb up to the next level. Finding myself checking out his arse in his tight jeans. Enjoying the view for a moment. Coming up to the top, the middle section missing and guarded by rails. Allowing my eyes to fall down to the dance floor beneath. Seeing the vampire in the middle with his new victim. Hoping it was just a flirty thing and he wasn't about to take her off and feed on her in an alley.

Shaking that thought from my head. Knowing it happens in this city from time to time and I had a different job to do right now. Heading down one side where the staff door sat. Seeing a small group of people sitting in the corner booth.

Two of them on the ends were massive men wearing leather jackets and sunglasses. They were his security. Leaning close to Dawson as we walked. "I think they've seen too many movies, dressing like that."

"I like it. Gives off that douchebag vibe. If this goes sideways do you want left or right?"

My eyes dancing between the two. "Might as well go left. I like his long hair." Downing the rest of my drink and placing it at an empty table as we passed by.

My eyes seeing the three ladies sitting around the little dude we were here to speak to. As we drew close I saw the gold rings on every finger. Thick chains hanging around his neck. Adorning himself with all that jewellery to seem more important.

I prepared to talk when I noticed the cushion he was sitting on to make him the same height as everyone else. A laugh bursting from my lips which made the guards stand with intimidation. Dawson quickly curled an arm around my waist, making it seem like I was unstable. Then he spoke with a lighter tone. Pulling a big smile like he was off his rocker with drink. "You'll have to forgive my friend here. She seemed to have taken our stash before I could grab a sniff."

The guards turned to the little man who waved them away. Both of them walking off but not venturing far. The man nodded and I was plopped down on the left end. Dawson taking position opposite.

I allowed my glassy-eyed look move over the two ladies beside me. They weren't dressed for the theme of the club either. Making it seem like they came with our drug dealer. Looking back over to him as he started the conversation. "What has she been partying with?"

"Just a little nose dust. She always gets super horny when she's high." Rolling my eyes and giving his shin a quick kick whilst keeping up my act. "I was hoping for something a little stronger though. You could say I've got a little resistance built up."

"I've got something that's pretty new. Still in the early stages so any hiccups are laid at your feet. You understand?"

"Completely."

"Got the cash?" The man leant forwards with

his elbows on the table. To my surprise the detective pulled out a nice wad of notes and dropped it on the table. Trying to count it with my eyes but it was snatched up quickly. "This should do for a couple of pops. Through here." The man shuffled which made the women move. Dawson quickly shifted to me and pulled me up to join them.

Seeing this man standing up and barely reaching to the rim of the table we were sat at. Following him with shuffling feet as he moved through the staff door. The little space getting more crowded as the two guards followed us in.

What used to be a storage cupboard for god knows what had been changed into a drug selling room. A safe at the end was opened and that's where the money was deposited. Then a small box was opened up on one of the shelves.

Seeing that there were many others. Varying in size. This one was the smallest, containing little packets. One of which was passed to the detective. The little man looked up at us both. "Of course, we expect you to take one of those pills now. To prove to us you're not cops."

My heart starting to pound. Knowing that we couldn't take that drug. It was killing people and I had plenty of life left to live. I had no idea if my werewolf side would keep me alive but Dawson didn't have that. My grip holding onto his wrist. "But honey, you promised we would do some when we got home. You know how I get." Leaning in and kissing his neck. "I'm not wearing any knickers." Licking my lips slowly.

Dawson's eyes drifted down my body like I was actually telling the truth. Then he smiled when our eyes met again. "Don't worry, I'll save the rest for when we get home. Bottoms up." My heart jumped into my throat as he tipped the bag. Then chucked one of those pills to the back of his throat. Swallowing it down before I could even catch my breath.

My mind raced through my thoughts. Knowing I needed to get him to throw that back up but as soon as I act the facade would be over. Turning with my hand on Dawson's shoulder.

Looking up at the guards. "Men, they really need to learn to share." Blowing out a sigh and then shooting my foot up into the groin of one. The werewolf strength making him drop with a red face. Seeing his veins bulging in his neck as the pain made him pass out.

The other rushed forwards but I grabbed his wrist. Spinning under it then bringing it down on my shoulder making it snap at the wrong angle. Grabbing his fingers and spinning again. Making that arm twist sharply. Those fingers snapping with ease.

Then I shoved the ball of my palm into his face. The first hit breaking his nose, the second knocking him out cold. Spinning to see the little man with his hands up in defence. About to move forwards to deal with him when Dawson dropped suddenly.

I managed to move fast enough to catch him and lower him down on my lap. Giving his cheek a quick slap. Watching his eyes roll back until I could see only white in them. Giving him a harder slap but it was no good. He was fitting and shaking like I had experienced in my ghost dream.

Looking up at the dealer. "Do something."

"What do you want me to? He took it on his own. He knew the risks."

"That excuse won't sit with me." Going to move from under the detective when he suddenly came back to life. Gasping as he sat up. Breathing in and out heavily. "Dawson. Are you okay?"

"Are you kidding? I've never felt anything like this before." He stood and I followed. Grabbing his arm. "I don't even understand how this is possible."

"What do you mean?" Spinning him around. Eyes going wide as I saw his face. My gut twisting with fear as I saw those teeth. Two fangs hanging down over his bottom lip. "You're a vampire?!"

CHAPTER 4

"What?" He laughed. The drugs making his eyes dance around.

"You're a vampire."

"Okay. How is that a problem? You're not human either."

"I…." Blinking. Looking at him with no words to speak. My two sides cancelled each other out. The only thing I should register in his senses was human.

"You gotta try this drug, Megan. It's unbelievable. I've never been able to see sounds before." His eyes dropped like something was slipping from his lips.

I shook my head and pushed him to the side. Grabbing the drug dealer by his shirt. "What is that stuff?"

"It's just a new drug." Seeing how he was looking at the vampire. Wide eyes, his voice shaking with fear. "What the hell is going on here?"

"You've never seen someone like him?"

"Of course not. He can't be real."

Grunting as I spun us around to gain his attention. "Where do you get this stuff from?"

"Another dealer gave me some to spread out for

him."

"And what's his name?" The man tried to look over his shoulder but I slapped his cheek sharply. "Focus. The dealer's name?"

"Vincent. I met him at RDJs the other night. He didn't mention anything about this affect."

"It's not a side-effect, you moron." Looking up as Dawson stared at his own hands in wonder. "Is there anything else you can tell me about it?"

"No. I just sell it. I don't know anything else."

"That will have to do then." My grip tightened before swinging his head into the shelving. Blood trickling down as he flopped to the floor. Blowing out a breath as I looked at the detective. Those fangs still poking out of his gums.

My anger wanted me to walk over and smash those teeth from his mouth. Instead I turned and gripped hold of the safe door. Fingers ripping that metal dial and allowing me to reach in. The lock not standing a chance as I pulled it free.

Grabbing the wad of cash that had recently been exchanged and handing it back to Dawson. "You and me are done."

"Why?"

Ignoring him and turning back for another handful of cash. Slipping it into my purse before shoving past the vampire and out the door. Shouting over my shoulder. "Don't want to see you ever again."

He came out with me followed by screams from those three girls. Jumping around to witness him leaning over the table and glamouring them to be quiet. Telling them to forget what they saw. The three of them settling and sitting there, having a normal conversation.

Next time I saw his face those fangs had slipped back out of sight. Stomping off but he grabbed my wrist. Turning me around. "Explain."

"I don't need to explain anything." Pressing my hand to his chest and shoving him back.

But with a blur he was already there blocking my way when I turned. "I'm not getting out of your way without an explanation. It's really fucking rude to just get up and leave someone when you're working together."

"You don't have to worry about that any more. Get out of my way." Going to move past him but he refused to shift. "Out of my way before I do something about it."

"The only thing you have to do is explain."

"You're a vampire. A scum sucking shadow of a person. You give in to your lust and thirst." My words pushing me harder. Jabbing my fingers against his chest, making him step back. "You honestly expect me to trust you now I'm know the truth?"

"It's not my fault you didn't figure it out. I knew you were different pretty early on. Werewolf I'm guessing."

"I'm not in the mood for any wet dog smell jokes, Dawson."

"You should lighten up." The smile he pulled just made me even angrier.

"I should snap your neck and rip your heart out

of your chest."

"That's a touch violent." That silly smile still written across his face.

Blowing out a sigh, chewing on my cheek. My teeth digging in too hard and that sharp pain threw me into action. Swinging my fist into his jaw. Sending him tumbling into the railing. Denting the metal with his body. "We're done. End of."

Pushing my feet across the carpet. Down the stairs and out into the open air. Not bothering with a taxi. I simply walked and walked. My feet killing me by the time I arrived back at the apartment.

The cool air filling my lungs helped with my rage but it hadn't completely gone away. Thinking about Dawson. Knowing I didn't want anything to do with him any more. Which meant going at this case alone with little to no information.

I had the club, RDJs, to hit another night but if that came up with nothing there wasn't much else I could do. My heels smacked against the steps as I moved up the floors. Getting to my door I didn't have enough energy to talk to my friends.

Opening the door to the living apartment and heading straight into the bathroom. Washing my face with cold water and drying it off. Slinking out of my dress and nicking Ivy's bathrobe from the back of the door.

Standing in front of the mirror I stared into my eyes. An idea popped into my mind but it was something I hadn't done on purpose. I had always stayed away from my ghostly abilities. Never having explored them out of fear of what could happen.

However, I needed more information and I felt more comfortable trying this than spending another day with that detective. So I slowed my breathing. Allowing my heart rate to drop. Closing my eyes and thinking about the young woman. Picturing her face in my mind.

It wasn't long before my fingers started to turn numb. The sink I leant against freezing against my palms. Opening my eyes to see the mirror getting layered with ice. My face vanishing behind that blue tint.

My breath visible. The air in the small room surrounding me in cold. I lifted my hand and brushed it across the mirror. The ice shifting and revealing that girl. Her vacant eyes staring into mine. My lips quivered as I spoke. "I need more information."

"I want to show you something."

"No." Shaking my head. "I don't want to see your death again. Information. I need something else to go on otherwise I can't help your mother."

"Let me show you." The girl reached forward and I gasped as her arm came through the mirror. Fingers wrapped around me. Her touch colder than the air. Seeing her skin pale and dead. I struggled to pull my wrist free. Backing away and pulling. The bathroom shifting on the tilt as something gave way and I fell back. Hitting my head had me seeing stars. Looking up, my mouth gaped in horror as the young lady that had overdosed was standing right there in my bathroom.

Not a reflection or a memory. She was right there looking at me with glassy eyes. Like her dead body had been hung there to scare me. I stood slowly. Looking at her. "Unbelievable." Looking at the mirror which showed my own face this time.

"Why did this have to happen to me?" Her voice coming out weak like a whisper.

"What do you mean?"

"Why me? I was dancing, having a great time. And this guy came up to me. I had bad breath so I asked my friend for a mint. The guy offered me one. Told me it would taste amazing. Something about his eyes had me trusting him."

A vampire. She was glamoured to take it. "You did nothing wrong?"

"Then why am I dead?"

"Wrong place, wrong time."

"What?" Tears started falling down her cheeks making her look even more horrifying as they froze on her skin. "But I wasn't even drinking. I was the designated driver. I was going to have lunch with my mum the next day. I was..." Her voice lost to the sobbing. The bathroom filled with loud cries.

I moved forwards and cuddled her to my chest despite still being freaked out by her presence. Stroking my fingers through her clumpy hair. "I'm sorry this happened to you. I can't offer an explanation. But I can promise to you and your mum, that I'll find the guy responsible."

Her face tilted back, cheeks stained with ice. "Trevor. The man who gave me the mint."

"Can you picture his face?"

She closed her eyes for a moment. "Yes."

"Show me. Show me his face." My eyes meeting hers when she opened them. Thinking about that memory of hers. Opening myself to it. My hand finding hers and gripping it tight. That touch of skin seeming to link us together for a flash.

Getting that image from her memories. The vampire smiling down at her. His face etched into my mind so I let go of her. Breathing in and out. The effort taking it's toll on my body.

The young lady sobbing again. Moving towards her when the door opened suddenly. Air kicking all around me and that victim vanished in a blink of an eye. Ivy stood there looking at me with a blank expression. "Megan."

"Yeah?" Still trying to regain my breath.

"Did I just see something?"

"Depends." Looking back at her, not able to believe what I had just done myself.

"Was there a girl right there? And then she vanished." Her eyes moving around the tiled walls at the ice. "Did I just see a ghost?"

"You did."

"I don't understand how that's possible." Then her eyes landed on me. "Is that my robe?"

Looking down, cracking a smile. "You got over seeing a ghost pretty quick."

"Well." Ivy let her lips curl into a smile. "I thought you could only see their deaths."

Walking out of the bathroom and into the

kitchen, my room mate following me closely. "Me to. But I hit a snag with the case. I needed more information from her so I figured I would give it a try. Communicating with her. But then she came out the mirror."

"Sounds like a horror film."

"It felt like one at first. But then she started crying about how she died. Telling me she wasn't even drinking that night. I'm sure she was glamoured by a vampire to take the drug."

"Really? That's a horrible thought."

"I know. She showed me what he looks like. If I can find him I can make him pay for what he did. I promised her."

"Understandable but will this detective you're working with be okay with that?"

Feeling a pulse of anger at the mention of him. "I'm not working with him any more." Grabbing a glass of water and taking a couple of gulps.

"What happened?"

"Turns out he's a vampire."

"Oh. But..." Flicking my eyes to hers, making her pause. Then she said it any way. "Don't you think you can look past one vampire?"

"Of course not. Vampires are evil."

"You know that's not true."

"I know what it feels like to see one lose control. To see them hurt someone you love. Make you think they're going to be taken from you."

"I know, I know. We all have our baggage."

"Yeah." Finishing off my glass. "I've only got

one more lead. I might not be able to finish this case and give Mrs. Clark the closure she needs."

"Megan."

"I don't want to hear it. This is how it's going to be."

"Alright. I won't push it."

"Thank you." Avoiding eye contact with her. "It's Wednesday tomorrow, I'm off to see my father."

"Right. Get some sleep. Conjuring a ghost like that must take its toll on your body."

"It certainly feels like it." Downing another glass of water before I headed to bed. Sleeping in my underwear and happy that the night didn't bring any nightmares after opening myself up to that ghost.

Waking up I grabbed a quick shower and headed out on my bike in my jeans and leather jacket. Pulling up outside Ling Medical Home. Parking up amongst the other vehicles for visiting hours. Moving through the entrance and getting greeted by one of the loveliest nurses I've ever met. "Good morning, Megan." She ticked her clipboard before standing up and stepping in beside me. "You know you don't have to obey the visiting hours any more."

"I know. But it's routine and I don't want to change anything for him."

"I've told you countless times. Your father is doing better and better each day. He hasn't relapsed in just under a year now. Truly. I know I shouldn't say this but I'm hopeful that his mind has fully recovered."

"Thank you." Giving a soft smile but I knew I

couldn't let myself be hopeful. I've thought the worse was behind my father countless times already. It broke my heart more and more each time it wasn't true. So now I never let myself hope.

We moved through the large canteen area where visiting hours took place. Looking around at everyone. Seeing their loved ones. Some of them over the moon with joy. Others barely registered them sitting opposite. It reminded me of my first few visits here. I was in my teens and seeing my father so vacant was an image that always haunted me.

The nurse led me out through the patio doors and down into the gardens that stretched on for ages. It was looked after by a nice group of people. Some of them were ex-patients here and that included my father.

Seeing him raking up some leaves in a thick dark green jacket. Wearing white trousers just like the others. His thick hair was pulled into a ponytail with a hat sitting atop. When he saw me his face lit up. The rake was placed on top of his wheel barrel and I was pulled into a tight hug. "Is it Wednesday already? Seems like I saw you a couple of days ago."

Pulling back and looking into his eyes. Checking to make sure the sparkle was still there. Grinning, "Nope. A whole week."

"It's great to see you, little one. Come and sit down."

The nurse touched my shoulder. "I'll bring out a coffee for you."

"Thank you very much." Turning back to my

father as he drank some water from his bottle. "So how has the week been?"

"Great apart from the weather. We've had to dig up the last of the flowers that were clinging on for life." He pointed to the flower bed in front of us. "They've given me my own area now. This is mine, all of it." Seeing the joy in his smile. "I planted these on the weekend. They'll snuggle through winter and bloom as it gets hotter."

Looking over the flower bed as he pointed and spoke. "That's really good, Dad." Catching his eyes as they looked off into the distance. My stomach twisting a little as he stared at nothing. Swallowing and touching my hand to his wrist. "Dad?"

He blinked and was right there with me again. "Sorry. I just thought….doesn't matter. So what have you been up to?"

"Doing cases here and there."

"I'm really happy you've stuck with it. The police wouldn't have been a good fit for you." His memory wasn't the best. Even though I had left the academy years ago. For him it seemed to be a recent event.

"And why do you think that?"

He pulled a big grin. "Because the first time your superior shouts at you. You would knock him out in one punch."

Laughing with my father. "That's definitely true." Laughing again as the nurse came back with my coffee. Sipping and enjoying the hot liquid. "I've hit a little snag with my current case though."

"Fill me in." Off came his thick gloves. He placed them on his lap then wrapped a hand around one of mine.

"A mother came to me. Her daughter died of an overdose. She wanted me to pick up some information, find out who's responsible. Maybe give the police a kick up the arse."

"They often need it."

"Very true." Leaning against his shoulder as he wrapped an arm around me. "I've been working with a detective. Things were going good. I was actually getting used to him when I found something out that I didn't like. I can't trust him but without him I don't think I can finish the case."

"I don't even have to ask what the problem with him is, do I?"

Looking down as I sipped my coffee. "Probably not."

"The V word?" Nodding in response. Not wanting to look at him because I knew he would be pulling that disapproving expression. "Megan." My hand being lightly tugged. "You can't let the past control your future."

"I'm not letting it control me."

"If this detective was human. Would you gladly take his help?"

"Obviously."

"Then your prejudice against a whole species for what one of them did is controlling you. It's stopping you from possibly closing this case and helping this woman." Forgetting how strong willed my father could be. "Has this detective given you any reason not to trust him?"

"You know far more than me that trust has to be earned. It isn't handed out."

"I agree with you completely. But you can't take away his chance to earn it. Has he done anything that makes you think you could trust him?"

I thought back. "He helped me with the case but that's his job." Remembering what he was like at the club. How he took control. "Okay, he was quite helpful. Without him I wouldn't have gotten the autopsy report. Or found the clubs that were dealing in this new drug."

"Sounds like he's been a huge help. And did he ever tell you he wasn't a vampire?"

"No. He assumed I figured it out since he suspected I wasn't human."

"Then it sounds like he's pretty good at his job and was being a good partner."

"Yeah." Chewing my lip. Finally looking up into his eyes. Blowing out a sigh. "Maybe I could give him another chance. He did manage to look past my anger issues."

"He didn't run away at the first sign of them?"

"No."

"Sounds like a good friend. If he didn't judge you, maybe you shouldn't condemn him so easily."

"Alright, alright. I hear you, okay. I'll give him another chance."

Feeling his fingers gripping my shoulder tighter as he hugged me. "Now that we've sorted one problem. Let's do another."

Blowing out a breath and shifting from him. "I know what you're going to ask and the answer is no."

"You need to speak with your mother. You can't stay mad at her for something that she didn't do on purpose."

"I've managed to do it for the last bunch of years. I can keep it going."

"You'd be better off if you just spoke with her."

"No. We go through this every single time I come here. Apart from my birthday last year."

"You do understand why I keep asking, right?"

"Honestly, no. I don't. I've made myself very clear."

"Megan." My father removed his hat and pushed his fingers through his hair. Seeing the bald patch where the thick scar ran across the side of his head. A memory hitting hard of him laying in a hospital bed.

Tubes coming out of his arms and mouth. Machines keeping him going. He was beaten so hard by his wolf pack that he couldn't recover by himself. The brain damage he had received was why he had been transferred here in the first place.

And if that wasn't bad enough. His beast had been beaten into submission. Losing his power as the alpha of his pack. The physical punishment and now he was like me. He could no longer shift into his wolf form. The full moon no longer held sway over him.

Apart from his strength he was practically human. Even that healing ability he possessed was constantly working to keep his mind from snapping again. Slowly building up his mental health.

His deep voice coming again, "What happens if tomorrow you don't have the option to see her?"

"Then it'll be exactly the same as it is right now."

"No. It won't. Right now you have a way back." His hand coming to rest on my knee. "You can still see her. But if she was gone or heaven forbid, you are. Then there will never be a way of turning it around. The decision will no longer be there."

"Dad." Seeing the plead in his eyes. Holding my words as I looked into those pools of colour. Giving him a little smile and nodding. "I'll think about it and that's the best I can offer."

"That's good enough for me." My father stood up quickly and tugged me to my feet. His smile huge as he jogged over to his flower bed. "First I'm going to tell you each one of my little flowers." Laughing as he acted like a little boy on Christmas morning. "Then we can walk around and I can show you where I've helped and what the others have been up to."

This wouldn't be the first time he's shown me around but I wasn't about to say no to a tour with him. His joy was infectious when he was talking about the gardens. "Please do. It's so good to see you so…."

He turned and looked into my eyes. Seeing the sadness making his eyes glisten. "I'm really sorry for not being your father since….you know."

"You don't have to apologise."

"But I want to. Because I missed out on a chunk

of your life. Memories that should have been made were lost. Even ones the ones I have are still a little murky."

"Dad." Moving closer and cupping his hands in mine. "You don't have to apologise. I don't blame you."

"You can't blame her either." Biting my lip. "It was my decision that threw me on this path. Not hers."

"Dad." Blowing out a sigh.

"No, Megan." Seeing a tear drop down his cheek. "I mean it. Each night I get some shards of memory back. The last couple of nights it's been one particular moment." Another tear dropping. Going to wipe them clear but he backed away. My stomach twisting. "I was so horrible to your mother. Looking back on it, what happened, I can't believe it was me."

"Dad."

"Don't. Don't you dare forgive me so easily. Not when you've given your mother such a hard time. There were two of us when we broke up. Two of us when we fought. Her on one side. Me on the other. We both felt the pain."

"But she moved on."

"And why shouldn't she have. She deserved to be happy. They allowed me to be part of your life after everything I did. All the bad choices I made."

I quickly moved to him and cupped his cheeks. "You're my father. End of, okay."

"And she's your mother."

My thumbs rubbing those tears from his cheeks. Giving him a soft smile and a nod. Taking a deep breath. "Show me your flowers. Please."

For a moment he stared blankly. Seeing the pain in his eyes. My father's lips curling slowly as he came back to me. A nod and a quick sniff. "Okay, sweetheart." Then he was back to that giddy boy. Pointing and telling me all about flowers. Showing off his newly found database of gardening.

It was a great morning with him. Grabbing a piece of cake at the end of it all before saying my goodbyes. Telling him I would see him next week and he can show me everything all over again.

My father went back to his gardening as I left. Thinking about what he had talked about. How it was his decisions that pushed him into the life he had. Like he held no ill will towards my mother like I did.

Walking through the canteen I saw that visiting hours had been over for a while. Getting on my bike and heading back into the depths of the city. Happier with my life after spending some time with my father. The non-breakable decision not to see Dawson again was on much weaker ground.

Changing my journey from my apartment to his. Pulling up outside that building. Heading up the stairs, practising my apology and my speech on how I may have over-reacted. But I was stopped when I noticed his door was slightly ajar.

Breathing in and out slowly. Sorting through the smells coming from that small crack. Getting mostly him. Other scents drifted off higher up the stairway. Pressing myself to the wall and sticking my nose in for another sniff.

Not bothering with the headache of using my leeching ability. Focusing on what my werewolf sense of smell got. Getting a lot from Dawson. Some perfume still lingered from his previous visitor when we first met but that was it.

Then I caught a whiff of something that had my hair stand on end. Riding the air was a thick bloody smell. So strong it made my nose wrinkle. Blowing out a breath, knowing there was no one else in here I pressed through the doorway. Closing it softly behind me. My eyes taking in the mess. Paintings had been torn and ripped to pieces. Laying on the floor in tatters.

Pressing forward I saw contents of drawers thrown about the place. His sofa turned over. All the kitchen cupboards were open. Food and cutlery tossed everywhere. Looking like someone had gone on a rage filled rampage through here.

My gut twisted. Thinking of Dawson doing this had me second guessing my decision change. Then I started worrying about him being in danger. Pushing further through the apartment. Finding a large bedroom. Sheets thrown on the floor. Drawers of an old looking desk hanging open.

Papers and files covering the carpet and wood. Letting my nose follow the bloody scent. The door next to his bedroom led to the bathroom. Gasping as I entered and found blood splattered over the bath. Streams of it clinging to the porcelain. Turning and finding the sink full of the stuff. Looking clumpy and gooey.

Worry hitting my gut like a sledgehammer. Digging out my phone and giving the detective a call. Ringing and ringing but no one pick up. Making me worry even more. So I rang his precinct. Asking for Dawson but when the officer came back to the phone he told me the detective hadn't been in for a few days.

Looking at all that blood covering the bathroom walls. Knowing I couldn't do anything more but I couldn't stop thinking about him. Worried that he was hurt. Even more worried that he was dead. Maybe he was out on the case, following a lead.

My mind putting him somewhere safe where he wasn't being harmed. But then, someone had attacked me at the park. Only I had no proof. He was carrying a knife covered in silver. Only he had no clue what I was. This case was starting to become bigger than I first thought.

CHAPTER 5

I was still in a panic when I got back to my apartment. Having given him another ring on my way up the stairs. Still no reply so by the time I got inside and found Ivy in her studio I was panicking bad. "Something has happened." Seeing the shocked look on her client's face as I came barging through the door.

"Whoa. What's happened?" She put down her tattoo gun and came over to me. Snapping off her black latex gloves. "What's going on?" Her eyes moving over my body like I was the one who got hurt.

"Dawson. I went to his place. The bathroom was covered in blood. There was so much of it."

"Dawson, the detective?"

"Detective?" The client started to sit up in the chair. Looking worried at the mention of law enforcement. "Look, I don't want to get into trouble."

Ivy gently placed a hand to his shoulder. "You won't. No detective will be coming here. You're safe."

Giving her a confused look as she ushered me into the hallway. "What's his deal?"

"He's a witch. Came for one of my special tattoos."

"Oh. Well he has nothing to worry about.

Dawson wouldn't care even if he was here to witness it."

"So why the sudden change with this vampire?"

"My father but that's not important right now. I can't find him. He hasn't been at the precinct. He won't pick up his phone and there was so much blood."

"You're jumping to the conclusion that it's his blood. Maybe he just had a feeding frenzy?"

"Right. Yeah, of course. He was just hungry after getting high on that drug." Rubbing my hand over my face as I laughed. "You're right, jumping to conclusions." If he was that hungry it might explain the state of his apartment as well. Vampires aren't all that reasonable when they're hungry and who knows what that drug did to his system.

"Come and have a seat. I need to finish off this guy's tattoo."

"What's up with him?"

"An inoperable tumour. My little concoction should give him a few more years of life to enjoy."

"Damn. I feel bad for barging in now."

"Come on, check it out. You'll like this one." Shaking my head as we went back inside the little room. My eyes picking out the bright purple colour of the flower head on his left shoulder. Vines coming back over and down his back. "See, what did I tell you?"

"You've certainly got talent I'll give you that."

The client rested his head back on the chair as the buzzing of the gun filled the space. I found my heart still beating fast so I took some deep breaths as

I walked around the chair. Looking at the art on the walls that she drew. Pictures of tattoos.

Then I came to the small shelf that sat above the much bigger one holding all her colours. These were her little concoctions. Tattoo potions she liked to call them. Seeing the one sitting on her table on wheels by her side for healing.

Some of the others I had no clue what they did. She wasn't too open about it to keep me safe if there was an investigation. My eyes landed on a little vial. The liquid giving off a blue glow. Reading the label and my eyes widened. Grabbing it off the shelf and giving it a closer look. "Ivy, what do you use this for?"

She peered over her shoulder. "That's for vampires."

"How so?" Asking the question but my eyes were running over the small amount of ingredients. One of them standing out from the rest.

"It limits their healing. Means the ink actually stays in their skin otherwise there wouldn't be any point in them getting a tattoo."

"And this ingredient." Using my finger to point since it was too hard for me to pronounce.

"That's the main ingredient. That's the one that affects the vampire."

Reading the name of it over and over. Remembering that strange word I had seen in the autopsy report. "And what if this was given to a human?"

"Small amounts of it are found in medicines these days so it wouldn't do much. A large amount however would cause the immune system to shut down."

"Mix that with drugs?"

"The body wouldn't be able to regulate and an overdoes would be inevitable." Seeing her expression suddenly catching on to what I was thinking. "No way. They're using that in a new drug?"

"Idiots don't know what they're doing with this stuff."

"I'll never truly trust humans. Not even Leon. Man cheats at board games like his life depends on it."

Turning around as she carried on with the tattoo. Seeing the ink being punctured into this person's skin. Remembering the pattern covering Dawson's chest and back. The card I saw on the fridge that first day.

The link forming in my head. "He might have figured this out already."

"What?"

"I might know where he is. Thank you." Giving her a peck on the cheek before running out of the apartment. Taking the stairs two at a time whilst fiddling with my phone. Using the internet to locate that tattoo shop.

My bike helping me cut through traffic and getting there within ten minutes. Parking up out the front. The massive sign above the door like a treasure map. Dotted lines leading to the X in the word extreme.

The door let off a little ping as I entered. Leather sofas to my right were empty. A hatch sat in the wall with frosted glass. Not hearing any buzzing coming from behind. I tapped the little bell that sat on the side to gain someone's attention.

A blurry figure came forward to slide that window open. A man stood there with a band t-shirt. Long hair pulled back into a neat ponytail. His stubble covered chin matched his rough voice. Every inch of exposed skin was covered in tattoos. "Can I help you?"

"Yeah. I was wondering if my friend had popped in. He's a detective, name is Dawson."

"We don't know a guy by that name."

His reply sounded a little shifty. "His chest and back are covered in a dragon tattoo. I think he may have popped in here because of a case. Is it possible he came around to ask some questions?"

"Like I just said, we don't know anyone by that name. We're busy, please leave." The window was shut quickly and he moved off out of sight. I took a deep breath. Concentrating on my leecher smell.

Fingers pressing to my forehead as that ache formed. Sweat trickling down my temple as I reached out within the building. One big blip hit my radar. Positioned by the back wall. I moved closer to the window, cracking it open and using my werewolf nose.

The smell of blood was the thickest scent. Then I caught Dawson's. It was unmistakable. They had him back there and the smell of blood was never a good sign. Hitting the bell on the shelf once again.

The man took longer to answer and he did with an annoyed expression. The window was slid aside and he opened his mouth to talk but I grabbed him by his hair and slammed that rough face into the wooden shelf.

The smack knocked him out so I pulled him through. Settling him down on one of the sofas. Hearing a sudden commotion I looked up and spotted a camera pointing down towards me. Cursing I quickly rushed to the door in the wall.

It wouldn't open so I slammed my shoulder into the wood. Catching movement as a fist was swung at me. Moving faster than I thought. Hitting me in the shoulder I spun with the impact. Shooting out my elbow into my attackers face.

His head snapped back so I swept his legs out from under him. Grabbing his throat and slamming him to the floor with enough force to kill his consciousness. Looking up and seeing three more men.

Sucking in air I caught that ashy smell. All of these people were vampires which meant I was outnumbered and definitely outgunned. My eyes flicking between the three of them. If I had been training my leeching abilities. I would be able to tell how powerful they were. Right now, I just had to hope I was stronger and better trained to fight.

Calling to the beast within. Feeling my claws extend, turning them into lethal weapons. Standing and giving them a deep growl. The vampire at the back moving away from his buddies. His voice shook with fear, "This isn't worth dying over."

Calling to him. "It's the afternoon. If you're

quick the sun won't fry your brain."

"I'm out of here. You guys are crazy." Seeing him shoot out the back door with a jacket pulled over his head. Leaving me with the last two standing.

They pushed forward at the same time. Waiting until they were closer before gripping one of the tattoo chairs and throwing it towards the vampire on the left. He caught it but was knocked off balance.

Giving me a one on one fight. Dodging two attacks but not seeing the kick against my shin. Dropping me to one knee I looked up and grabbed the arms swinging down towards me. Fingers gripping those wrists tightly as I dropped back. Using my foot to swing him over me and through the door to the reception area.

The second vamp caught hold of my ankle and started to drag me across the floor. Kicking out hard enough to dislocate his jaw. Making him pull back in pain. Stumbling so much he crashed into the counter.

I quickly jumped to my feet and slammed my claws through his shoulder. My other hand grabbing his head and smacking it down through the counter. Splinters flying into the air as it was destroyed.

Arms grabbed around my waist and I was pulled back. Throwing back an elbow but it did little to stop him. Seeing the tattoo shop moving past me. Instinctively throwing my hands out as the door frame came into view.

Muscles tensing giving me a moment to think. Wrapping my leg around his then reaching back with my thumbs. Two claws slicing through his eyeballs.

Blood pouring out as the vampire screamed. Pushing harder until those screams quietened.

The pain must have made him pass out because his body leant back until it hit the floor with a crunch. I didn't know which ones were still breathing and which were dead but I didn't care. Wiping my hands on my jeans as I moved back through.

Dawson sat on one of those tattoo chairs. His face was covered in bruises and blood. His lip busted up, blown up like he was allergic to their fists. They must have had him here for a while because he was still wearing the same clothes from last night.

Only now they were ripped and stained red. Injuries covering him. Fingers on his left hand snapped in odd directions. Just moving him was going to cause a lot of pain. Watching as his body seemed to get worse.

Lifting a hand to his cheek which made him wince even in his half passed out state. "Why aren't you healing?" A finger pointed to a bottle of glowing blue liquid. The same kind that I saw in Ivy's studio. "Shit. We need to get you somewhere to recover. Do these vamps know where you live?"

"No." Dawson's voice was little more than a puff of air passing between his lips.

"Look, this is going to hurt but I need to get you out of here with the least amount of trouble." One eye moving to look at me since the other was swollen shut. I brought back my fist and slammed it into his face.

His one good eye shutting as his head flopped

back. With him out cold I wouldn't have to worry about him crying in pain. I just hoped it would last by the time I got him back to his apartment. There he could drink blood and regain his healing.

Pulling him up from the chair and over my shoulder. When I got to my bike I sat him behind me. Holding onto his arms around my body so he didn't go flying off at a corner. I couldn't ride as fast as normal but it wasn't such a bad journey.

Getting back to his building and carrying him up the stairs easily. Luckily no neighbours stuck their faces out of their apartments. Kicking his door open since I hadn't shut it when I left earlier. My ankle knocking it closed before I pushed through the mess and into his bedroom.

Settling him down softly and picking up the sheets from the floor. Covering his legs I ripped his shirts to rags and chucked them away. Grabbing a few towels from his bathroom and a bowl of water from the kitchen.

Acting as nurse as I cleaned up that excess blood. Trying my hardest not to disturb those wounds but there were so many of them. Once he was as clean as I could get him I went routing around for blood bags.

Finding a little fridge built into the wall behind his bathroom mirror. Snapping the plastic head and letting it trickle into his mouth. At first it seemed to come leaking back out but his mind must have sensed it. Dawson woke up with a groan. Both from pain and pleasure from that bloody taste in his mouth.

He polished off five bags in a few minutes before he settled back to rest. I shifted off the bed and looked around at the mess. Picking up case files from the floor. Starting to put them in the right places. Ordering them when I noticed in one of the drawers there was a bundle of letters.

The paper looked so old on them. Stained from age and some were fallen apart. As I pulled them out I saw it was from being opened again and again. The flaps hanging on for dear life. I took off the elastic band and shifted through them.

Seeing there were a few different addresses for Dawson. None of them this building or even this city. Opening up one of the first and reading through slowly. Surprised that they were love letters between him and some lady. No name. She signed off with a little hand-drawn picture of a rose.

Reading through a few before getting to the more recent ones. Whereas the ones before had been full of love and sweetness. The language in the letters started to turn sour. They argued back and forth. The relationship started to break down.

Opening one of the envelopes it didn't have a letter inside but a handful of photos. Showing Dawson and this mystery woman cuddling taking selfies. On holidays, mountain sides. They seemed like the adventurous type.

Then they quickly changed. Being only of the woman. Still going on adventures but without the detective. The content of the letters showed that they drifted apart. Then things were ended by her. Saying how she had met someone else. That she needed to love someone fully and have them in her life.

Dawson's last letter back to her simply said. *I hope he makes you happy because you deserve every possible second of it. You will always be in my heart for all eternity.* Singing off with his name and a huge kiss in the corner.

I quickly wiped a tear from my eye when I heard Dawson shifting behind me. Moving my hands quickly so he didn't see me going through his private stuff but it wasn't quick enough. "It's rude to go looking through other people's things."

"Would you believe me if I said I was clearing up?" Grouping the envelopes together but not putting them away.

"I guess I made a little mess."

Turning on the small chair, "That drug must have hit you pretty hard."

The detective sat up which produced pain in his face. "I've never felt anything like it. I drink heavily and I've never gotten that buzzed before. And it hit so hard. Like trying to stop a runaway train."

"Imagine that but on a human body."

"I know. It's inevitable they'll overdose on that drug. I'm surprised more bodies haven't been cropping up."

"It's only a matter of time. Did you see how little the dealer had? Must be in low supply."

"Which means we need the next one up the ladder."

"RDJs. The little dealer told me he had

a connection with the supplier there. I don't understand how the tattoo shop is involved though."

"They aren't." Turning more to face him. "When I finally calmed down. My brain started working. The only experience I've had where my healing factor was stripped was getting my tattoo done. I stopped by to ask some simple questions. They thought I was investigating them for illegal tattooing on humans."

"They didn't take kindly to that."

"No they did not." He moved again which made him cry out. My eyes seeing that some of the smaller wounds were beginning to heal. His swollen eye opening more now. "How did you know I was there?"

Getting up I moved over, fingers still gripping onto those letters. "My room mate is a witch and a tattoo artist. I saw this glowing blue bottle and read the ingredients. The same one that appeared in the autopsy report."

"Still. How did you find me there?"

"I went to visit you before figuring all this out. Maybe I got a little worried. So when I realised tattoo artists use this stuff on vampires. I remembered your ink and I spotted the card for that place on your fridge when we first met."

"You could do well as a detective." Laughing at his compliment. "Last time I saw you, you were having a go at me for being a vampire. Clearly there's a story behind that."

"You first. These letters. Who's the woman in the pictures?"

Those eyes filled with sadness as he looked at the bundle. His fingers twitching like he wanted to hold them but couldn't bring himself to do it. "Her name was Donna. We were madly in love. Beat out all kinds of odds like her father hating me. Thinking I wasn't good enough for her."

"I can understand his point of view." Making the detective smirk.

"Please keep all rude comments until the end."

"Yeah, right." Grinning. "Please continue."

"We were in love and everything was amazing. One night we were walking home at night. A guy jumped out. Mugged us but then attacked me with a knife. I was at death's door when a stranger came along. Promising me that I could live if I gave myself to him fully."

"That's when you were turned."

"Yes. I thought he was a good Samaritan. Using his vampirism to save my life. But it turned out to be staged. As soon as I started disagreeing on the things we were doing, horrible things. He threatened Donna. So I sent her away. She understood but the plan was to come back together once I had dealt with my nest. Only I had gone down a dark path to accomplish this and I wasn't the same man she fell in love with."

"I'm really sorry to hear that."

"Thank you. Donna eventually found someone who could give her the life I couldn't. So I gave her my blessing. That was thirty-five years, four months and ten days ago." Surprised to see tears starting to fall down his cheeks. They dribbled until turning to ash and flitting off onto his sheet.

I reached for his hand and gripped it tight. "You're a good man."

"I'm not a man any more though. She would have aged and I still look the same."

"A good vampire then." Swallowing after my statement. Disbelief that I had even thought it let alone said it.

"Which leads us to your disdain for my kind? I shared so it's only fair."

"I think your injuries have made you delusional. You should get some rest." Pulling up his sheet like I was a mother tucking in my child. Giving his forehead a kiss. "Now get some shut eye. Otherwise no ice cream for you."

"You will tell me. However, some sleep actually sounds good."

"I'm glad you agree." Replacing his letters and giving the desk a bit of a tidy up before heading out into the apartment. My first stop was the fridge where I found a carton of orange juice. Filling up a large glass I started organising his kitchen.

Throwing out the food on the floor and restocking his cupboards. Surprised at how much he had since his diet was sustained with blood. Turning his sofa back over then finding his music collection. Putting on something rocky which helped motivate me to move faster.

Getting through most of the lounge before looking through the bathroom door. Deciding to shut it and staying away from all that blood. The detective may be growing on me but clearing that up was out of the question.

I headed back to the kitchen to top up my orange juice when I heard the door open. Holding my breath and freezing. Expecting to hear a skinny blonde calling out for Dawson but there was nothing.

Honing my hearing and catching footsteps tapping over the wood flooring. Pressing my back to the wall adjacent to the little hallway. Sniffing, gaining as much information from my senses as possible.

Four men. One staying by the door, the other three moving deeper. Hearing the clicks of guns, smelling the gun powder. Taking a deeper breath but forgetting it as one of their arms came into view.

My hand shot out and grabbed that wrist. A loud gunshot making my whole body jump before I thrust my shoulder into the man's side. Flinging him over and onto the dining table. The thing creaking but didn't give way.

I turned and sped for the next in line. Grabbing a handful of his jacket and using him as a battering ram to hit against the third intruder. He was sent to the floor and I took out the forth with a flying body.

Both of them knocked back through the door and into the hallway. I followed quickly, the two men climbing to their feet. Blocking a punch by one and throwing out my foot to knock the other down the stairs. The thuds of his body impacting until he came to rest on the landing below.

Getting knocked back but I soon regained my

balance and twisted my body. Bringing the man over my hip and dropping my weight onto him as we hit the carpet. Fingers gripped my hair and I screamed as he yanked my head back.

Throwing blind elbows until I felt it crack into his face. Hitting a second time and his body went limp. Pulling my hair from his fingers as a gun came out into the hallway. Hearing the bangs as bullets dug into the wall behind me.

Pushing with speed. Feeling the burn of metal puncturing through my right arm before I knocked the gun from his grip. Slamming my hand into his throat making him gasp. The man struggling to breath as he fell back.

There was one left so I stepped over the body. Hearing the cock of a gun and seeing him standing there. Gun pointed at my chest. They might not be firing silver bullets but a heart with holes would still be fatal.

Raising my hands high. "Who are you?" Trying to take control of the situation. "Who sent you here?"

"We get paid to do a job. That's all we know." My heart leaping into my throat as he pulled the trigger. Seeing a sudden blur of power as the man was shot against the wall. The impact impairing his aim but I still felt that bullet rip through my right shoulder.

The pain flooding every single thought. Dropping to my knees. "Damn that hurts like a bitch."

Dawson came over to me. Looking worse than I did and he hadn't just been shot twice. He inspected my shoulder front and back. Then my arm. "Your arm went straight through. But you still have the bullet in your shoulder. Here." He placed my hand over that wound. "Keep pressure."

Looking into his eyes and seeing the lines of red starting to form in the whites. Seeing his need for blood in his weakened state. Licking my lips before speaking. "Are you okay? With this." Nodding to the blood slowly leaking through my fingers.

"Don't worry. I have yet to lose my cool around blood." Seeing the struggle in his voice. Feeling vulnerable but I needed his help right now. "Keep pressure. I'll be back with a knife."

"Take your time." Leaning back against the wall on my arse as he rushed off into the kitchen. Bringing back a wooden spoon and a knife that looked like it could chop off my arm. "Big enough?"

"I haven't had any complaints yet."

Tensing my jaw so I didn't laugh at his joke. "Now is not the time for your stupid jokes."

"If you can't laugh at the most terrible of times, you don't deserve to laugh at the best of times."

Smiling, "Don't tell me you came up with that."

"Donna did." Seeing the flash of sadness before that big smile was shining brighter. "This is for you." Feeling like a rabid dog as he pressed that wooden spoon between my lips. Biting down so hard the thing snapped in two.

My jacket was pulled off my shoulder. "This is going to hurt." Without another warning he shoved the point of his knife into my flesh. Cutting through the hole. Then he started digging around with the point.

Holding off for as long as I could but soon I was screaming out in pain. Knocking his hand away. "You don't have any tweezers or something?"

"This might shock you but this is my first time doing this."

"Dawson." Growling his name. "Just do it."

"If you say so." Groaning as he pressed fingers into that hole. The bullet getting shifted about. Feeling his grip getting hold but it slipped causing more pain to shoot down to my fingers. "I can't get a good enough grip."

"I'll just do it myself." Pausing as I allowed my fingers to grow those lethal claws. Looking down and pressing them in to find that projectile. Going slowly I gripped it between two. Pulling until I felt the metal come free.

Blood leaking out quicker until Dawson pressed a tea cloth to it. And there we sat. Both of us breathing heavily. I looked around at the bodies. Dawson gave the nearest one a nudge with his foot. "You certainly cleaned up. Any clue who they are?"

"This is your place they visited. I was hoping you would know."

"I haven't pissed off any husbands lately." Rolling my eyes at his joke. "They could be working for the drug dealer. We left him alive after all."

"Clearly a mistake on my part."

"Just means we're getting close." The detective shifted as footsteps came by the front door. He leant his head around the corner. "Hey, Carl." Looking myself to see an elderly gentleman carrying a couple of grocery bags. "Don't mind the mess. It'll be cleared up in no time."

"Are you okay? You both look a bit worn out."

"You could say that but we'll be fine. How did your granddaughter's play go?"

"She was superb. Got it all on tape to rewatch over and over."

"I'm glad for you. I'll let you know when the next poker night is."

"Maybe clean up first."

"You bet, old man."

Leaning my head against the wall as the elderly man left to head up the stairs. "How are you so calm?"

"Is this the first time you've been attacked?"

The memory of the attack in the park had me shaking my head. "No but.....talking about poker?"

"I enjoy a game or two with some of the guys in the building."

Looking at his serious expression made me burst out laughing. Unable to hold it in, not even sure why this was my reaction. But I revelled in it. Feeling the happiness in such a random moment.

Dawson took his hand away from my shoulder and replaced it with mine. He crawled over to the nearest body who I had chucked over his dining table. Watching as he rummaged through his pockets. Finding some of those drugs that had sent him off like a kite. "We were right. Looks like they were going to plant these in my apartment."

"Lucky I was here. Looks like you owe me."

"Technically if you hadn't rescued me from the tattoo parlour, I wouldn't have been here to frame any way."

Looking at him with a dead pan expression. Raising an eyebrow as he looked back in confusion. "So you owe me twice then. Saving you from the tattooing vampires. And again right now."

"You were right the first time. I owe you once. Let's leave it at that."

I pulled the tea towel from my shoulder. Happy the bleeding had stopped. The small hole starting to seal up. "We should get going. Head somewhere safe."

"Obviously my place is compromised. Have to move yet again. Maybe this time I'll just buy new furniture. Beats packing up all this stuff."

Climbing to my feet I chucked the towel into the sink. "How many times have you moved?"

"You mean since moving to the city?"

"Never mind." Blowing out a sigh as I cradled my arm to my body. "We'll head to my apartment. My room mate can help you heal with some light magick."

"Your room mate is a light witch? Wow, I've never met one before. She must contrast well with your meanness."

"Until she gets sarcastic. Then she gives me a run for my money."

"Duly noted. Let me get a top on first. I'll call this in as well."

"I'll just hang out here." Bending over against one of the chairs. Taking deep breaths. Willing my healing to jump into overdrive. The pain was starting to make me feel sick. Thinking I heard movement I held my breath.

Dawson's voice came from the bedroom but I ignored it. Feeling a presence. Mustering all my strength and turning. Throwing my fist but freezing as I saw a girl. She looked early teens. Such an innocent expression on her face.

She would look like an angel if it wasn't for the blood pouring down her neck. Seeping through the flowery dress she wore. Seeing those puncture marks. Non-stop bleeding. My bottom lip shaking as I tried to speak.

The little girls voice coming out soft, playful. "Are you friends with the detective?"

"I guess."

"I've watched him for so long now. He doesn't have friends."

"I've noticed." Looking over my shoulder but Dawson hadn't emerged yet. Turning back and jumping as she was so much closer. Close enough I could reach out and touch her cheek. Her eyes looking bigger. Her blood looking darker.

"I don't think he deserves a friend like you."

"What?" My breath slowed. Making me suck in harder but it was no good. The air started to turn cold. Feeling something around my throat pressing hard. My body slipping down until I dropped to my knees.

Looking into her eyes as they flashed black for a moment. The invisible grip around my neck getting tighter. "What are you doing?"

"He doesn't deserve another friend."

"Stop." I reached up but there was nothing to pull away. Feeling my eyes getting heavy. My mind starting to shut off. A blink lasting for minutes. That black pulling me under.

CHAPTER 6

My eyes shot open. Dawson was crouched in front of me looking worried. His hand tapped my cheeks as I regained my breath. I reached up to touch my neck. Feeling the ice clinging to my skin. Brushing it off with a shiver. Clearing my throat. "I'm alright, stop fussing over me."

"Excuse me. I come walking in and you're on the floor not breathing. What am I supposed to do?"

Looking into his eyes but all I saw was the girl. The blood covered ghost who just tried to kill me. "I've got something to ask you and you need to tell me the truth."

"Can we make sure you're okay first?"

"I'm fine." Pushing up to my feet but almost losing my balance. Hitting back against the kitchen counter.

"You don't look fine."

"I am. Just…." Putting my hand out to stop him from coming closer. "Do you know a little girl. Flowery dress. She was attacking by a vampire." Looking at him. Seeing the realisation in his eyes. Feeling my heart breaking. "Did you attack her?"

"Look. I think I've shared enough for one day

don't you?"

"No. I need to know this."

"Why?"

"I need to know you're not another monster. Prove to me that not all vampires are the same."

Dawson moved back, using one of the chairs to lean against. "No. You share first. Why are vampires monsters in your eyes?"

"Apart from the obvious?"

"I'm very, very aware of the obvious. Trust me." Anger laced in his words as he spat them out. The first time I've seen him like this. The sight of it shocked me silent. Looking at him as it slowly slipped from his features. "You need to share as well."

"I was eleven. My mother is a leecher. She married a vampire when I was a baby." Just starting this story had memories rising to the surface. "Someone from his past came back. Decided she wanted to destroy the life the two of them had made together. So she kidnapped my step-father when he was away on business for the vampire council."

Dawson stood there listening. Not showing any emotion. "She held him for a week. Starving him, injuring him. By the time she dropped him back off to us. He was only just holding on to his control."

The detective's hand coming to cup mine. "It's okay if you don't want to finish the story."

"Um…" Licking my lips as tears started to fall. "My mum now has a scar down the side of her face, down her neck an across her chest. And I." A cry taking away my words. So I lifted up my top. Showing him the jagged scars that wrapped around my whole right side.

"What the hell?"

"He ripped and tore."

"Megan. I'm sorry for pushing." Dawson wrapped me up in is arms. Clinging to him tightly as I let the tears fall. Seeming like they would never end. My repressed feelings bubbling to the surface. Not letting me stop crying.

Clinging to him for what seemed like hours. When I finally calmed enough to speak I pressed my hand to his chest. Not to push him away but to rest it over his heart. "I'm sorry."

"For crying?"

"No, for treating you how I have. You weren't the one."

"I get it, Megan. You don't have to teach me about past trauma. It sticks with you for a long time." The detective pulled back and pushed my hair out of my face. Wiping my cheeks with the sleeve of his shirt. "We all have it."

Nodding to his words. "Look. You don't have to tell me about the little girl."

"How about we get out of here before more men show up. Then you can decide whether you want to know or not. You can ask me anything. Okay?"

Smiling. "Sure." Looking into his eyes.

"But I'm not a monster. I can promise you that." The softness of his expression making me believe him.

Sniffing and rubbing my nose with my jacket

sleeve. "We should get going. Both of us could use some rest."

"I know I could." We both helped each other out of the apartment. Feeling his arms tight around my waist as I we rode my motorbike. Keeping an eye out for any tails but there didn't seem to be anyone following us. Taking a much longer route just in case.

Getting to the apartment I led us through into our sleeping apartment. Hobbling the detective into my bedroom and laying him down on my bed. Placing the bags of blood we brought from his on the side. "I'll get Ivy to have a look at you. She can use some magick if she thinks you'll need it."

"No, it's fine. A little pain never hurt anyone."

"I think you've got that wrong."

He let out a soft laugh. "I just need some rest and some blood. I'll be right as rain by the morning."

"Morning." Looking at him. After all the information I had received I had completely forgot about his reaction to the sun. "How do you walk out in the sunlight without it frying your brain?"

"I'm sure you know the world of magick changed when Luana was defeated twenty odd years ago."

"Of course." It was hard to forget something that was told during bedtime stories almost every night.

"I found a light witch. Very good at protection spells. She made something for me." He took my hand and pressed my fingertips to the inside of his arm. Feeling a little lump there. "It's an implant that protects me against the sun."

"Wow. It's horrifying to think there could be young, impulsive vampires out there during the day."

"The witch did it as a favour. Plus it cost a lot of money." Dawson rested back on my bed. Popping one of those blood bags into his mouth. Letting it hang out as he drew in that liquid like a straw.

I used the bathroom to clean myself up. Happy that the bullet wound in my shoulder wasn't as deep. The one through my arm had completely disappeared. I took off my jacket, pissed off there was now a hole in the leather. Exchanging my blood soaked top for a nice baggy hoody from my bedroom floor.

Heading across the hall I found Connor sitting watching television whilst playing some kind of video game on his handheld console. Expecting to find Leon at the stove but it was Ivy. "Is he out again?"

The witch turned, braids swinging wild. "You don't look too good."

"Getting shot will do that to a person."

"Oh my god." She dropped the spatula and came rushing over.

I placed my hand to her arm. "I'm okay. Already started healing. Dawson is worse off than me." Her eyes looked past me to the door. "I left him on my bed."

"Is that why he looks worse?"

"Grow up, Ivy." Pushing past her and picking out a piece of mince from the pan. Munching it down with a groan. I hadn't eaten since my piece of cake with my father which was a long time for me since I enjoyed food far too much. Especially when it came to meat. "When will it be ready?"

"Ten minutes. I was going to put some in the fridge for you but since you're here."

"Thanks." I grabbed some plates and set the table for three. Connor came and sat up with us. We chatted about school. He tried to get details out of me about my case but I kept them secret. Telling him he needed to hold onto his innocence for as long as possible.

After the food was done with, me and Ivy shared the clean up. She washed up whilst I dried and put it away. That's where our conversation carried on as Connor went back to his video game.

Filling her in on everything that had happened. Every detail of the case. "So you're telling me that I might get my stuff from the same guy supplying these drug dealers?"

"I doubt it. I've met the witch you get it from. He's more straight and narrow than you."

"Agreed."

"Also, the people supplying it, probably don't know what it's being used for." Putting away the pile of dishes. "Our next step was to head over to RDJs but I think we both need the night to recover."

"You're not going anywhere dangerous tonight."

"Have I ever told you, you're like a big sister?"

"Countless times." Ivy looked at the clock on the oven. "It's past eight and he's still not back."

"I'll put Connor to bed." I enjoyed spending time with Connor. In these apartments we're practically family. But seeing him want his father there was heart breaking. Leon needed a life away from being a father but his son was still the most important thing. Or at least he should be.

Grabbing the boy from the sofa I threw him over my shoulder. Whilst he had a shower I poked my head into my bedroom. Dawson was out cold. Taking a moment to watch him sleep. Connor came up behind me. "Who's that in your bed?"

"He's a detective." Turning and ushering him away. "And someone you don't need to worry yourself over."

I took him into his little section. The wall covered in football stars and comic canvases. "Can you tell my dad to come wake me up when he's back. I want to tell him what I did in my game. It's really cool."

"I'll happily take a look." Crouching down beside his bed as he brought up the replay. Watching the video with a smile before the screen went dark. "That is very very cool and Leon will love it as well." Taking the handheld console and placing it on is shelf. "I'll make sure he comes in to see you."

"Thanks, Megan." He leant up and gave me a tight hug.

"Get some sleep. Your father will be back soon." I switched his night light on and then turned the apartment light out as I left. Poking my head into the other apartment. "Hey, Ivy." Her young face appearing. "I'm just popping out. Don't suppose…"

"Clifford's. The bar a couple of streets over."

Smiling. "Thanks."

"I would say be gentle with him but I don't think he deserves it."

"Definitely not." Making my way a few streets over. Coming up outside Clifford's. The place was quite empty since it was a weekday. Some day drinkers were sleeping at their tables. My eyes spotted Leon and his new friend by the window.

I didn't want to head in and make a scene. So I tapped on the glass to get their attention. Leon's face dropped when he saw me. Crooking my finger for him to come outside. Pacing back and forth as my annoyance rose. Happy that he motioned for Wallis to stay seated at the table. "Megan?"

"First." Slapping him across the cheek. Seeing his skin going red immediately. "That's for Connor. You're missing out on him. You're his father, the only one he has after Kevin passed."

"Passed? He was shot during a mugging."

"Even more reason for you to be there for your son. Not out having drinks and wasting your time with him." Waving my arm in the air which made Leon flinch. Biting my lip at how I was making him react. Knowing it would bring back memories but I was too angry to cool off.

"Look. I'm finally having some time to myself. I'm finally having a laugh. With a man." I looked through the window at Wallis watching us. "You don't understand how it feels to actually feel it's okay to smile. To trust someone."

"We all have our problems so you have no right

to tell me what I haven't felt. I put Connor to sleep tonight. He told me, to tell you, to wake him when you're home. So he can show you a clip he's recorded."

"He did?"

"Yes. I know for you this is all new and amazing. But he's had just as much trauma as you. He lived through all that as well. The biggest difference is, he's twelve. He's still a kid. His trust issues will affect him deeper and for longer than yours will."

"You don't know that."

"You're out. Having drinks with your new friend. When was the last time you heard Connor ask if he can go over someone's house. Do you remember the last time he wanted to go to another kid's birthday party?" Leon's face went blank. "He's missing out and when you're not there. He's missing out on a lot more."

"I hear you. But I'm already out. Having a good time. I'll come back and tomorrow will be different."

"You sound like a junky asking for one more hit. This starts right now. You're coming home with me."

I reached for his arm but he pulled it back sharply. "Don't treat me like I'm a child."

"Don't make me carry you back. You know I can."

Worry filled his eyes. "Don't ruin this. What if it doesn't happen again?"

"Then you'll have the three of us to support you through it. Like you always have."

"She's right." Wallis came walking out of the bar. Handing Leon his jacket. "Megan is right. You can't miss out on Connor's life. But it doesn't mean we have to miss out on each other."

"What do you mean?"

"We can take it slower. Spend time together with less alcohol. I'm not saying thrust me into your son's life from the start. But maybe I need to realise that at some point, it will happen. And I need to act like a good role model when that time comes."

"Just, wow. You are wow, you are." Leon leapt and planted a kiss to his lips.

I turned, already starting my way back. "Come on, let's go."

"Coming." Looking over my shoulder I noticed that Wallis was joining us. It was better than nothing and at least Connor could show his father what he wanted. Getting back to the building we climbed the stairs.

Not paying attention until I got to the very top. Seeing a man leaning against the wall. My eyes moving to the doors. Both of which were still intact. Turning to warn Leon but he was already there. Seeing the horror spreading through his face. Instinctively he pushed away from Wallis who gave him a confused look.

Turning back around I took charge of the situation. "What are you doing here, Paul?"

"I want to see my son."

"He's not yours." Leon spoke up but hid back behind me when he was shot a look.

"Leon is right. He's not your son."

"I raised him for years. He's part of me just like

I'm part of him." The man pushed off of the wall. Standing right in front of me, making me crane my neck back. I refused to budge. Standing between him and my friend. "So are you going to let me in?"

"He's asleep. You honestly think I'm going to let you in to see him?"

"Why are you talking? This is between me and Leon."

I pressed my hand to his chest as he tried to push past me. Holding him back but putting on the fake strain. Letting him believe I was human. "You only want to do that because you can intimidate him. You can't do that with me and I'm already quite pissed off so I wouldn't push me."

"Your tough talk has never scared me, Megan. Do I look scared?"

"You look like a knob." Paul looked passed me to Wallis. Feeling the new man in Leon's life stepping froward next to me. Seeing the size difference between the two. Wallis was toned but he was nowhere near the size of Paul's body-builder physique.

"And who's this? Your new boyfriend, Meg?"

"Actually he's mine." Leon's voice was strong. "He's my new boyfriend."

Paul's eyes shifted past me. "You'll never replace me."

"Why would I want another man like you?" Paul went to step forwards again but I kept myself in his way. "You're never going to see Connor. He's not your son."

I wasn't the only one surprised at Leon's

actions. This was the first time he had ever stood up to Paul and you could see that written all over his face. The angry man gained his composure. "This isn't going to go the way you want it. Even with your new boyfriend protecting you."

Feeling Leon backing down a step from this moron. About to push back with words when Wallis suddenly erupted into action. He grabbed Paul's wrist and twisted his arm around his back. Thrusting him face first into the wall.

My mouth gaped open as I watched him manhandle someone almost twice his size. Seeing Paul's muscles tensing but it was no good. He was pinned to the wall. Wallis leant in close. Whispering something that we couldn't hear. Judging by the man's face it wasn't anything nice.

As soon as he let go Paul ran for the stairs. Both of us moving out of his way. He didn't look back, he just kept going. All the way down until we heard the front door open and shut with a bang.

I turned to the new man with a smile. "What the hell did you just say to him?"

"It's not important."

"The hell it isn't." Leon leapt on him like a monkey clinging to a tree. Laughing as he smothered him with kisses. "That was amazing."

"It was nothing." Wallis put him down.

I moved past both of them to the apartment door. Opening it with my keys. "Wallis, why don't you come in for a little bit?"

"No, I don't want to shove myself into your lives

like this."

"Not at all. I wouldn't have offered if I didn't mean it. After what you just did to that dick. Ivy won't believe it if it comes from us."

"Yeah, come on. You can teach me how you did that arm twisting thing." Laughing as Leon tried it on Wallis without warning. The toned man easily pushing him off. "You can stay for one drink, champ. First I need to chat with, Connor. Apologise for my behaviour." Leon disappeared into the other apartment. Leaving me to lead Wallis inside where Ivy heard all about what happened.

She thought I had put him up to it until Leon came over and confirmed exactly how it happened. After the story we sat around chatting at the table. Wallis didn't seem as bad as I first thought. Having him with us in the apartment, Leon was acting like his normal self. We even cracked out a board game and had a good laugh before I started to feel tired.

I headed over the hall leaving Leon to cheat his way to victory. I checked on Connor to make sure he had gone back to sleep after his father had popped in. Happy to see him out cold. Moving to my bedroom I found the detective sprawled out like an idiot. Like he expected me to sleep on the floor in my own bedroom.

I was tempted to lift up the mattress and pour him out and if he had been one hundred percent healed, that's more than likely what I would have done. Instead I stripped out of my clothes. Put on a baggy t-shirt that smelt mildly clean. After setting the fan off I climbed under the sheet.

Having to shove him over a little which stirred him half-awake. Laying down on my back. Our bodies pressing together. Feeling the strength in his thighs as they tensed when he rolled onto his side.

Looking over into his eyes with a smile. "Don't you dare think about copping a feel."

Dawson's eyes sparkled as he softly chuckled. "You're the one climbing into bed with me." His grin showing off those teeth. Seeing the sharp points of his canines even when not extended.

"It is my bed after all."

"Whatever you need to tell yourself." The vampire lifted up the duvet and had a peek underneath. Tempted to give him a punch in the arm for it but resisting the urge. "And there was me hoping you'd be in just a thong."

"I get all dressed up for you and you don't like it?"

"I never said that. It's a very cute look and lucky for you, cute works for ya." Laughing as he wiggled his eyebrows at me.

Happy to see even without me saying no. He didn't make a move. No hand touching my thigh or his lips pursing for mine. Feeling quite safe right next to him in bed. "How are you feeling?"

"A bit battered but I'm getting there. The blood helps a lot."

"Good. I'm glad you'll survive. I've been getting used to you being around."

"You make it sound like I'm a bad smell."

"Don't worry, you can have a shower in the

morning."

"Cheeky. Just like a thong."

I rested my head back on the pillow. Looking up at the ceiling. "If you like them so much maybe I'll let you wear one of mine tomorrow."

"I know I want to get into your knickers but I think that's taking it too far."

"Bet you'd look good though."

"Such a perv. I'm trying to sleep over here." Grinning as I looked over to him. "Night, Megan. If I take up too much room just lay on top of me. I won't mind."

"I bet you won't." Getting myself comfortable and slowly drifting off. Half asleep I found my hand drifting to my side. Just resting it against his. Feeling him there was nice. Having someone in bed with me.

Finding it easier to get to sleep. The dream world taking me under. Having quite a hot dream to start off with. Feeling a man's hands. His lips. Not able to make out his face but it was extremely hot. Jolting awake as I felt him thrust. Breathing heavily and feeling myself ready to jump someone.

I gave Dawson a quick look but my movements hadn't woken him. Laying back down to drift off again. This time opening my eyes to find myself in a strange place. Instead of an apartment bedroom. This place was much nicer. Hearing the sound of waves not far away.

Looking around the small room. Moonlight flooding through the open window. Then a crash came making me jolt up. Hearing it again I swing my legs over the edge and stepped down. Finding everything so much bigger.

I grabbed a nice fluffy robe and wrapped it around my body. Moving out through the door and onto the landing that also looked out over the living area and kitchen. Realising it was a beach villa.

My eyes looking around in the dark until another crash came. Seeing a figure down below. My hand moving to hit the light switch. Downstairs getting illuminated. Seeing it was Dawson. Looking just like he did now. Injured and bloody.

My bare feet tapped down the stairs. Grabbing hold of him as he slumped onto the sofa. He tried to speak but he couldn't get any words out. My whole word jolting as a loud bang came when the door was smashed open.

Blurs of speed as the place was filled by vampires. Seeing them coming to a halt. Some of them had bloody knuckles. Others, bloody chins from feeding. One came to a stop in front of me and my Dawson. "Did you really think we wouldn't be able to follow you home?"

"Don't. Just leave. I'll do what you ask."

"You will. However, we need retribution for what you did." A hand grabbed my robe and I was lifted off the floor. Kicking my little legs and I realised who I was. Dawson's ghost, the one that had attacked me. This was her.

My eyes going wide as I felt teeth sinking into my neck. Blood leaking out, feeling so cold as it washed over my arm and chest. Those teeth yanking out. His hand dropped me to the floor like I was a piece of meat. The world dimming slowly until there was nothing but dark.

The only feeling was a touch to my arm. Something that slipped around my hand. Fingers entwining with mine making my eyes shoot open. That girl standing beside the bed. Fear starting to leak into my thoughts. Remembering how she grabbed my throat so tight before.

Moving my hand to wake up Dawson but she put a finger to her lips shushing me. My whole body tense with her standing so close. The little girl moving her lips. A soft voice coming out. "Don't wake him."

"Are you going to try and kill me again?"

"No. Sorry. I didn't know who you were and you're the only person who has seen me."

"You can't attack others?"

"I didn't do it on purpose. I was just angry about someone taking him away from me."

"What do you mean? He doesn't know you're here?"

"I thought you were there to take me away. No one has ever seen me before."

"I'm not going to take you away from him. Honestly, I haven't paid this part of my abilities that much attention. No offence but chatting with ghosts isn't my idea of a good time." Looking around the room. Surprised there wasn't ice coated over my bed sheet or the walls. No breath visible like smoke. "It's all quite new to me."

"Oh." Her big eyes moving to the vampire

laying next to me.

"You're his little sister, right?"

"You saw?"

"Yeah, in my nightmare. I'm sorry that happened to you."

"Thank you."

"Have you been with him ever since?"

"No." She shifted and sat on the edge of the bed. "It took a while before I found this place again. I'm not sure how long had passed but he was living by himself. No Donna and he didn't have anything to do with other vampires."

"He clearly blames himself for what happened."

"I did for a long time. But the actions of those vampires weren't his to control. He was tricked into this life. He never asked to become a vampire."

"Can you see what happened to him in the past?"

"No. I eavesdropped on a lot of his therapy sessions."

"Therapy?" Looking over to Dawson. "I never thought about a vampire in therapy."

"It's not an ordinary therapist. They chat about vampires and all that."

"Wow, didn't even realise there were that kind out there. I suppose supernaturals need someone to talk to as well."

"Speaking of which. It's actually really nice to finally have a conversation with someone. It's so frustrating when no one can hear you."

"I bet." I reached out to her. Touching her skin,

surprised it actually felt warm. "I don't know much but I know you can't be happy being stuck around here."

"It's all I know."

Thinking about the things my mother used to tell me about the ferryman. The being that would transport a soul to one of the afterlives. "Was there someone when you died? He wouldn't look like anyone in particular. I've been told his look changes."

"I don't remember seeing anyone. But there was a voice. It came out of nowhere. It freaked me out."

"That's the ferryman. I had nightmares about him when I was younger. My mum thought it was a good education to tell me all about him. Did he give you an option of staying?"

"Yes, I didn't realise it would leave me like this. But I picked it straight away."

"I think that was the wrong decision. I know you were worried I was here to take you away from him. But I think that's what you need to do."

Her big eyes looking over to the detective. "But I can't leave him. What if he forgets about me?"

"That's not possible. I've only known you for a moment and I'll never forget you."

"You're sweet and nice." She pulled a smile which chubbed her cheeks out. "You're much better than the others he spends time with. So many with blonde hair."

I laughed. "I think that's a way of him coping being a vampire. Dawson seems to have as much trouble with what he is as I do."

"You don't seem like there's something wrong with you."

"How many can speak to ghosts?"

She giggled. "Maybe there are more of you than you think. Someone out there might be able to help you understand."

"That's a really good point." The only other person I knew who could chat with the dead was someone I didn't want to speak with. "How come you're so smart?"

"Spending all this time watching my brother. I guess his smartness rubbed off on me."

"Do you want to speak with him?"

The little girl's eyes went wide. "Can I?"

"I'm not sure how but I can definitely relay a message. Anything you want to tell him?"

She took a moment to think about what she wanted to say. Her eyes glued to her older brother as he slept. "Um. You know what. When he wakes up in the morning. Tell him that he was the best big brother I could ask for. Tell him it wasn't his fault and he needs to let go of his guilt. Please tell him that."

"Of course. It would be my pleasure to give him your message."

"Thanks." The ghost quickly shifted around the bed so quick she was hard to follow. His little sister leant over and placed a kiss to his forehead. The way he shifted when she did had me believing he could actually feel it.

I slipped out from under the covers and stood there for her to come back. "I'm new to this so I'm hoping this will work."

"What should I do?"

"Just think about somewhere you love. A place that feels like home to you. We'll see if that works." Cupping her little hands in mine. Closing my eyes and thinking about pushing her on. Not even sure if I was doing anything right. Thinking about the ferryman. The description my mother always gave me of him.

But nothing was happening. Opening my eyes to see the optimistic look on the little girls face. "Is everything okay?"

"Let me try again."

"It's okay if you can't make it work."

She was being nice but I could see the disappointment in her eyes. "Let me try again." Before I could I heard Dawson shifting in the bed. Looking over as he opened his eyes. "Dawson."

"What are you doing up? Are you talking to yourself?"

"Not exactly." Looking at his little sister and turning back. Only he wasn't moving. His face frozen. Looking quite funny with his mouth hanging open. "I don't think I did that."

"He's frozen." She started to look around my room. Only she couldn't see what I could. Seeing a man standing there. His skin changing tones. Eyes changing colour. Hair slicked back, spiking behind him. Shifting from blonde to brunette. Then red and blue. So many colours shining down those strands of hair.

Despite knowing all about this being. Seeing

him was like watching Santa Claus putting presents underneath the tree. It was hard to believe. Swallowing then licking my dry lips. "You're the ferryman?"

Surprise hitting his features that kept changing. "You can see me?"

"Yes."

The little girl turned to look at the blank space. "Who are you talking to?"

Placing my hand on her shoulder. "It's the ferryman."

"I can't see him."

"That's the way it is." The girl looking excited at what was going on. "Usually, any way." The being's eyes coming back to me. "There has only ever been one person who could see me."

"Yes. My mother has told me stories."

"You're her daughter? I'm so happy she managed to have a family."

"Not exactly a family."

"Oh?" The ferryman walked forwards.

"Not something I want to share with a total stranger."

"Understandable. So what is going on here?" His eyes shifted down to the girl by my side. "I remember you. It's been a very long time. I hope you've been happy with your decision."

"I was happy that I could still see my brother. But Megan said that maybe I should move on."

"And you agree with her?" Seeing how he reached out with his hand. Touching her shoulder and making her jump out of her skin. The bedroom getting filled with laughter from all three of us. "Usually ghosts don't get a second visit from me. I told you that your decision would be final."

"So you can't help her?"

His colour changing eyes flicked to mine. "I didn't say that. I don't follow certain rules. Death is never so black and white."

The little girl kept looking around, trying to see where this figure was standing. "So, you can take me somewhere?"

The ferryman crouched down. A hand going to her cheek. Angling her head so her eyes met his. "I can and I will." The strange looking being peered over to Dawson as he laid there frozen. "Since you look really beautiful in your flowery dress." His hand shifted over her shoulder where the blood had stained her outfit.

The red faded away slowly until she looked brand new. Like she had never died. "I look pretty again."

"You sure do." The ferryman giving her cheek a little pinch which made her giggle. "Now, do you have a message for your brother?"

"I do." The little sister looked up at me.

Giving her a nod and a smile. "Go on. Tell him yourself. It'll do you both some good. Go on." Taking a step back as the ferryman guided her over.

I turned and exited the bedroom. Shutting the door to allow them time to themselves. Moving into the kitchen. Opening the fridge to find some little sausages that Connor enjoys eating in the night.

Munching on them until the bedroom door opened. Dawson came walking out with ash covering his wet cheeks. His fingers quickly wiped them clean as he smiled. A long sigh slipping from his lips. "I have no idea what that was. But I feel like I have you to thank for it."

"It was a group effort."

"Well, thank you. I don't think anyone has ever done something like that for me."

"You don't get a lot of niceties when you're a vampire?"

His eyes met mine. Worrying that he took it in the opposite manner that I meant it. But then he smiled wide. "I think you're warming up to me."

"I did let you sleep in my bed."

"And I'm very appreciative of everything you've done. Especially letting me say goodbye to my sister."

"It's my pleasure."

"So." The vampire came closer, snatching one of those little sausages from the pack. "You can talk to ghosts?"

"We all have our secrets."

"I don't think mine are as interesting as yours."

"I'll take that as a compliment."

"You should. It's a very impressive gift to have."

Laughing softly. "I don't know if I would call it a gift myself."

"You allowed my little sister to move on. And you let me see her one more time. I always hated myself for what happened. It was my fault and I'm not saying I suddenly forgive myself. But hearing her say that it wasn't. Goes a long way in how I feel. That's a gift to both of us, from you."

"It's the first time I've ever done something like that."

"Maybe you should look into developing it. You could help a lot more people out there."

"I guess." Looking at this vampire. Someone I disliked on more than one occasion. Now I was looking at him as a friend. Someone that I could trust with my life in a dangerous situation. Moving a little closer.

Placing my hand on his chest. Tapping those hard muscles with my fingertips. "You're still injured so this is all you're getting." Leaning in and giving a gentle kiss to his lips. Pulling back and seeing the surprise in his raised eyebrows. "Don't get any ideas."

"I wouldn't dream of it." A massive grin coming across his lips.

"Good. I need more sleep." Moving past him to my bedroom.

Dawson still stood by the kitchen counter. "Look. I can sleep on a sofa or something if you wanted."

Turning slowly. "Come on. I'm not going to jump you. Don't be scared now." Laughing as I reached over and took his hand in mine. Taking him to bed where we laid. Resting my head on his chest, my arm draped over his body. Falling asleep even quicker than before.

CHAPTER 7

When I woke I woke alone. Looking around my room I noticed Dawson was nowhere to be seen. A little worried that my kiss had scared him away. Moving out of the bedroom and across the road in my baggy t-shirt. Finding my room mates sitting around the table with the vamp in the kitchen. The smell of breakfast filling the whole apartment.

Connor giving me a wave with bacon hanging out of his mouth. Laughing as I walked over to the table. Dawson turned with a frying pan in his hand. My eyes taking in his muscles and how they strained against the t-shirt he was wearing. Grinning as he slipped a mushroom, two sausages and a tomato off onto a plate waiting for me. "Nice t-shirt."

Dawson's eyes flicking to mine. Seeming softer than usual. "Leon let me borrow it since my shirt was a little bloody."

"It's truly my pleasure." Giving Leon a quick smile as he sat there admiring Dawson in a t-shirt that was clearly too small for him.

"Sit down. I got some beans on the hob." As I sat he came back and scooped some onto my plate. Grabbing my fork and digging in. The food tasting so good and having it cooked for me by Dawson was a nice surprise. The vampire took a seat between me and Connor. "Hope you enjoy it."

"It tastes great." Taking a moment to watch him messing around with Connor on his handheld console. Feeling someone prodding me with a fork which made me yelp. Turning to see Ivy giving me a massive grin. "What?"

"Don't be so coy." She nodded to Dawson.

Switching my look between them. Noticing Leon leaning in as well. "The only thing getting grilled right now should be the sausages. Can't I enjoy my breakfast?"

"By all means." She leant back with a mug in one hand and a piece of toast in the other. Her eyes on me with that smirk.

Ignoring her the best I could whilst munching through my plate. Grabbing a coffee halfway through. Finishing it all off I took my plate to the sink. Rinsing it and placing it with the rest of the dirty dishes. Ivy called over. "I'll sort that out before my first client gets here."

Leon stood up, "I have to get to work. Come on, buddy."

Connor pulled a face and whined. "But we haven't finished our game yet."

I was about to speak when the detective piped up first. "Me and Megan can drop him off. We're having a really gruelling match here."

The three of us looked at each other. Giving them a smile. "Like he said. We don't mind dropping him off."

"Alright then." Leon leant over and kissed Connor on the cheek. Then he did the same to Dawson who just carried on playing the video game. I got one as well and Ivy was last before he disappeared for his shift at the library.

I leant back against the counter with my coffee mug in my hands. "And where are we heading off to today?"

"I figured we would head down to the precinct. Instead of just visiting RDJs and hoping for the best. We can check to see if that little drug dealer has any friends. And maybe those bodies at my apartment can shed some light on our case."

"Sounds like a good idea." Watching as my distracting question made him lose the match. Connor chucked his hands in the air with a cheer. "I hope you're not a sore loser, Dawson. I'm not spending the day with you if you are."

"I think I can handle losing to a kid." The vampire watched as Connor jumped off his chair and ran around the table waving his arms in victory. "However, that is hard to take without getting a little grumpy."

I laughed. "Alright, kid. Get your stuff together and we'll head off." Giving Ivy a tight hug. "Have a good day, will see you later."

"You have a good day with your vampire."

"That's enough out of you." Jabbing her rib playfully which made her yelp in surprise. I quickly grabbed a pair of jeans and my black denim jacket from across the hall. Filling my pockets with everything I needed before grabbing Connor's bag, then we left. Walking two streets down and one over to drop the kid off at school. On our way back the two of us chatted about my friends. Sharing about Leon's past with his ex. And mentioning the new guy on the scene.

We jumped onto my bike and headed for his precinct. Parking around the back, Dawson used a code to gain access to the building. Moving through the short hallway then out into the bullpen where there were rows of desks. Cubicle walls surrounding each one.

Further across the room were offices which is where we were heading. Finding the one with his name written across the frosted glass. "You get your own office, huh?"

He opened the door for me to enter. "I'm an important man around here."

"I doubt that." I pulled a chair around his side of the desk as he booted up his computer. As he waited he pulled open a drawer and pulled out a shirt. My eyes watched as he slipped off Leon's top. Eyes moving over his muscles slowly. "Take your time."

Dawson flashed me a look with a big grin. Shaking his head, "Such a perv." The vampire sat down with his shirt left open. In went his login and password then we had access to the police servers. First he searched for any known accomplices for the little drug dealer from In The Ruff.

Only one came up but he was deceased,

currently residing in the morgue. The cause of death was a knife wound to the neck. "I suppose that happens all the time in their line of work."

"I'd be lying if I said I hadn't seen it before." He made another search for the bodies that had been picked up at his apartment. Names and previous addresses came up. Who they were affiliated with.

When Dawson went to probe a little deeper we hit a wall. Access denied came flashing up on his screen. My gut sank. Knowing that if the detective on the case couldn't gain access. It meant the government was involved. And not just any department. The supernatural one that was headed by someone I didn't want to speak to.

I looked at Dawson who seemed to understand the message as well. "That's a bugger. It'll take me ages to get access and that's even if they allow it."

Biting my lip. Remembering how sad Melanie's ghost was. That smug look on the vampire. Letting out a deep sigh. Chanting my father's words in my mind over and over. "I might be able to help with that."

"How so?"

"I know someone in that division of the government. Pretty high up."

"How is that?" He turning to me with a smile. "You never told me you had friends in such high places."

"There's still plenty I haven't told you." Turning back to the flashing message on the screen. "I wish I didn't have to but it seems we've hit a dead end in our case."

"If it's something you don't want to do, we can find another way. We still have RDJs to check out. We might get lucky."

"Or we might just walk into another situation without thinking about it. Those men at your apartment are clearly involved with the drug. The little dealer probably sent them after us. I should have killed him when I had the chance."

"It'll work out in the end, don't worry."

My eyes still moving over the screen I noticed something in the bottom corner. "What's that?" Tapping where the file sat. The name of which was what caught my eye.

"That's the name of my snitch." He closed the access denied message and clicked on the file. Bringing up a picture of the man we had gone to see. The same kind of knife wound in his neck. "What a coincidence."

"What's that attached to it?" He clicked and a photo of a body showed up. Seeing the head sitting atop it. Leaves still covering most of him. Numbered yellow tags dotted around the area.

"Looks like someone took care of the killer already." His eyes scanned through the writing in the file.

Mine were still on that photo. "Do they have any leads?"

"Not by the looks of it. He had his head torn clean off. Had to be someone supernatural."

"It was me." Biting my lip after confessing to

him. "He followed me on my bike from the snitch. Attacked me with a silver knife. I didn't have much of a choice. If he killed the snitch then they might be tying up loose ends. I bet that little drug dealer will be next."

"You're probably right. That's his problem now. The drug ring must be protecting themselves with the overdoses coming to light."

"Then it looks like we don't have much of a choice. We need the information in that file to make our next move."

"Agreed. Do you need to make a call or something?"

"No, we can just drop by."

"Must be a good friend."

"Yeah." Laughing at his comment. Running through my brain how long it had been since I last spoke to my mother. It hadn't been the best of conversations either. My father's words running through my mind. Telling me to give her another chance. "Let's get going." Wanting to get this over and done with as quick as possible.

We left his office after he buttoned up his shirt. As we moved through the bullpen someone called out his name. Both of us turning as an officer came running over to him. A thick black ponytail bouncing left and right. Her face pulled into a stupidly big grin.

Then her eyes landed on me and that happiness disappeared quickly. "Megan. What the hell are you doing here?"

"Working on a case."

"Oh really. And you roped sweet Dawson into helping you? He just can't say no to a damaged kid."

Dawson pulled a confused look. "You two know each other?" The vampire took a step back but hid it by turning towards me. "How so?"

The officer grabbed the reigns of the conversation before I could. "We were in the academy together. Megan here was near the top of our classes. Just below me. But she had a huge problem with authority. Often landed her in trouble."

Dawson was still looking at me. "I didn't know you were in the academy."

"Yeah. Best time of my life." Putting on a fake smile. Wanting to get away from this woman.

"Megan butted heads with anyone better than her. Afraid she wasn't going to be first. Such a sore loser."

Curling my fingers and digging my nails into my palms. Gritting my teeth as the anger tried to rise. Blowing out long slow breaths. "It was nice seeing you again, Tammy."

"Truly." She pulled one of those fake smiles before turning her attention back to the detective. "So how have you been?"

"I've been alright. Been working with Megan the last few days."

"You're always helping people out. Such a sweetie." She started running her hands over his shirt. "Have you been working out?"

"Not lately, no. I spent the night at Megan's. Had to grab one of my old shirts from my office just now."

His fingers tugged at his top. Making her grip loosen on the material. "It's a little out of style but it came in handy in a pinch."

"You two spent the night together?"

"Yes we did. Megan showed me something that I had been missing for a very very long time. No other woman has managed to come close to that." Smirking as I saw her smile vanish. Her eyes moving to mine then back again. Looking like she was about to be sick. "Anyway, we best be heading off. The case awaits."

"Okay." The officer's hands pulled back slowly. "You let me know if you need any help, with anything."

"That's okay. Megan is more than capable. Have a great day." Flashing her a wink before we turned and made our way back out into the car park. As soon as the door was shut I launched into a hug. "What's this for?"

Pulling back with a huge smile. "Tammy was the most annoying person in the world at the academy. Kept boasting how she was the best. Rubbing it in my face. Always singling me out. Making me feel like I didn't belong there."

"Essentially she was a typical bully in school."

"Yeah. She should have grown out of it by now but I see the uniform hasn't changed anything. Thanks for sticking up for me back there."

"There was me thinking you would hate me for implying that we slept together."

"If that's what she wanted to think that's on her. As far as I'm concerned everything you said was true." Leaning in and giving his cheek a kiss. "So thank you. It felt so good to see that look on her face."

"Well, I'm very happy that's the case." We walked over to my bike. Straddling the seat. Before starting it up I looked over my shoulder. "So you two slept together?"

"Please don't remind me. I was wasted and just wanted some company. If I knew how clingy she would become I never would have gone through with it."

I laughed and kicked my bike into life. Heading through the city and pulling off into an underground car park beneath one of the tallest buildings here. The front sign listing names of companies. Some of them claiming to be charities.

Coming up to the little hut where a guard sat. His head poked out the sliding window. "How can I help you?"

"We're here to see the lady in charge."

"Of which business."

"All of them. The very top." His eyes moved between us. Weighing up his options. Seeing his shoulder shift and knowing what he was about to do. Looking over my shoulder. "Put your hands up."

"Huh?" Dawson's confusion getting replaced with surprise as four guards in full tactical gear came out of two doors either side of the hut. Surrounding us with assault rifles aimed at our heads.

We both put our arms up as the guard came out for a chat. Holding a pistol in his lowered hand. "Do you have an identification?"

"Sure. I keep it in my back pocket. Can I get off my bike and get it out?"

"No, stand up. I'll get it."

"You don't have the right to put your hand in her back pocket like that. Feeling her up isn't part of your job." Dawson's hands went to lower but that made the guards start shouting at him.

"It's okay, Dawson. If I feel him grab my arse he'll get a bullet to his knee from his own gun."

The guard's eyes shifted to me. A slight smirk written across his lips. "That would be the last thing you do."

"Ditto." Giving him a big smile, acting all cheerful like it would be pleasurable to make him suffer. Standing up, my arms still raised. "Oh, you would also lose your job and never get another in this city."

"You've got a mouth on you."

I looked up at the camera sitting above the hutch. Knowing that when the guards are called. There are a small group of people who get notified. One of those people was who we came to see. "I'll give it five more seconds."

The guard's hand hovering in mid-air after my comment. Counting down in my head when the phone inside his booth rang. Cutting through the silence like a knife. He backed away and answered.

The voice on the other end of the line was loud and angry. Seeing the expression on his face like a puppy being told off for pooping inside the house. "Yes. Of course. I'll send them straight through." He put the phone down. "Back off and let them through!"

Giving him a cheeky wink. The guards retreated back into their little hideouts and the barrier was lifted. Giving the guard a wave before roaring through the car park. Getting a spot right near the elevator doors.

We entered with a push of the button. Noticing the top level was already selected. No one gained access to it without the fingerprint of someone who resided there. The box moved up with a whirr of electricity.

Looking over to Dawson who's eyes kept looking my way and back to the doors. "Just ask whatever question is running around your mind."

"So this friend of yours? She runs this whole building?"

"Well. She runs the whole supernatural division for the government, from this building."

"Oh wow. That's very impressive."

"If you say so." Blowing out a long breath. Bouncing back and forth whether to tell him the truth or not. Looking over as he gave me a soft smile. A sigh flowing between my lips. "You might as well know the truth. It's bound to come out any way."

"What truth?"

"The lady we're going to meet. She's not a friend. She's my mother."

"What?" The doors opened. His eyes wide and innocent like a deer caught in headlights. "I'm about to meet your mother?"

"Don't make it weirder than it already is."

"Sorry."

I blew out a breath as we walked out over the carpet. A large area with sofas and a coffee table sat to our left. A kitchen running along the wall behind them. Further ahead were offices that lined each wall.

Moving through I peered left and right. Seeing people at work on their computers and phones. My mother had the ambassadors for each species working up here with her. She wanted them close to handle any issues and for them to feel equal in the running of the supernatural unit.

We walked down the end where the walls opened up. Massive windows showed off the city landscape beneath us. Very few buildings were as high as we were right now. The young lady sitting behind the desk smiled. "She's expecting you, Megan."

"Thanks." We turned and headed for the massive pine doors. Hearing Dawson laughing under his breath. "Get it out now before we get in there."

"Sorry. You get treated like royalty around here, don't you."

"That's enough out of you." Hitting him with my elbow.

"How often do you come here?"

"When I was younger, quite a bit. Recently? Not so much."

"Oh. Why do I have a feeling this about to get really awkward."

"No doubt about that."

"I think I'll wait out here."

I quickly grabbed his wrist and yanked him

to my side. "Don't you dare. I'll need a buffer if the conversation is going to stay civil."

"Great. I'm a buffer now." Dawson started smoothing out his shirt. "I wish I had an iron at the office as well."

"Stop it. You're making me even more nervous." I pushed through the right door. The office was the kind of place you would find in a humble home. Unlike how the rest of this floor looked. Inside was darker thanks to the smaller windows. Just enough light to illuminate the place. Showing off the shelves of old looking books. The desk something you would find at a car boot sale. Nothing in here screamed fancy. It was all sentimental to my mother.

Getting a strong waft of lavender from the incense sticks burning on her desk. Dawson lifted his nose and sniffed. "Smells nice in here."

"You could say my mum has quite the nose. She finds the incense helps keeps the scents at bay."

His eyes casting around the space. "Not quite what I imagined."

Laughing as Dawson pulled a face like we had just walked into the sewers. "My mother always said. She spent so much time here she wanted it to feel like home."

"I'm surprised you still remember me saying that." Her voice came from the racks to our left. My mother came walking out slowly. Wearing a pure white skirt suit with black heels. Her brunette hair tugged back into a tight ponytail. Everything about her screamed professional.

Seeing that thick scar that ran down her face and disappeared under her collar had my heart pounding. "I remember a lot of things. This is..."

"Detective Dawson. I know all officers and detectives who are working cases that might leak into our jurisdiction." She came over. Closing a book into her left hand and reaching out with her right for a handshake.

Dawson took it, smiling wide. "A pleasure too meet you."

"Very polite. Aching to make a good impression I see." Her eyes shifted to me as she let go of his hand. "And you. Do I get a handshake or a hug?"

We shared a look before I turned away. Walking over to the shelving where my hand picked up an object that looked like a compass. Instead of the usual letters it held symbols of some kind. Running my thumb over them. "Did you know I was working this case?"

"No. I don't keep tabs on you."

Giving her a look before walking off down the shelving. Hearing her footsteps following slowly. "So why is this case leaking into you jurisdiction?"

"I can't talk about an ongoing investigation."

"There's a drug out there killing humans."

"People overdose on drugs all the time. As much as I would like it to stop, there's nothing I can do about that fact."

"But these people aren't taking it themselves. Not this one anyway." My eyes moving over the items on the shelves. Pretending to be paying them attention but all I could focus on was her footsteps. Fingers slowly turning that strange compass in circles.

"Let me guess. You've asked the parents. They claim their kid would never touch the stuff. They wouldn't be the first parents to not know what their kid is up to."

Looking over my shoulder at her. "This isn't about us."

"Everything in my life is about you. You're my daughter."

"I didn't come here for this." My footsteps moved quicker, taking me back into the bigger section of the office. Seeing Dawson standing there looking very awkward. I walked over to my buffer and turned. "I know for a fact she didn't take it herself."

"How?" My mother coming over to me. Plucking the item from my fingers and placing it back where it belonged. "A hunch?"

"No." Biting my lip softly. Trying not to let her get under my skin. "Can't you just trust me?"

"I want to know how."

Blowing out a breath that sounded more like a soft growl. "You know how."

"So your powers are getting stronger." This new train of conversation brought her back to us. "How strong?"

"It doesn't matter."

"It does." My mother lifted her hand to stroke my cheek but stopped just an inch shy of my skin. Her hand dropping to her side. "Alright. Fine. So this one didn't take it herself."

"No. A vampire compelled her to. I don't think he knew that she would overdose. But it still means people are out there dying and it's not their fault. And you can't just lump them in with the drug users and forget about it."

"I never said I was forgetting about it."

"Seems like me and Dawson are the only ones investigating at the moment."

"There's a bigger picture you need to see. We're aiming to bring down the people making this drug."

"And the fact you're involved means it's supernatural in nature."

"Yes. I'm sorry I can't just give you the information you need."

"You haven't even heard what information we need. What I want, is to be able to tell the girl's mother that she can rest. That I found the people who were responsible and stopped them."

The head of this division walked back and sat down at her desk. "So I give you this information. What do I get out of it?"

"What do you want?"

"I want you to come work for me."

"That's never going to happen."

"Why not?"

"Because I don't want anything to do with you." My voice rising as that anger started to grow.

"Why do you keep blaming me? I didn't do anything on purpose to make your life difficult. And it wouldn't even be difficult if you would let me help you."

"You're not responsible for my life?" Taking a few steps forward, leaning on the edge of her desk. "I couldn't have stayed with my father and his pack because I can't shift. Leechers would cast me out because I can't leech. When I was growing up. There was a point where I didn't know if I was talking to a real person or a ghost. I would wake up screaming because there was someone in my room."

"I remember every single night."

"So do I. I never fit in anywhere. Not as a werewolf. Not as a leecher and definitely not able to pass as human." Standing upright. Looking down at her and that scar. "You brought someone into my life who almost killed me. That was your choice."

"It wasn't his fault or mine."

"It doesn't matter. It was your decision to have him as your husband."

"And the fact I killed him doesn't mean anything to you? I killed him to save you."

"I wouldn't have been in danger in the first place if it wasn't for you. My father would have been fine if it wasn't for you leaving him. Picking that vampire over him." My words just spitting out. Not looking likely to stop any time soon. "You broke his heart. You pushed him to do things he never would have. And you've broken me too." Feeling the tears rushing down my face. Turning my back to her. Looking at Dawson. The vampire stuck between wanting to comfort me and wanting nothing to do with this argument.

Hearing my mother standing up from her chair. "You only feel broken because you believe you are."

"Maybe if I had a family. Somewhere that felt like home. I wouldn't have grown up like this."

"That wouldn't have changed anything."

"I would have had my parents, together. Teaching me."

"Megan." A hand touched my shoulder but I refused to turn. "Is this what it's all been about? The fact that me and your father aren't together?"

Blowing out a breath. Rubbing my eyes not wanting to cry any more. "No, of course not."

"Even if we were still together. You still wouldn't be able to shift and you still wouldn't have been a part of his pack."

"But we would have had our own pack." Blinking, the tears stopping for a moment.

"You do realise you can still have that. But not until you stop pushing me away. You would still have me and your father. We may not be together but we both love you very much. That's still classed as a family."

Biting my lip. Feeling a tear trickling down my cheek. Letting out a sigh as more followed. "I just wanted a proper family." I knew that need was the werewolf inside me. The need for a pack, to have close ones all around me. It's why I loved having Leon, Connor and Ivy.

My tears came in hard waves of sadness as I started sobbing loudly. Feeling my whole body shaking. A touch from my mother still had me pulling away. A sudden rush of wind and Dawson was right there next to me.

Arms encircling my body. Pressing my face to his chest and letting it all out. The office silent apart from my cries. All that emotion coming hard. Not letting me stop until it had all been released.

Pulling free of his grip and turning to face my mum. Looking at her sad expression. She rubbed a thumb across the bottom of my eye. "It's still possible to have that."

"Maybe." Sniffling then rubbing my sleeve across my face.

"But I think that's a discussion best for another time."

"Probably best if it was just us."

"Of course." As she let out a sigh I did the same. A weight lifted from my shoulders like the tears had washed it away. "Now, the information you want." Swallowing as she walked around to her side of the desk. A drawer was pulled open and a file was brought out.

Looking at the wad of papers. "Did you already have this ready?"

"As soon as I saw you two on the camera. I printed it off."

Taking the folder from her. "How come you've changed your mind?"

"I always knew I would give you everything you wanted as soon as I saw you. If you ever dropped by, I would give you anything. But, I was being selfish. I wanted to see if you would come back to me. To treat me as someone you might love again. I shouldn't be acting like the director. I need to act like your mother."

Swallowing past that emotional lump in my throat. "Thank you."

"Make sure you're both being careful out there."

"I'll make sure Megan stays safe." The vampire standing tall like he was getting inspected.

My mother leant in, "He's cute."

"Mum."

"Too soon? I understand." I gave a soft smile. Thinking about going in for a hug but backing away a step instead. "I'm here, if you ever need me."

"Yeah. I know." Turning and walking away with Dawson beside me. All the way to the elevator it was silent.

As soon as those doors shut Dawson burst out with his words like he was holding them in the whole time. "So that's your mother?"

"Yep."

"I see there's a bit of a strained relationship."

"You figured that out with your keen detective skills?"

"Sorry."

"It's okay." Looking at the numbers as they slowly changed. "I'll give you until we get to the car park to ask any more questions you have." Eyes on his reflection in the elevator doors.

"The rumour is that the head of the supernatural division is the one that saved the world twenty odd years ago."

"Is that a question?"

"I think I can figure out the answer myself." Seeing his eyes on me before he looked straight ahead. "Won't bring it up again."

"I would appreciate that." The box pinged and the doors opened to the car park. Walking over to where I parked the bike. Sitting on the edge and flicking through the papers. Handing some over to the detective.

Scanning through the information. "Seems they've been keeping track of these dealers when the drug first hit. Obviously they didn't do anything since they're human."

Turning a piece of paper around for him to see. "Looks like the owner of RDJs is one of the shot callers. Possibly the man in charge of the whole distribution of drugs around the city."

"Glad we didn't pick that one to visit the other night. He'll have security coming out of his arse. Doubt we would have made it out of there alive."

"Maybe a visit during the day would be a better idea. There won't be any customers. We'll see everything clearer."

"I think that's probably best." His eyes scanned across the paper I was showing him. "Doesn't have any information of where he's getting his drugs from. You don't think he's making it himself?"

"Not according to this. They've tracked shipments to and from the club but can't back-track it to the origin. These guys are really careful if they're fooling the division."

"We'll just have to work on our detective skills then. Let's go visit this guy. Put the squeeze on him so to speak. Get some information out of him."

"And what if he doesn't want to share?"

"I can be quite convincing you know. Plus I can just glamour him to spill all his secrets."

"Sounds like a plan. We need to go in soft though. Spook him too early and he'll get a message out to his buddies. We'll never find them."

"Best let me do all the talking then."

"What's that supposed to mean?" I stood, whacking him with the pile of papers.

"Your people skills could use a little work. That's all I'm saying."

"Get on the bike before I kick you in the shins and leave you here." He laughed as we climbed onto the bike. Leaving the car park and heading through the city. Heading into the more populated area where the night life lived.

The place looked deserted at this time of the day. The front of nightclubs that would usually be lit up with queues running for miles were bleak and bare. Finding plenty of space right outside RDJs.

Looking up at the circular neon lights. Spelling out those letters with a cocktail glass sitting below them. Climbing off and locking my helmet to the handlebars. Spotting an alleyway that ran down between this place and the bar next door. "What do you think about me going around back and sneaking in whilst you distract the owner?"

"Don't you think they'll have cameras?"

"Hence why you need to distract him. Be your usual self. It'll work like a charm."

"I was thinking of being a dirty cop actually. See if he's willing to play ball."

"That might work. Think you can pull of being dirty?"

"One night in bed with me you'd never ask that question again." Seeing the big grin and the little wink he gave me. But seeing through all that and seeing Dawson for the person he was. He was fun and carefree.

Licking my lips before giving him a wink. "You're not the only one who can be dirty."

"Megan, why I never." Giggling as he pulled a shocked face. Fanning himself as he walked towards the front door. I moved along the path and waited by the corner.

The door opened and Dawson flashed his badge to gain entry. Giving it a few minutes before I started moving down the alley way. Acting casual until I spotted the back door. Pressing my ear to it I couldn't hear anyone nearby. Judging by the cigarette butts on the floor this is where the staff come for a smoke.

I waited until I heard footsteps, someone chatting on the phone. Giving the door a thud and it was opened. When a head poked out I gave the door a quick kick. Slamming it into his face and smacking his head into the door frame. Lowering him down quietly before pulling him out into the alleyway.

I deposited his unconscious body behind some bins. Lifting his phone to my ear. Some woman asking if he was alright. "The boss wanted to speak with him. He'll ring you back shortly." Hanging up and chucking the phone onto his chest.

Moving inside the building I walked along the hallway that ran across the back wall. One door led out behind the bar. Another that would bring me out by the toilets. A massive dance floor looking miserable with no one dancing on it. The place completely lit up with boring white lights. Like seeing a holiday park during a rainy winter. It just didn't look right.

Moving further along I came to the break room. Looking through the small window I saw two men wearing black shirts and trousers. Pouring themselves cups of coffee in the little kitchen. I opened the door and rushed them. Kicking one of the tables into the first body.

The second turned as I knocked his hand up. Pouring the hot liquid over his face. A swift punch to his throat made him stumble back gurgling in pain. Dropping to his knees trying to breath properly.

The first climbed over the table. Swinging my leg to trip him up. His shoulder hitting the table before landing on the floor. Swinging my foot across his face and knocking him out cold. Turning to the wheezing man who was still struggling to gain his breath. Grabbing a fistful of his hair and slamming his face into my knee.

The body slumped back lifeless. About to leave when I noticed the little basket of biscuits. Grabbing one and munching it down as I went back into the hallway. Coming across the locker room next.

Hearing the faint noise of music playing. Spotting a cleaner dancing about with his earphones in. Deciding to leave him to it. Moving further along until I came to a dead-end. The door to my right led out into the main area of the club.

Pushing through cautiously I couldn't hear anyone. Stepping through I peered up as sunlight shone down through a stain glass ceiling. Seeing the colours and motions of the sea. Waves crashing down, creating that wash of white.

The vision the ghost showed me. I saw the sea like it was actually there. The drug must have gotten her high as a kite whilst she choked on her own vomit. She saw it moving. She died right there on the dance floor in front of me.

Hearing a sudden cheer from behind a set of double doors. Running over silently. Picking up three different voices. Two men and a woman. The female not sounding like she was having fun. Begging to leave. Pressing my shoulder to the door. "You're not going anywhere. We deserve our money's worth and since we're paying your wages, get that arse moving." Hearing her yelp after a sharp slap.

Turning the handle I barged in. My body moving so fast as I pushed it to its limit. Seeing the lady rubbing her cheek as she hugged the pole in the middle. The two men sitting and laughing on the other side of the room.

Getting to them before they even knew what had happened. Punching one in the face so hard his head snapped back and his body shifted limp to the side. The other was raising an arm as I got to him. Grabbing the wrist and spinning him down to the floor. Ramming his face into the cheap carpet.

He grunted in pain as I twisted his arm even further. Pushing until I felt his shoulder pop out of joint. Slamming my fist against it causing it to dislodge even more. Reaching around, wrapping my hand across his jaw. Then I snapped back. His neck breaking. Head flopping to the carpet with a thud.

Blowing out a few deep breaths before the lady hugged me tight. Thanking me over and over before she ran for the door. Hearing her footsteps taking her out onto the dance floor. I followed but ducked back when there was a loud bang. A bullet skimming past and breaking into the wooden door frame.

Peering out I saw three men. The distance was too great. As soon as I pop out of cover they'll put a bullet in me. The man with the gun called to me. "We already have your partner downstairs. Come quietly and you won't be harmed."

Looking around but there was no escape. This was the only option which would allow me to live. Even if it's just for a short time. "I'm coming out. I haven't got any weapons."

"Out you come then. I won't shoot." Peering out again to see him still holding that gun. His other hand waving for me to come out. "I won't shoot. I promise."

"Okay." Taking a deep breath and coming out slow. My hands up, body ready to react but he kept his word. A hand wrapped around my elbow and I was pushed through a door labelled private. Coming to a set of stairs that went down to the right. Lowering ourselves into a vast room right under the dance floor.

Looking up through the glass. Able to see the ceiling high above us. "That's just pervy."

"It's a good way to keep an eye on my customers." Looking over to the man behind his desk. A black suit adorning his athletic build. Bald head shining underneath the lights.

"Remind me to never wear a skirt or a dress to your club."

"Why don't you come in and have a seat next to your partner." Seeing the vampire sitting there. No harm was done to him so I took the spare seat. The man in charge dismissed his three employees that had escorted me in. "My name is Mister Carver."

"We know."

"Boy, it's impolite to interrupt someone." The man stood up, suit tailored to his tall stature. Watching as he walked over to the glass cabinet. The doors were opened and he pulled out a nice wooden box. Stained dark. A gold clasp being opened before the lid was lifted up.

Out came a long cigar. The end getting clipped off before a lighter was revealed. The man not saying another word until the end was gently glowing orange. Smoke leaking from his lips as he leant back in his chair. "I could tell your man here was a cop of sorts when he came walking in. Claiming he was looking for under the table work."

Dawson gave me a smile. "It was worth a shot."

"That it was. You get top results for having

balls. But you." His hand grabbed a small remote. At the press of a button a projector came to life. Shining onto the only blank wall his office. Showing me sneaking down the hallway. Cutting to the break room. Seeing how I caught the two men off guard. "I wasn't one hundred percent sure here. But then I saw this part."

The video changing again. Feeling like this man couldn't get any seedier when I saw they had a camera in the private room. In I came. The first going down. Looking much harsher from this angle. Then the second was took to the floor. Me snapping his neck. Looking to see Dawson's reaction. "Impressive."

"Shut it." Biting my lip so I didn't smile at his comment.

"Watching you kill those men cleared it up for me. You're not part of any law enforcement. Which begs the question. Who are you?"

We needed to play this smart otherwise we wouldn't be walking out of here alive. "I'm a PI. I'm looking into the overdose that happened in your club."

"There are no drugs here."

"I'm not here for you. I'm here for the man that gave her the drug. Now, my plan was to have the detective here distract you. I would sneak in and steal the security tapes for that night. Hoping to find the guy responsible."

"So you thought the best option was to assault my men?"

"Granted, I may have gotten a little carried away. But those men in the room were treating that girl like crap. As far as I'm concerned they got what they deserved."

"One way of looking at it." The man's eyes studied me as he sat there puffing on his cigar. "The other would be that you're looking into more than one overdose."

"You've got someone on the force." Dawson's voice was especially smooth compared to the man opposite.

"Indeed I do. I also know that you recently visited a bumbling idiot who does his work out of In The Ruff. You see I've been tracking you for a little while now."

"Were you the one who sent someone to kill my snitch?"

"You mean the man that was found in the park with his head ripped off?" Eyes lingering on the detective before slipping to me. "Which one of you managed to do that?"

"Me."

"An amazing feat of strength. But a total waste of blood." My brow creasing as I looked at him. Studying his face. "And such a despicable way of disposing of the body. Just leaving him there under a pile of leaves." He stood up and my whole body tensed.

Looking over my shoulder to make sure those men hadn't returned. Checking the corners and finding no cameras. My heart rate hiking quickly. "You don't seem at all surprised. A little girl like me ripping someone's head off." Looking over to Dawson who seemed to now be catching what I was getting at.

"You could say I've had my eyes opened recently. Introduced to a new world." My heart raced as he came walking around his desk. Sucking on that cigar. The smoke leaking from his lips more than being pushed out. "It's amazing the kind of gifts my new friends have bestowed upon me."

My fingers gripped the chair to push me up but he vanished from sight. My heart skipping the beat it took for him to move and grab Dawson's throat. That cigar getting rammed into his eye. The detective screaming in pain.

I rushed over and dug my shoulder into his gut. Like hitting a brick wall it hurt me more than it did him. Feeling him hooking an arm under me and I was sent flying into one of his book shelves. Dropping down through the wood to the floor. Groaning as thick books landed on me.

Dawson was pulled from his chair and pushed back, furniture getting kicked out of their way. I got up and followed. Grabbing hold of the vampire and pulling him from my friend. Dawson shooting out harsh punches to his gut.

I rammed my foot into his knee ditch. Pushing him down. Dawson cracking fists into his face over and over. Sucking in air just as an arm flung out at me. Feeling his punch hitting my ribs hard. A loud crack filling my ears as the bone snapped.

Hitting the floor with a groan. Holding my side. My friend getting tossed back into the wall. A blur of speed and the man was back behind his desk. Sitting in his leather chair. His cigar sitting in his lips.

I got up to my knees but had to stop there. Breathing shallow to avoid a pulse of pain. Seeing those sharp teeth as he opened his mouth to take another puff on that cigar. "I was terrified when this new gang came into town. Telling me they're going to take over and kill anyone who gets in their way. Needless to say I bowed out. But instead of gaining my territory. They gained a worker. And I gained a new boss."

"Is there a point to this?" Pushing myself up on my feet as my bones started to heal.

"They gave just as much as they took. Turning me into a vampire opened up so much of my life. I didn't realise how much I was missing. Incredible speed. Strength. Never getting ill. The ability to heal almost anything with enough blood. Even the ability to make people do what I want. I haven't had this much sex in decades."

"Could you be any more of a creep?" My hand still touching to my side. Pressing to see how painful it would be to fight.

"Name calling is very uncalled for. Plus, they enjoy themselves." He placed the cigar into an ash tray. His fingers moving over to an electronic pad on his desk. "The best thing are the gadgets though. Little things to make my life easier when someone comes calling. They knew the government would start investigating. Sending their little agents along."

"I'd be very happy if you told me your bosses were packing up their things and heading for the horizon." Dawson came to stand next to me. That burn mark swelling up one of his eyes.

"Not quite. I have my orders. To kill anyone who sticks their noses into our business. Drain the bodies of all pints of blood then dispose of the bodies."

"I've killed vampires before." A gush of air kicked up as Dawson rushed forward. A loud thud erupted around the room as a sheet of glass shot down between us and that desk. The detective stumbled back rubbing his head. My eyes seeing that it didn't make a mark in the glass. "What's this?" The detective pressed hands to the divider. "Hiding back there? You've trapped yourself."

I looked over my shoulder to see that another pane of glass had come down over the door. Meaning we were trapped down here as well. Turning back to the owner of the club. "What are you planning?"

"I'm going to watch you being ripped apart by your partner. Then I'll put him out of his misery when he realises what he's done."

Dawson laughed, "You'll never get me to kill her."

"You won't have a choice." Another button was pushed and red light filled the room. Feeling the heat of it against my skin.

Watching Dawson slowly turn. A look of worry on his face. "What is it?"

"It's like the sun only ten times worse."

"But your implant. It won't affect you."

"I don't think it's strong enough." He flexed his jaw. Seeing points coming out of his gums. Growing in length. The vampire shaking his head. "Megan."

"Dawson. You can fight it."

"No, I can't." He took a deep breath before blurring over to the exit. Bashing fists so hard against the glass his knuckles bled. "This isn't good."

"What can I do?"

The room fell silent. His hands pressed flat to the glass. Heavy breaths fogging up the glass. The detective turned and I saw his eyes. The red lines coursing over that white. Pupils huge. My whole body shaking in fear. Bringing back memories I had buried deep. Bringing my worse nightmare to life.

CHAPTER 8

Backing away slowly until I pressed up against the wall. Swallowing again and again as I looked into those eyes. Dawson's muscles straining against his shirt. My mouth opening to speak when he came for me. Gasping at the sudden movement.

Just able to dodge out the way, tumbling to the floor. I spun over as the vampire jumped against the wall then launched at me. Laying flat as his body came down on mine. I pressed up a knee between us. Keeping him from chomping those teeth into my neck with an arm across his chest. My other hand grabbing a fistful of his hair.

Using all my strength to hold him back but it still wasn't enough. His biting jaws lowering closer and closer. My whole body sweating as I feared for my life. The wolf wasn't enough so I called to that dormant part of me.

Awakening my leecher ability and focusing on his ashy scent. Finding it quick since he was all over me. Reaching mentally. Trying to grab hold of it but it was like trying to keep sand in your fist.

Feeling it slipping through again and again. Trying so hard my eyesight started to go blurry. My head pounding. Gritting my teeth, feeling them grow sharper as I pulled on more of my werewolf strength.

Looking around frantically. Seeing the broken shelves laying on the floor. Looking into Dawson's eyes as I reached for a piece. Fingers wrapping around it I slammed my attack into his side.

The vampire coiled up in pain. His arm twisting to try and grab that piece of wood as it reacted with his blood. Like silver on mine, his vampire blood started to boil with the contact. Kicking out with both feet to send him crashing to the wall.

I rolled over and crawled across the floor but I felt his weight on me again. Then his bite as he tore those teeth into my neck. Hearing him sucking up that blood greedily. Trying to pull my arms from underneath but he held me down.

Crying out as he shifted his jaws. Tearing open my neck even more. Sucking in a breath as he pulled me up into the air. Still feeding as he slammed me into the glass divider. Pinning me there as he fed.

Feeling my fingers going numb. Spreading up my forearms. My eyes open wide, seeing how the drug dealer watched with a sick smile. Puffing on his cigar. Feeling my body getting weaker. Then the sensation of cold coursed through my body.

Not realising it wasn't blood loss until I could see my breath hitting against the glass. Blinking a few times until I saw a little boy. Wearing a wet suit. A single red flower in his collar. Eyes staring at me.

I pressed my hand to the glass. Concentrating

on that little figure. Calling to him mentally. Making him come closer until he vanished from sight. Appearing next to me with a tug on my top. Looking down out the corner of my eye. "How can you see me?"

"I...." Spitting blood out over the glass. "Who are you?"

"My name is Billy. That's my older brother." He pointed to the man behind the desk.

Bringing in all my strength and calling out. "Billy!"

The red light suddenly vanished. That heat disappearing making me feel even colder. Teeth pulled out of my flesh and I was dropped. Taking a moment on my knees, shaking. Feeling blood coursing down my neck. Putting my hand there which was quickly covered.

I looked over my shoulder. Dawson was wiping his mouth with the back of his hands. The look of pure fear written across his face. Turning back to look up at the dealer who had walked around to me. I hadn't even felt the glass sliding back into the wall. He placed a hand under my chin. "How do you know that name?"

"He was your little brother."

"How do you know that?" Getting words growled at me in anger.

"I can see him. He's right next to you." Looking past him to the little boy. His expression full of rage. "What happened to him?"

"He got what he deserved."

The ghost suddenly shouted. "I didn't deserve to be killed! He was responsible for our mother falling down the stairs. I saw him push her. And to shut me up he drowned me in our pool. My father thought I committed suicide. Believing him that it was all my fault she died."

"What?" Feeling a bit more strength as I joined him in anger. "You drowned him because he knew you killed your mum?"

The vampire's face was blank. Eyes blinking down at me. "There's no way you could know that."

"You took away his mum. Then you took his life."

"He took my life!" The little boy screamed. Making the leather chair fling into the wall hard enough the arm snapped off.

The vampire spun around in shock. "How are you doing this?"

"It's not me." Another scream and the desk was next. Getting destroyed against the two-way ceiling. Bringing down a section in a rain of glass shards.

The dealer backed away from me. "Make it stop."

"I can't." Pushing myself to my feet. Walking over to the little boy and placing my hand on his shoulder. The vampire stared with wide eyes. Noticing his look was down to my right. He was seeing this boy. Feeling the cold against my palm through the wet jacket. "It seems that you're the one who needs to get what you deserve."

The little boy stepped forwards so I followed. The older brother dropping to his knees. Tears starting to fall and turn to ash. "Please, I was young and stupid. I didn't know what else to do."

"You knew what you were doing." Feeling the ghost getting colder as his anger grew. "And this is what you get. Die!" Feeling the whoosh of air as a piece of wood flew through the air. Seeing it pierce through the vampire's chest.

Slamming him back into the wall. Pinned there as he writhed in agony. Screaming out in pain as the blood boiled out of his wound. Watching as his skin started to melt. Pieces of his body dripping off.

Hearing the cries of horror from above when his men came to see what was going on. The three of them running. Horrified by the sight of their boss turning into a gooey mess. The screaming turning to gurgles as he drowned on his own liquefied flesh. Slowly turning silent. His skin had shifted so much I could see his bones shining through.

Turning around and crouching in front of the boy. Keeping my hand over my leaking neck. "That was very brave of you."

"Thanks. I've wanted to do that for so long. You made it doable."

"I don't think I did much."

"You did." He came in for a tight hug which surprised me. Feeling the warmth of his body. When he pulled back he smiled. Seeing how his clothes were no longer drenched. His hair dry and neatly combed to the side. "What do you think happens to me now?"

Giving him a big smile. "Someone will come. You won't be able to see him. But he's a friend. He'll take you somewhere peaceful."

"Thank you."

"Thank you, as well. You saved me." Giving the tip of his nose a little bop with my finger. "Have a great afterlife." I pushed away the thought of seeing him. Letting him fade from my sight for him to meet the ferryman.

I stood back up and looked at the remnants still pinned to the wall. This was a mess for my mother to clean up. The supernatural unit are good at cover-ups. So I moved through the office to Dawson.

The vampire was leaning back against the wall. Breathing in and out heavily. He had found something and was wiping his mouth and neck with it. Trying to mop up that blood but it was still there like it had stained his skin.

Stopping a few steps away when his eyes flicked to mine. They weren't blood shot any more but his stare had my fists clenching. My mind tossed back into that nightmare. "I'm sorry. I'm so sorry, Megan." Seeing the flakes of ash dropping from his wet cheeks.

"It's okay." My words didn't have a believable tone. I wanted to move forwards and tell him I was fine. That it didn't affect me. But I couldn't move my feet. Swallowing past the lump in my throat. "How are you feeling now?"

"Better. I never want to feel like that again." He pushed away from the wall to come towards me. Holding my ground until he lifted a hand towards my neck. Flinching as he did. My head falling after seeing the disappointment in his features. "It would be silly of me to think you could let me touch you after that."

"It's just…"

"I get it. I really do. You don't have to explain it. Honestly." He took a step back. "I could do with a little time by myself actually. You don't mind if I head off, do you?"

"No. Of course not. You need time to recover." Jumping on the opportunity to have some space between us.

"Yeah. Um…" He looked everywhere but in my eyes. Looking like I had just told him his dog had died. "I'll give you a call later today. So we can discuss what to do next."

"Maybe change your top." Letting out a soft chuckle that was more reflex than actual laughter.

Dawson smiled but it held his sadness still. "Good idea. I'll call this in to the supernatural unit. They'll want the…" A finger was pointed to the horrible mess against the wall. "Whatever the hell you would call that."

"I was thinking the same. Thanks." Smiling as he left the office. Waiting a few minutes before making my own way out of the club. Grabbing a tea towel from behind the bar. Lodging it under my jacket and over my neck. The bleeding had stopped but it was still an open wound and it hurt like hell.

Something this severe could have ended my life if his teeth had caught an artery. Still, it could leave a nasty scar if I didn't get to Ivy quick enough. She could help me heal and hopefully she won't insist on doing it with a tattoo.

Riding my bike back to the apartment. Getting

inside and making my way to her studio. Opening the door just as she was cleaning up someone's thigh. My room mate's eyes lifted to mine. Seeing the blood on my neck. The way I was holding it. "Uh, just give me one moment." She came rushing over to me. Lifting up the material of my jacket and removing the tea towel. "Bloody hell. What the hell happened to you?"

"Maybe we could talk a little more privately. Possibly whilst you give me something for the pain?" Trying to shut it out as much as possible.

"Alright, you okay for a couple of minutes?"

"Don't rush on my account." I walked over to the little chair in the corner. Leaning against the wall. Watching as she finished up her client by cover her tattoo up with some cream and then wrapping it up.

I got a quick look from her before she paid and went on her way. When Ivy came back she tapped the chair. "Up you come."

"Don't get any ideas about tattooing me. You pick up that gun and I'm heading to a hospital."

"Don't be a baby." I watched as she moved around the little room. Picking out things from the higher shelf. Pulling a pestle and mortar out of a locked cupboard. Mixing it together, crushing the ingredients until what she came back with was a paste. "No wincing, you're a werewolf after all."

I gritted my teeth as she applied that stuff over my wound. Pushing it inside and wiggling her fingers about. "We still feel pain you know."

"Oh, be quiet. When I've been laid out with a hangover from hell. You've been jumping about the apartment."

"Totally not the same thing, Ivy." Gritting my teeth again as she applied more. Feeling the cool mixture pressing to my mangled skin. "It's not my fault alcohol doesn't affect me the same way."

"It is your fault." She pressed around the edges, making sure she did a proper job before using her little sink to wash her hands. Washing the utensils she used. "I'm guessing you came across a vampire."

"That obvious?"

"Wounds on the neck tend to be in that area of the supernatural spectrum. Although this was less of a puncture and more of a tear."

"That's what happens when a vampire hits blood lust." She spun around quickly. Drying her hands before scooting close on her wheeled stool. There she sat with an eyebrow perked high on her forehead. Arms folded across her chest. "It was Dawson."

"Explain before I storm over to wherever he lives and kick his arse."

"You don't need to do that. He feels so bad about what happened. It wasn't his fault."

"Like I said, explain, quickly."

"We went to visit a drug dealer. We entered the club thinking he would be human. Turns out the people supplying him with this new drug is a group of vamps. They turned him more than likely to gain his loyalty. You know how younglings and masters are like."

"They follow orders like good little children."

"Exactly. We thought we had him cornered. But he switched on this red light and it acted like the sun. Even with his implant Dawson couldn't stop himself. The red light triggered his blood lust. His instinct to survive."

"And that's when this happened?"

"Yes."

"How did you stop him?"

I leant my head back against the chair. Flexing my neck and feeling the ache from my wound. "I didn't. There was a ghost there. The dealer killed his mother, then killed his little brother who had witnessed it. He helped me. Killed the vampire actually. Never knew ghosts were so strong."

"I think it's linked to their anger. The reason why they're still here."

"Whatever reason, he saved me. And I guess Dawson. He looked so upset."

Ivy pulled on my hands, placing them inside hers. "I'm not worried about him. I'm worried about you. You told me what happened when you were younger."

"I told Dawson as well."

"Then he knows what happened must have shook you up."

"It did." Giving her a smile. "It really did. I couldn't let him near me. But...."

"But?" Her lips curled. "You must really like him to still want him around after this. Childhood trauma isn't something you just get over."

"You don't have to tell me that. But."

"There's another but." She grinned. "You're all ready to go if you want to find him. Confess your love for him."

"It's not love." Wanting to playfully swat her but knowing it would cause my neck pain. "I like him. Not just the way he looks I mean. Him, the person."

"No point talking to me about personalities. You know I think the body comes first."

"Well, you haven't seen his body."

"Megan." She pulled and pinged her glove at me making my neck hurt when I tried to shift away. "Oh, sorry. That was silly of me." She made sure the paste hadn't been disturbed.

"Dawson said he needed time."

"A sensitive man is hard to find. A sensitive vampire?"

"I get it. You think I should jump his bones."

"No I think you should date his brains out."

"You definitely have a way with words."

"I've been told I have a talented tongue." Ivy wiggled her eyebrows at me.

Turning away and pretending to throw up. "Too much information." Sitting back, lifting my arm up a little. "How long will this take to work?"

"It should be doing its job as we speak. Depending on how badly you were injured, could be a couple of hours to a day or two. It's magick, not a miracle cure."

"I thought that's exactly what magick was?"

"Maybe before the ley lines were damaged. Not any more." She wheeled herself over and dumped her gloves into the bin.

I sat up to the edge of the chair. "Speaking of that event. I saw my mum today."

"Really?"

"Yep. It went about as smooth as you would think."

"No duh. The case took you there?"

"Yeah. With the vampires involvement it was a logical place to stop by."

"Stop by?" She stood and walked over to the fridge she had installed. Grabbing a bottle of water. Chucking it into my lap. "You stop by a cafe or a diner. Not your mother's after not talking to her for years."

Laughing as I took a few gulps of water. "It wasn't as bad as I thought it would be. She may have pointed something to me."

"And what was that?" She took the bottle for her own swig.

"That I was blaming her for my parents not staying together. I feel that if they stayed together I would be more normal."

She rolled her eyes. "Megan. That's what I've been telling you for months, years I think."

"Ivy. You're supposed to support someone when they have a break-through."

"I'm your friend not your therapist. I tell you how it is and what I think. Just like you do with me and Leon."

I stood up and pulled her into a tight hug. "Thanks for always being there."

"I'll always be here for you, Megan. Friends for

life. Plus you won't find anyone else willing to patch you up."

"I have other friends you know."

"I doubt that very much. No one would put up with you."

"Oi." Jabbing her in the ribs which made her jolt then giggle. "Be nice, I'm injured."

"You get no sympathy from me."

"You have the bedside manner of a Rottweiler." I pulled back and gave her cheek a soft kiss. "I'm going to lie down and let my shoulder heal. Maybe I'll give Dawson a ring later in the day."

"A rest is a good idea but you should definitely give him a call later."

"Yes, nurse." Moving out the way of her swatting hand. Making my way into my bedroom and laying down. Not even bothering to remove my clothes. Just wanting to relax and drift off. Shutting my eyes and feeling my mind slipping away.

About to slip into a dream or a nightmare when something grabbed hold of my wrist. Jolting awake, sitting up and wincing in pain. Seeing the ghost of the overdose girl standing there. Her grip tight around my wrist. Her features filled with anger. "What the hell are you doing?"

"Do you mind letting go?" Trying to tug my wrist free but her grip was too tight.

"You should be out there finding the guy that killed me. Instead you're having a lie down."

"I got injured." Yanking my arm from her icy grip which made my neck pulse in pain. "Had a vampire sucking down on my neck for blood."

"A vampire?"

"Yes. Vampire. You're a ghost. I'm a werewolf. The detective helping me is a vampire. There are many, many more beings out there. Welcome to the world you never knew existed." Pushing myself back up the bed. Sitting against the headboard. "Sorry to tell you but being a ghost isn't all that special."

"How dare you!" Her scream created a rush of power. One of my picture frames flying from my chest of drawers.

"Hey!" Moving to stand up but settling at the edge of my bed when the pain was too much. "You can't come in here and start throwing things about. This is my life. You think I want to see ghosts?"

"You think I want to live in a place where you're the only one who can see me? This is torture."

"It's no picnic for me either and I'd like to point out. You're not the only ghost I see."

"It wouldn't be such a terrible imposition if you weren't a horrible person."

"Excuse me?"

"If you actually wanted to help people you would be happy about seeing us. You get to help people no one else can."

I finally stood, ignoring the pain. "I didn't ask for this gift or all the other crap that's happened in my life. I never asked for any of it."

"So you just want me to hang around. Watching life going by without the ability to affect it. To watch others living. Going out and having fun."

"It's not my responsibility." I had lost myself to the anger. "You come to me. Showing me how you died. Pleading me for help. Interrupting my life. Telling me I need to help you. I'm sorry but I have my own problems. The guy I was starting to like turns out to be a vampire. I get over that. Then he attacks me and tries to drain me of my life. I'm still not sure if I can get past that."

"At least you get to decide. To choose which way your life goes. Mine just came to an end. It's not fair!" Cold air filled the room. Knocking my drawers to the floor. Books from my shelf being chucked across the room.

I stepped to the ghost. "Hey! Stop that!" Grabbing her wrist my brain was flooded with coloured lights that were blinding. My mouth dropping open, sucking in air as best as I could. My eyes going wide until the inside of the club came into view. It was the night she had overdosed but earlier.

She was at the bar doing shots with her friends. Mirrors opposite showed the rest of the club. Taking it all in until I saw that vampire named Trevor. He was in the distance but it was definitely him. "Stop." The image freezing. Liquid pouring down my throat, feeling the burn of the alcohol. "That's him."

"Who?" The ghost's voice filled my mind.

"The vampire that gave you the drug. He's right there." Wanting to point with my finger but my body refused to move. "What's he doing?"

"He looks like he's handing something over to that man."

Looking at his hand. The packets of white in them. "The drugs. Wait this vampire is the drop man. He's part of the gang. I thought he was just some random vamp. It's important we find this guy."

"That's what I've been saying all this time."

"I know, I know. But this guy will lead me to the group making it. I can shut down the whole operation. Make sure no one else overdoses on this stuff."

"What do you want me to do?"

"Can you fast forward to when he speaks to you?"

"I don't know. It wasn't me who stopped it."

"It was me?" Thinking about this memory pushing forward. My mind shifting through time slowly. Watching as she enjoyed more drinks. Chatting with her friends before they moved to the dance floor.

Dancing around the massive crowd before that vampire showed up. That tall figure looking down. "Freeze it there." The world coming to a halt. "I can't see anything that could lead me to him. Back it up slowly." Speaking to the ghost like she was in control. My words pushing back that scene bit by bit. The view shifting as the girl spun to the music. Seeing that tall figure a little further away. "There."

My hand trying to shoot out like it was going to hit a pause button. Looking at him. One of his hands dipping inside his jacket. Seeing the badge that was hanging from his inside pocket. The symbol like two blue waves crashing over two letters. "I can't make them out."

"Wait, I know that symbol." Hearing her excited words bouncing around my brain. "It's a company, I've passed by that place so many times. Down by the river. That massive thing floating in the water. That's their symbol."

"If he works there. That could be where they're making this stuff. Do you know what they're doing in the water?"

"The story is that they're studying it. Finding out ways to purify it for drinking."

"Which means they might have containers, labs. With the flow of the river they could be powering that place with the current. Self-sustaining drug lab off the grid. Sounds like the perfect place for their operation."

"So what do we do now?"

I pulled myself out of her memories and let go of her wrist. Looking into her eyes. "I finish this. And kill that vampire."

"Thank you." The ghost peered around my room. "I'm really sorry about the mess."

"Don't be. It's seen worse. At least it's not covered in ice this time." Moving around and picking up that picture frame. Looking at the photo of me and my father cuddling together when I was a baby. "How do you get here?"

"How do you mean?"

"When I find this vampire. I'd like you to be there. To watch."

"I would love to be there. Sometimes I hear you. Like you're calling to me."

"It might be when I'm weak or my guard is down. I lose my control over this ability and you hear it. Would explain why other ghosts have appeared when I'm asleep or injured. I promise you, I'll call to you when I have him."

"Thank you, again." She hugged me which made my whole body shiver. "And sorry, again."

"Don't mention it." I gave her a smile before she faded from sight. Leaving me in my room all alone. I checked my neck in the mirror. The paste was still intact. Blowing out a sigh. "No time to rest, Megan. Get your arse moving."

So I quickly jumped into the shower. Taking the head off the wall and soaking myself. Watching I didn't disrupt the paste. Cleaning myself up of blood and giving my hair a quick wash. Flinging it back into a ponytail before getting dressed in my room.

Picking a baggy top that would hang off my injured shoulder. Leaving my wound space to heal. Chucking on a pair of black jeans a nice black hoody. White patterns on the left shoulder woven down the sleeve. I looked very casual but it'll have to do for now.

I moved from one apartment to the other. Letting Ivy know what I was up to just in case something happened. Heading down to my bike. Before heading off I called Dawson but he didn't pick up.

I had no clue if he didn't hear it or if he was avoiding me. If it was the latter I didn't want to impose myself on him. So I sent over a text message letting him know what I had learned and where I would be. Maybe a hint of danger in my upcoming day would push him to get in contact.

Using my bike I dodged through traffic. Pulling up alongside the river. Stopping my ride in the little lay-by where a nice food truck was always parked up. Grabbing a tray of chips and walking along the river.

Seeing the massive white structure sitting in the middle. A walkway running from the side to the middle platform. Two dome structures either side. Doors leading into both visible from where I was. There were a couple of people up top smoking and munching on food.

Eating my chips as I walked past the gate that locked the walkway from any wanderers. I could get around it easy enough. Only I saw the cameras sitting at the other end. They would know I was there before I could find anything important. I looked down at the water. Seeing how murky it was. Not liking the idea of swimming through that just to gain access.

I parked myself on a bench. My eyes moving around the scenery of the river but keeping my attention on that water building. Finishing my chips and chucking the tray into the bin. Blowing out a breath as I couldn't think of a way in.

Pulling out my phone I gave Dawson another ring. It went on and on until the line picked up. Surprised that my heart skipped a beat at the thought of hearing his voice. "Hey." Hearing the slur in his speech in that single word.

"Been drinking I hear."

"It's the only way to rid myself of the

nightmares. Both past and more recent."

"Look. I don't feel...." Stopping myself. Realising that no matter what I said it was his own guilt making him feel this way. I could reel off a thousand reasons why he shouldn't be depressed about it but that was me, not him. "I've got a lead. Think you could sober up enough to meet me by the river?"

"I don't think we should work on this case any more. I'm a vampire and your history isn't very positive in that area."

Feeling a hole growing in my stomach. "It's my history to live with. I decide what I live with. All you have to do is respond to my decision. Don't make excuses based on what you think is best for me. I decide that."

"Megan."

"Look, you seem to have your own problems with drinking my blood. Don't use mine to cover up that fact. I'm getting over what happened. I want us to work together on this case. I want you in my life. So if you can deal with your problems then get your arse up here. We have a case to finish."

Leaving him with that thought as I hung up. Pushing my phone into my pocket. Looking over to that bright white thing in the water. The soft taps of steps on the metal gang way bringing my eyes to one of the men.

Seeing him discarding a cigarette into the water. His white coat giving him an air of intelligence. Pushing out my leeching radar. Breathing through the dull ache as I locked my eyes on him. Thinking about only him and reaching out. Catching that whiff of ash.

He was a vampire and that meant I would need to be quick about this. Marching after him, crossing the road a little further down. My eyes on his back. If I tailed him for too long there was a chance he would spot me.

Biting my lip, thinking I should head back when he ducked into a little corner shop. One of those places that tried to shove too many products into a small space so you could barely move. As I got to the door it swung open just missing my face.

A man came jogging out of the shop mumbling something to himself. Confused I stepped in and hands grabbed a hold of me. Pulling me through and flinging me through that small space. Hitting the back shelving and dropping.

Hearing the door being locked. Looking up as the vampire turned over the closed sign. "Why are you following me?"

"I love a guy in a white coat." As I pushed myself up causing my shoulder to ache. Pulsing pain but I gritted my teeth. Not wanting to show him my weakness. "Thought you were cute."

"You don't seem like a stalker to me. You have no idea what you're getting yourself in for."

Knowing I would only register as a human in his nose I pretended to be nothing more than a blood bag to him. "Obviously I made a stupid decision. Let me go and we can just forget about this."

"Not a chance. Doesn't matter why you were

following me. I haven't drank in a few hours. You were at the wrong place at the wrong time." The vampire came stomping down that thin aisle. Waiting until he got close enough. My hands grabbing the shelves that run up the middle of the shop and swung them across.

Catching him off guard so much he hit his head against the wall and tumbled to the floor. Crisps and sweets dropping on top of him. He flicked them away as I moved to his body. Slamming my foot down into his face.

The second one he caught and spun me off balance. He was up and coming for me before I could regain my balance. Hands grabbed my hoody and he lifted me up. My fingers gripped into his wrists. Claws growing through his skin as I swung my leg around his neck. Bringing my other knee up into his throat. Cranking his head back. "Looks like you don't know what trouble you've found."

Squeezing my legs together. Feeling in a position of power until he started swinging me around. Smacking me into the walls. Hitting shelving to the ground. The impacts just made me dig my claws in further. Blood running up his arms.

It wasn't until he cracked my shoulder against the wall that I let go. The momentum of his body sending me sailing to the floor. Hitting so hard my eyesight went blurry. Spots of sparkling stars filled my vision.

Eyes shot wide as fingers grabbed my throat. Lifting me up with ease. Swinging my leg around again but this time he blocked it. Holding me up like

I was nothing to him. Squeezing as I wheezed for breath.

I growled out as much as I could. Looking down at this vampire. His mouth opening and those teeth sliding out an inch. My grip around his wrist wasn't doing anything. So I grabbed his face with my hand. Curling my thumb and shoving it into his eye socket. The feeling of that pop as it shot gunky liquid over my hand.

I was dropped. Landing on my feet I shoved my shoulder into this vampire's gut. Pushing back until I saw the doorway and the stairs that led down to the basement. Grabbing him and chucking him backwards.

Hearing his body hitting those concrete steps with cracks and groans of pain. Seeing him thudding to the very bottom. His neck snapping as he landed. Bones sticking out of his skin. I slowly made my way down to him.

A snapped neck was a good way to incapacitate a vampire only it wouldn't kill him. Which would have to do for now. I grabbed his lab coat and pocketed that badge where no one could see it. I looked nothing like the picture but I would still need it to gain access to the facility.

Leaving him there and locking the door behind me. Making my way out of the shop, keeping the closed sign showing through the glass. I got back to the structure. Using the key card I gained access to the gang way.

Moving down the slight slope I got on top of the

fake research facility. Nodding to the two men still out here smoking. Using the key card for a second time and gaining access to the nearest dome. Moving inside where the noise of machinery filled my ears.

The place was less like a research lab and more like a factory. Machines pounding down below. Moving down two flights of metal stairs. Looking over the railing as I descended. Seeing vats of liquid being churned in circles. Something clear getting mixed with a white substance. A couple of men shuffling it in every now and again.

Further back was a massive generator that was being powered by the current of the river. The sound of rushing water joining the loud noises. Cables running from that machine to the lights sitting around the curved walls. Meaning it was a good start if I wanted to shut this place down.

But my first port of call was finding this Trevor. Once I had tortured him enough. I could move onto halting production. As I got to the bottom I started walking through. The sounds were deafening.

The only other person here was working near the back. A massive table was set up where he seemed to be splitting the finished compound. Trays in a row to squeeze out the liquid from the finished product.

The stirrers gave me a weird look for a few minutes before getting back to their job. Moving over to the back where it was a little quieter. Trying to stand tall with authority but he still looked down at me when I arrived. The air around me wafting with ash. I needed to get this done before they realised

I wasn't one of them. Hoping they wouldn't bother giving me a sniff since the white coat made me fit in with everyone else.

Clearing my throat. "You know where Trevor is?"

"He works with distribution in the other unit."

"Cheers." Turning to walk away but he grabbed my hand. "Is there a problem?" Looking up into his eyes. Not backing down as he squared off to me.

"My name is Freddie. Haven't seen you around here before. Are you new?"

"Sure am. My name is Denise." My hand extended feeling his palm slip down from my wrist to shake it. Taking a deep breath and releasing it slowly. The vampire's fingers grabbing my hand tighter. Yanking me forward but I was ready.

Throwing my shoulder into him so he stumbled into the table. Rushing forward I threw my knee into his chest sending him down to the floor. Swinging my foot into his jaw. Knocking him out cold but to make sure I had enough time I grabbed his head and twisted. Hearing his bone cracking.

Peering over to the stirrers who were looking for the commotion. Keeping low I moved behind the table. Making my way around the room quickly. One of the vampires walking over to see what was going on with his buddy.

Sneaking up behind the other I bashed his head into the massive metal bucket. Tipping him over the edge and inside to be swirled around. Picking up the metal pole he was using and scurrying across the room.

Getting to the vampire as he found his co-worker out cold. Smacking the end of the pole into the base of his neck. His spine cracking into pieces right there. His mind losing power over his body. Making him drop with a thud. Giving him a second whack. This time round the back of the head hard enough to cave in that section of his skull.

Walking to the generator I looked at the massive console it was connected to. Seeing the dials and the buttons. Not knowing what any of them did. So I decided to turn everything up. Pushing all the levers up, turning the knobs to the highest numbers. Seeing the dials starting to climb. Seeing the red areas they would eventually reach.

Hoping that will give me enough time to find Trevor and make him pay. Leaving the drug making half of the facility. Moving back up and over. The outside world not realising what had just happened inside. Entering the other dome with my stolen key card.

It was much the same. A metal stairway that led me down to the bottom level. Only this time there was a tunnel that connected the two domes together. A pile of that white powder sitting there. This side of the facility was more populated with vampires.

Many of them working on putting that powder into little plastic capsules. Bagging them up. Further across this little bags were being boxed up. As I got to the bottom step I noticed the different stickers on the boxes. Clearly this city wasn't the only place they were distributing this drug.

I made my way over to the nearest vampire. "Where's Trevor?"

The vampire too busy to turn around to reply, "He's not working today. The lucky bugger got called up for the party tonight."

"The party?"

"At the mansion you idiot. Not that we'll ever get an invite for it."

"How come he got one?"

"What?" The vampire finished sellotaping the box he was working on and went to turn.

I shoved my knuckle against his back. "Don't move. I've got a wooden stake sitting right behind your heart. You make a noise or a move I don't like and you'll be on the floor nothing more than a boiling pile of mess. Nod if you understand."

He nodded. "Who are you?"

"I'll be asking the questions." Shifting around so it looked like we were talking. The nearest vampire was a few metres away with his back turned to us. "Where's the party?"

"At the master's mansion in the city."

"There aren't any mansions in the city. Try again."

"Yes there is. The wildlife park for endangered birds. It's a front. The place doesn't go all the way to the middle. He's set up his estate there."

"That's impossible. People would notice. The amount of drones flying overhead."

"Have you never heard of magick? He's been

living there for decades. There might not be any more illusion witches but the enchantments they created still work to this day."

"How do I get in?"

"You would need an invitation. And they don't give them out to humans." Gasping as his arm swung for me. Fingers wrapped around my throat. His eyes dropping to my hand and he grinned. "That's a finger. Not a stake." His muscles tensed as he lifted me high into the air.

"Put me down and we can just forget about this."

"You're not in a position to negotiate."

My eyes moving around as the other vampires started coming closer. I didn't have much time. "I tried to do this the easy way." Bringing my knee up into his face. His head snapping back but his grip didn't falter.

Slamming my knee again brought blood pouring out of his nose. My throat getting squeezed harder. "You think that's going to work?"

"When all else fails." Shoving my thumb into his eye. He screamed and pulled back. Sucking in a huge breath as I dropped to the floor. Hitting harder than I thought, my legs buckling. I rolled onto my front.

A pair of feet already there. Crying out as a fist grabbed my hair. Tugging me to my feet before I got a punch square in the face. My vision shaking blurry as my head snapped back. Stumbling into the conveyor belt behind me.

Putting up my hands as my vision returned.

Three vampires standing before me. Two more not bothering to get involved. I let out a soft chuckle. "You don't think I can handle three of you?"

One of them stepped forwards. "We're going to drip all that blood out of your system and dump your body in the river. No one will find you for days."

"Why hasn't anyone created a vampire etiquette school. You lot are so rude." The first lunged for me. Kicking out his foot so he dropped. Not enough time to finish him off as the other two gripped my arms.

Lifting me up and slamming me to a table covered in boxes. Sending them flying as the wood snapped in half. Dropping through with a grunt. Groaning as my body signalled so much pain through every nerve.

A hand grabbed my ankle and I was dragged out of the mess. Pulled up into the air. Hands holding onto the lab coat. My head flopping left and right as my body tried to heal. My shoulder aching so much it felt like my arm would drop off.

A growl rolling up my throat as I saw teeth slipping from the gums in front of me. Swinging my arm over head and slamming my fist down into his chin. Snapping his mouth open, skin ripping. Blood pouring out as I was dropped.

Not enough energy to get up. A kick hitting into my ribs. Screaming as pain rolled through my core. Ribs were definitely broken. My body getting beat worse and worse as more kicks hit hard. Crying out. Hands trying to stop the onslaught but I was too weak.

Moaning on the floor when they finally stopped. My body in so much pain it was like a truck had smacked into me. Opening my eyes. Blurry from the impacts. Looking up as two vampires stood above me.

Not even able to move my limbs I was in so much pain. My hair was grabbed. The vampire lifted my head up. A sudden impact hit my face. Blood filling my mouth. Feeling it dribble out the corner of my lips. Spitting it out onto the floor groaning.

This was how my life ended. Getting beaten by a pair of vampires. Rolling my eyes as I thought about the decisions that led me here. As soon as the case turned supernatural I should have walked away. Preferring a more human lifestyle. Letting my head fall back.

One of the vampires spoke but his words were lost to the pain. Then a loud bang make the metal beneath me shake. Another hitting and the lights went out. Footsteps coming closer as all the vampires grouped together around me.

A third bang rung out and the ground seemed to shift. Making me roll to the side. Slanted as gravity seemed to lose control. Opening my eyes and looking around. Seeing the rush of water start coming through the wall. Vampires running for the stairs. Leaving me weak on the floor.

Cold water hitting my body. Sucking in a breath as it washed over me. Picked up off the floor as the river started to fill up this place. The cold water coming over my head and I started to drop through it.

The world around me being blanked out by the liquid. Opening my eyes but with the lights out I couldn't see anything. The weightlessness of my environment making it seem I was being dragged off to heaven.

The pain going numb in the cold. My body possibly going into shock. My head filling with memories. The real world lost to me now. Just my thoughts moving through my mind until they were taken away by the dark. By the lack of life in me and I dropped into the vast black abyss I found myself in.

CHAPTER 9

The pain rolled through me like thunder. Lightning bolts shooting through my nerves. Screaming out in pain as teeth raked through my side. Looking down and seeing my blood covering the vampire's face. So much of it pouring out he didn't even seem to be enjoying it. Just needing more of it.

I slapped him with my hands but it was no good. His eyes watched me as he fed on my side. Seeing the red lines filling up the white. The pupils big like saucers. Crying out for my mum. Needing to be saved.

Thinking it was hopeless until a broken off chair leg was stabbed down through the vampire's chest. Seeing the moment he realised it was over. Blood popping against the wood. Boiling out and turning darker.

Hands dragged me away as his skin started to melt. Cooked from the inside. The room spinning as I was pulled around to see the face of the woman who had saved me. Seeing my mother. The wound running down her face was pissing out blood. So much of it covering her whole body.

My sides feeling like it had been clawed out.

Trying to look but she wouldn't let me. Her soft voice coming to sooth my world. "It's okay. You're going to be fine." Tears cascading down my cheeks. Wanting to give up to that pain. My body trying to give in but my mother's voice was keeping me there. "Open your eyes. Please open your eyes."

Looking at her. "I'm still here."

"And you're going to stay here. I'm not losing you." She picked me up and took me to the kitchen table. Laying me there she grabbed her phone. Ringing someone who would turn out to be her close friend, Amara. The strongest healing witch. So strong she still looked like she was in her twenties despite being centuries old.

She's the one that helped me keep my side intact. Scars there to remind me of that horrible day. The memory of that day had never been this clear before. Laying on that table. My mum not leaving my side. Not checking on the husband she just killed. Not worried about nothing but me.

I stared at her until my vision started to fade. The silence of the kitchen getting replaced by rushing water. Bubbling water. My body freezing cold. Feeling a pressure on my chest pressing rhythmically. Shifting my body with each press.

A feeling rushing in my chest. Coming up and I coughed violently. Feeling a spray of water over my face. A hand turning me and I coughed up more. The water hitting the concrete. Feeling like my insides were coming out with it.

When I was done my body was turned back

gently. Feeling something cushioned under my head. Opening my eyes to find the burning light up high. Blinding me until a head came into view. Dark at first until my eyes adjusted.

My heart pounding hard as I saw Dawson staring down at me. His lips curling when we looked at each other. Coughing before speaking. "What are you doing here?"

"Pulling you out of danger, clearly." Looking at his shirt and jeans. Seeing they were soaked. "And what were you doing?"

"Clearly, I was putting myself in far more danger than I thought."

"I'm very happy to hear you knew how stupid you were."

"She really did care for me, you know."

His features creasing with confusion. "Who are we talking about now?"

"My mother. I never really thought back to that day. The hate blurred the memory. She killed him without a second thought. She knew I was in danger of losing my life so she took his. No hesitation."

"That's good. Isn't it?"

"In one way, yes. In another. I may have jeopardised my relationship with her. All those years I hated her. I could have had a mother. She was right. It wouldn't have been an ordinary family but it still would have been a family."

"It's never too late, she clearly wants to still be a part of your life." His arms sat me up. Feeling brick pressing to my back. Finding myself at the side of the river on the path. "But right now you need to tell me what's going on with our case."

"It's still, our, case then."

"Of course."

"I didn't think I would see you again after." Looking down at my shoulder. The paste had been washed away. Luckily it had done enough to seal it up. A mangled part of my skin as another reminder of a vampire losing themselves to bloodlust.

"I was ashamed of what I did. I knew that's what happened when you were younger."

"It was but….." Looking into his eyes. "I guess when you like someone it helps you to forgive them."

"You like me, huh?"

"Maybe a little. Or maybe I'm still a little funny from trying to drink the river dry."

He laughed. Rubbing his fingers across my forehead. Wiping away my wet hair. "You think you can stand?"

"Stand? Yeah I can manage that." Holding out my arms for him to pull me upright. Feeling a little weak in the legs but able to stand without falling. Stretching my arms up, my sides aching in response. Feeling my bones still cracked or broken. "I need to heal though."

"Let's get you back home then. Ivy will be able to help."

"She will." Looking into his eyes. Feeling my head going light. "You have to promise me though. You will not let her tattoo me."

"Why can't you tell her yourself?"

"Because I can already feel the world slipping from my mental grip. Yep. Here I go." My eyes shut and my body fell forwards into his chest. Arms circled around me. The last thing I felt was my legs being swung up over his arm. Carried away from the river.

When I came to I could hear the buzzing of a tattoo gun. My eyes shooting wide but I couldn't feel the pain of the needle. Twisting my head I found myself laying on the extra table Ivy had for back tattoos.

Shifting again and seeing Dawson sitting backwards on the chair. The tattooist was busy finishing off his amazing tattoo. Blowing out a sigh. "I had a really worried thought that you were doing me."

My room mate flashed over a smile. "What makes you think I didn't?"

"Because you're not that mean." Smiling but it faded when I saw the look Dawson gave her over his shoulder. "What was that?"

"Nothing. He was just checking me out." She let out a soft laugh as she carried on with the black ink.

"No, that was something. If you have put a tattoo on my skin you are going to pay for it."

"Usually my clients pay me." Another giggle had worry settling in.

"Alright. Where's a mirror?" She quickly came over and pushed me back onto the table when I tried to move. "Get off. I want to see what you've done."

"You are not moving until I'm sure your bones have set properly. You were damaged. Like, really damaged."

"Vampires were using me for football practice. Maybe they had a company match coming up against werewolves."

"I'm glad your humour has stayed intact. Let's just hope you see the funny side of me tattooing Dawson's face on your back."

"What?!" My head twisting. The urge to bite at her coming quick. "I will tear my skin off if you've done that."

"Way to hurt my feelings, Megan." Flashing him an angry stare which made him go quiet but it didn't stop him from laughing.

Looking up at Ivy. "Please, just tell me what you did."

Her face turned serious. "I just want you to know that I didn't have a choice. You would have died from the damage if I hadn't intervened. Even with your werewolf healing."

"Just show me." Resting my body on the table. No energy to fight her weight on my back. Hanging my arms down either side of the table.

"Here." Ivy positioned herself to my left. Holding a mirror up to show my shoulder. Running down my upper arm were four wolf prints. They were small and quite dainty which I liked. Biting my lip because I didn't want to tell her how much I loved them. "There are four. You, me, Leon and Connor. I suppose I could put an extra one on there for Dawson if you like."

"I wouldn't go that far for the guy." Eyes shifting up to her then back down.

"You don't have to say it but, you're welcome."

"Uh-huh." Looking to Dawson who was sitting there staring right back with a little smirk. "Ivy, why have you added a giant penis to his dragon?"

The vampire just laughed and turned to my room mate. "She does realise, she's not actually that funny."

"I don't think she does."

"Hey, you two. I'm right here. I'm not dead." Giving her the evils.

Ivy let out a soft laugh before replying. "Luckily you have us to thank for that. Get some rest. By the time you wake up you'll be good as new with some ink on you. Free ink, might I add."

"Free ink against my will." Sticking my tongue out but doing as she suggested. Placing my head down and closing my eyes. Hearing the buzz of the tattoo gun going again but soon that drifted off into the distance.

Happy it was sleep undisturbed by memories. Opening my eyes and finding myself in my bed. Rubbing my eyes with my palms before looking around. Sad I didn't find Dawson in here with me. My whole body feeling great. Better than great.

Throwing off the cover and climbing out. Since I was in my underwear I checked myself out in the mirror. Pressing on my ribs which provided no pain. No mark where they had booted me. My face was completely clear of blood or injury.

My eyes finding those paw prints. Running my hand over them. It felt like they had been there for years. Taking a step back and standing sideways. Looking at them and pulling a little smile. I would have to thank Ivy properly one day.

But today I needed to thank Dawson and maybe have a little fun in the process. Chucking on my robe and walking across the hallway. Finding Leon sitting around the table with Wallis. Making googly eyes at each other. "Hey."

Both of them turning and saying in unison. "Hey."

Finding it a little creepy. "You seen Dawson?"

"He popped out. Left you this." Leon waved a piece of paper which I walked over and grabbed.

"Thanks." The letter told me that he had something to take care of. That he wouldn't be very long. Feeling my happiness taking a slump. I was in great shape and really wanted to celebrate being alive. "Don't suppose he mentioned where he was going? Or what time he would be back?"

"Not a word." Giving them both a smile before making my way down to the tattoo studio. Popping my head in but Ivy wasn't there. Coming back out. "Ivy offered to go pick up Connor."

"Alright then." Walking back past the table I noticed they were playing cards. Have a quiet game like that was not what I wanted to do right now. "I'm going to head out for a run. Get rid of some of my energy." Mumbling the last sentence.

Going back to my room I chucked on a pair of jogging bottoms and a hoody over a sports bra. Heading down the stairs I turned right and started jogging. It wasn't something I enjoyed doing since my werewolf body would keep itself in shape for most of my life.

Trying to think of anything but Dawson but it was no good. My stamina taking me for a long journey. Taking a right every now and again. Coming back around in a large circle. Blowing out a breath as I leant back on the wall. Looking at the people walking by. The cars sitting in traffic.

Then I noticed Dawson come walking down the street. Wearing a fancy black suit with a bow tie. Hanging over his arm was a royal blue dress. Not able to tell the style. Stepping from the wall as he came to my building. "You're looking very handsome."

"Thank you very much." His hand straightened his bow tie as he stood there posed like a secret agent.

"What do you have there?"

"A dress. For you."

"A special occasion?"

A soft laugh rolled out of his lips. "When you were out of it you mumbled. Mostly about your mother and what happened. Something about a witch that never aged as well. Interested to meet her one day."

"Watch it, mister."

Dawson cracked a smile. "But, you also talked about a party. This Trevor fella you're trying to find. To exact revenge on him for what he did to the girl."

"Sounds like a did a little more than just mumble."

"It was cute." The detective stepped back as I

went to swat at him. "So I did a little research on the mansion where the party is being held."

"Anything?" I turned and offered him my arm.

He took it with a killer grin. Making our way inside, the conversation carrying on up the stairs. "Officially there isn't anything about a building at the centre of the wildlife park."

"I'm guessing you checked unofficially?"

"I did, which meant getting in contact with the supernatural unit. They do specialise in unofficial business after all."

"That they do. Who did you chat with?"

Feeling his eyes on me. "Not your mother, if that's what you're asking."

"It might have been."

"I figured. No, I chatted with the vampire liaison. Considering this is vampire business. The only thing they can tell me is that the land the park is on belongs to one Carlton Vaskez."

"And what kind of guy is he?"

"One that enjoys drinking blood. He holds a lot of land and magically, they all hold some kind of endangered species. Meaning that he has his own rules about who can and cannot venture on his land. He's been very very clever."

"Sounds it. But he didn't count on a drunk detective and a PI with anger issues stumbling onto his operation."

"That he did not." I opened the apartment door to the living quarters. Leading him inside. Slipping off my hoody and showing him the black bra underneath.

Leaning with my back to the kitchen counter like it was nothing. Seeing his eyes running over me. His speech stopping for a moment before he carried on. "So I put on my detective cap for an hour. Dug around, called some companies. Figuring they would need supplies or catering for the party."

"Catering? I don't see them standing around eating finger food and chatting about the weather."

"Not that kind of catering. Blood banks. Even though they're not supposed to. Some of the smaller ones make extra cash by doing bulk deliveries. I may have found which one delivered a van load to the wildlife park last night."

"Really?"

"Yes. So on the way to picking up my gorgeous suit. I gave them a little visit. Showing my badge, throwing my weight around. Telling them I won't call them up on charges with the supernatural unit if they gave me all the information they had."

"And?"

"It wasn't a lot. However, I got the code for the back gate. They said every time they have delivered, it hasn't changed. That's our way in without disturbing the guests."

Standing there for a moment. Long enough to make Dawson ask, "What's up?"

"You're willing to venture into a mansion full of vampires."

"That's the case. We bring down the bad guys. No matter what they are. If it was a mansion full of humans with guns. I'd still be heading in."

"But you would have back-up."

"I've got you."

"I'm serious. This is highly dangerous. I have my reasons for doing this."

"So do I. As a detective my cases involve helping humans. Which is fine, it's why I got the badge in the first place. But whilst I'm helping people. Supernatural beings are out there dispatching them in much higher numbers. To bring down a drug ring and whatever else this Carlton is involved in. That's a huge win in my book."

Moving from the counter to him. Reaching up and cupping his cheek. "You know. The way I feel right now it's hard to believe I couldn't stand you a few days ago."

"It's hard to believe a one night stand with you isn't all I can think about right now."

"What are you thinking about? The second night?"

"Breakfast in the morning. You wearing one of my shirts. Waking up and seeing you there next to me."

"Careful." Giving his cheek a gentle rub with my thumb. "Sounds like you might have caught feelings."

"No might of. Megan. I like you enough to not want this to be one and done." Feeling him step back.

"Dawson. I'm not offering a one night stand." Stepping back myself. Pushing down my jogging bottoms. Standing half-naked in front of him. "I'm offering you me. And everything that goes along with it."

"In that case." The vampire checked his watch. "We've got a few hours to spare."

"Will that be long enough?" Grinning as he slipped off his jacket. Folding it over one of the chairs around the table. The shirt coming off next. Nice and slow. Revealing that tattoo wrapped around his toned torso.

Biting my lip as it seemed to take him forever to push down his trousers. Tight black boxers not leaving much to my imagination. Watching him come closer. A hand slipping around my neck. Sliding up into my hair which sent a shiver down my spine. My ponytail getting tugged free. Hair falling across my shoulders.

Looking into his eyes as my heart raced. Breathing starting to become heavier. My eyes locked on his. Hands touching his bare chest. Running over those bumps slowly. Pressing my thighs together tight. Rubbing them back and forth.

Letting my hands slide down lower. His grip making them stop where his underwear started. Looking into his eyes. "Look, I don't want to push things too fast."

"Dawson." I looked deep into his eyes. Pulling from his grip I shoved my hand over his natural bulge. "Fuck me." With that he claimed my mouth with such hunger I whined. Pushing my tongue into his mouth as he lifted me up. Feeling my arse dropped onto the table. His body coming over. Making me lay back.

Lips locked together as my hands ran over his skin. Feet pushing down his underwear frantically.

Needing to feel him. Feeling that hit of flesh smack against my thigh. Feeling so hard. Making me roll my hips, letting out a low groan. Biting into his bottom lip as I growled. "What's taking you so long?"

A sudden blur and I felt my knickers snapping against my hips. The fabric lost to the floor as he pressed himself back to me. Pushing out my legs around his hot body. A grind making me whimper. Legs locking behind him. Pulling him closer with need.

Feeling his member gliding over my lips. Growling out, digging nails into his back and raking them down. Gripping his arse and pulling just at the right moment. Flashes exploding before my eyes as we connected in the most delicious way.

My thighs shaking as I tried to catch my breath. Dawson pushing and pushing until he sat hilt deep. Biting my lip before my jaw dropped open with a loud moan. Hands grabbing his face and pulling his lips to mine.

Our kiss deeper than before. The link between our bodies driving up the passion as he started to move over me. Feeling his hand slapping against my thigh. Fingers digging in as it was lifted. Feeling him moving my body. Getting a better angle as he slid back and forth.

Pushing heavy breaths of moans out of my mouth. Shutting my eyes and feeling every inch. Every touch of his skin on mine. Feeling his hot breath hitting my lips. Pushed higher and higher as my mind flew.

Arms loosely wrapped around his body. Hands rubbing over him. Electric charges sent through my nerves. Not able to think about one point or touch. Everything rolling into one surge of energy building in my core.

Licking my lips, puffing out air as my moans grew louder. Able to speak just two words as he moved faster. "Oh god." My eyes flying open. Looking deep into his as I reached my peak. Tightening, holding onto that feeling for an eternal, blissful second before falling.

My whole body shaking as I drenched him. Moaning out in screams. Over and over. Dawson not letting up. Still going as fast. Pushing me through the hot explosion of pleasure. Shutting my eyes as the last ripples of it ran from my head down to my toes and back up between my thighs.

Shaking out a weak breath as he slowed. My whole body flopping flat. Feeling him stop. His body pulled back until he slipped free. Wanting to curl up as my nerves were still firing. My skin tingling as I looked into his eyes. Grinning up at him as he stood.

His eyes running over my body. Heavy enough to feel it moving across my bare skin. "That was...." Breathing in and out. "Wow."

"That good, huh?"

"It's been a while so maybe I just needed it so bad." Feeling him slapping my calf. "I was kidding. I think it's pretty obvious how I felt about that." Blowing strands of hair out of my face.

Going to sit up but my body refused once I

was half way. Making Dawson grab hold of my arms. Pulling me to the edge of the table. My hands found his waist and I pulled him to my body. Feeling my nipples ache as they rubbed across his chest. "I feel the same way. Just so you know."

"Good." Pressing myself to him for a kiss. Gentle and soft. Teeth nipping at his bottom lip. "I hope you've still got some gas in the tank."

"I'm not done with you yet." Feeling that tingling between my legs heighten with his words. "That's the kitchen ticked off."

Giggling through a grin. "What's next, the hallway?" Nodding towards the apartment door.

"Maybe somewhere less daring, for now." Grinning as he picked me up. Holding me so easily I could let my hands glide across his skin.

About to lean in and kiss him when I heard keys in the door. Breathing in to speak when there was a sudden gush of power. My head spinning a little. Realising I had my back pressed against my bedroom door.

Clamping my hand over his mouth as we waited. Hearing the door open I heard Connor's voice. Then Ivy mentioning the need for something to eat. But her speech was cut short. Biting my lip as Connor made a comment about the clothes on the floor.

Ivy made up an excuse and seemed to rush him out of the apartment. Giggling as I removed my hand from Dawson's mouth. "That was close. You were very fast."

"I can't take my time with everything."

"Is that what you plan on doing? Take your time with me?"

"Absolutely." Feeling his lips on mine as I was slowly laid down on my bed. That pursed touch moving to my neck. Sending shivers down my spine as they kept moving lower. Those kisses teasing and touching. Squirming underneath him as he headed south to that most intimate part of me.

Moving my legs out wide for him. That touch hitting right on target making me gasp, then moan out with a sigh. Not able to think straight for the next couple of hours as it was filled with his touch. His lips, that hard piece of him. All of it filled me with joy and I was well and truly satisfied by the time he finished for me. Even for a werewolf.

My whole body void of any energy. Knackered I couldn't even tell you how I fell asleep. All I knew I woke up cuddled to his body. Practically laying on top of him. His breathing lifting my head up and down.

My hand made a trail up his leg and over his chest. Enjoying the bumpy road of his abs and pecks. A soft, gentle sigh leaving my lips as I looked at his face. Unhappy with him still being asleep I pinched his nose gently. His breathing slowly getting heavier until he gasped awake. "What the hell?"

"You're awake." Giggling as he threw me a look. "You were snoring."

"I don't snore." Dawson grinned down at me. His fingers coming to touch my bare back. Trailing up and down which made me squirm against him. "I think this should be a ritual from now on. Any time we're awake. We should do that."

"I absolutely agree. Traditions are very important in life." My hand curled my fingers against his chest. Following the black lines of his tattoo. "So this party."

"Yes?"

Biting my lip as he dug his fingers into my back a little harder. "We have our way in. We have our outfits. What do we do once we're inside?"

"You know, I wanted to chat to you about that. But something distracted me from my train of thought."

"I have no idea what that could have been."

"I'm sure."

Biting my bottom lip as he smirked at me. A circle of his touch making my body squirm. "The question is. Do we detain these vampires? Call in the cavalry and get them arrested?" Pausing as I looked into his eyes. "Or do we kill them?" Eyes searching his. Knowing my answer already. "What do you think?"

"You clearly already have your answer."

"Oh?"

"I can tell just by looking at you."

"I wish you were easier to read."

A large sigh lifted his chest up and down. My fingers tracing his tattoo as I waited. "If it wasn't for you, I wouldn't be alive right now."

"Actually I think I owe you one still."

"In that case I know you'll have my back when things go sideways." His stare finding mine. Smiling as we looked at each other. "I stand by what you decide. Whichever way that falls. I'll stand by you."

"You should definitely leave your badge at home then."

"I think that's a good idea. But we still have the problem of all those vampires. Even if it's a small gathering. It'll be more than we can handle."

"You think we need help? I'm not asking my friends to come along."

"No, silly." Yelping as he jabbed me in the ribs. "I was thinking someone more official."

"My mother?" Thinking about it for a moment. She was the head of the supernatural unit. She had politics and the rest of the government to worry about. "The less she knows the better."

"Alright. So just me and you. Against all those criminal vampires."

"Yeah." My eyes on his chest. Watching it rise and fall. So soft and relaxing. Fingers stretching. Pressing my palm to his skin. Focusing on the tattoo. A slow smile curling my lips. "We use the same drug against them."

"V-Dux? Your plan is to get them high?"

"No, you idiot. The drug that strips away your immune system. We put it in something we know they'll drink. Add some poison. Should do the job."

"It would but what do we put it in?" Dawson's face lighting up. "The blood delivery. We pump it into the blood bags. They'll drink it without realising. We poison the whole lot of them and we're home before the night is over."

Laughing as he wiggled his eyebrows. "Clearly

for some more fun."

"With the dress I got you? It'll be hard not to start the celebrating early."

"Behave." Giggling as he pulled my body to his. Kissing his gorgeous lips. My body going flat so I can feel as much contact as possible. "Where are we going to get the drug from?"

"I know exactly where. The tattoo shop. You ran those guys out of there. I doubt they dared to come back if they thought I would grass them up to the government."

"Alright. What about the poison? Be a bit suspicious buying a whole load of that in one go."

"Rat poison."

"From a shop?"

"No from a pest company. They stock the ingredients for this stuff. Some of them can kill a human. If not then they'll at least be vomiting and shitting themselves. Easy enough to kill a vamp doing that."

"You can go near those ones." Giving off a little laugh as his fingers tickled my side. "If you think it'll work. I'm game."

"Sounds good. I'll round up the stuff we need. You need to shower and get that dress on."

"And do my hair."

"Lucky we've got plenty of time then."

"Cheeky sod." He caught my wrist as I swung it. Rolling us over so he laid on top. Feeling him nudging my legs apart. "I don't think we have enough time to fit that in as well."

"Probably not." Dawson groaned as he got off. Standing there for me to enjoy the view. "Shall I meet you by the back gate of this estate then."

"Sure. Party starts at half eight. We should get there at eight. Drug the blood before it's distributed."

"Perfect." His eyes moving over my body as I laid there. "So not fair to be leaving that in bed."

"Off you run. Before I jump you again."

"Promises, promises." My hand wrapped around his neck as he leant down to kiss me. Holding him there, deepening the kiss with my tongue. Finding myself licking my lips as he pulled back. "Can't wait to see how you look in that dress."

"It'll be a nice surprise." Watching him leave to grab his clothes from the kitchen. Letting my body drop back and fully fall into that blissful feeling. Running what happened through my mind over and over.

Hearing the door open and shut I jumped into action. First I showered. Washed my hair and whilst in my towel I started scrunching it up in my hands. Putting in tight curves. Using my towel as a dress as I got myself ready.

Putting on some natural make-up. Adding blue eye shadow to match the dress. Finishing off my hair by heaving it back into a loose ponytail. Plenty of strands hanging down either side of my face. Using some hair spray to keep those curls exactly the way they were.

Then it was time for the dress but I didn't want to put it on just yet. So I exchanged the towel for my robe and headed across the hall. Ivy's eyes hitting mine as I appeared. Feeling my cheeks flush red but also my lips turn into a huge grin.

She rolled her eyes. "Are you eating here?"

Knowing I wouldn't be eating a vampire's diet at the party. "Definitely. I could do with some meat."

"By the sounds of it you already got some." Throwing Leon a look as he laughed with Wallis. Noticing Connor had his headset on whilst shooting bad guys.

Walking to the table and flicking his ear. "I don't talk about my conquests."

"Since when?" Leon pulled a massive smile. "Come on. He's a hunky piece of meat. At least tell me everything matches that description."

Looking to Wallis who seemed just as interested. "Yes." Turning around to see the mince meat in the pan. Pasta boiling on the back hob. "You need a hand?"

"I got it." Feeling her eyes on me so I turned my head. Staring right back. "I'm not going to say it."

"We both know you are. Out with it."

"Connor shouldn't have to worry about walking into an apartment and catching you two at it on the table."

"I know, I know." Looking over my shoulder as we whispered to each other. "Thanks for not telling, Leon."

"I did. He doesn't seem to care." I gave him another look. The two of them sitting there chatting. A single glass of beer being passed to and fro. "And he's barely spoken to Connor."

"He's definitely acting weird." Turning back to watch the meat being pushed around with onions and mushrooms. "What do you think of the new guy?"

"Seems nice enough. He could use a little practice having a kid around."

"Do you think he's a good influence? The strange behaviour started when he arrived on the scene."

She flicked a piece of meat at me which landed on my shoulder. Flicking it back at her. "Don't think about interfering."

"I wasn't. Leon deserves to be happy and if Wallis does that then fair play. But Connor doesn't deserve to be left behind."

"I agree with you completely. We'll see how it goes. If it gets too bad then we'll say something. Together."

"Agreed."

Ivy added in some tomato paste and stirred. "So what's happening tonight?"

"We're finishing the case. Drug distribution was hit hard. Now we take out the men at the top."

"You sure you need to do this?" Shooting her a look. "You're a private investigator. You're not a cop and you don't work for your mum. Do you really need to put yourself in this much danger just so a woman can get closure for her daughter's death?"

"It's much more than that. The girl was so scared and frightened. Her life was taken away from her because some vampire came along and decided to give her a drug."

"That's not your responsibility."

"But Connor is, in small part. What happens when he's older and something like this happens to him. Or even now. There are people out there both human and otherwise that enjoy ruining people's lives for money or for fun. If I can help by taking some of that danger out of this world. Then it's worth the danger."

Ivy looked at me with a smirk. "You've changed a little."

"Hopefully for the better?"

"If you come back in one piece tonight. Then yes." She handed me the spatula and wiped her hands on a tea towel. "I've got something for you." I heard the door to her studio open and close. She came back with a little vial of clear liquid. "This is just in case you get into a tight situation."

"What does it do?" Taking it and rolling it between my fingers.

"It'll give you a massive boost in adrenaline. And for a werewolf I don't have to tell you what that would be like."

"Thanks. We've got a plan that should take out most of the vamps without a problem. But I'll definitely keep this close." Leaning in and kissing her cheek.

"When is tea going to be ready?" Both of us turning and scowling at Leon. "Sorry. We're just hungry."

"Me to." Connor came over to the table still

facing the TV killing bad guys.

"Coming right up you greedy lot." I giggled as Ivy dished it out onto plates and I brought them over. The five of us sitting around and munching through our meal. Garlic bread being brought out a few minutes later but the look of charred bread put me off giving it a try.

Once I was full I headed back over to get ready. Slipping on the blue dress I marvelled at myself in the mirror. Dawson actually had some great taste. The top half clung to me like I was wearing a corset. Pushing my curves up to attention which was no doubt his intention.

The bottom half draped at an angle. Looking like I was spinning without turning. A slit letting my leg breath. Enough room to throw a kick when I needed to. The perfect dress for elegance and danger.

I took a photo of myself and sent it to Ivy who gave me a thumbs up. Not bothering to walk across since I needed to get moving. I folded up a few notes into my cleavage for the taxi. Not bothering with my phone just in case this went sideways. I didn't want to give them a way to hurt my friends or my family.

My taxi dropped me off outside the wildlife park after convincing the driver I would be okay by myself. It wasn't long until another came driving past. Dawson climbed out in his suit. A flash of hotness as I remembered him stripping out of it.

As soon as his eyes landed on me he grinned. Seeing how his stare moved over my body. Lingering on my chest where I knew it would. "I sure know how to pick out a dress, don't I?"

"There was me thinking I would be the one getting the compliment."

He grinned wider. Took up my hand and placed a kiss to it. Eyes lifting to mine. "You look beyond beautiful tonight."

Giving him a little curtsey and a smile. Fanning myself. "Thank you, kind sir."

"Now who's being funny." Laughing just before he pulled me into a gorgeous kiss. Melting against his body. Loving those lips on mine. Tempted to rip his trousers off right here.

Pulling back as my ears picked something up. Looking over towards the thick gate that sat between the tree lines. Seeing a figure shifting about. Tapping Dawson's chest to send his attention that way.

Blinking my eyes I brought up my night vision. The slight glow of green covering everything. Including the ranger that stood by the gate with his hand on his pistol. A strange thing for a park ranger to be carrying around with him.

A sudden flash of light covering us made me wince, switching from my night vision. "What are you two doing out here?"

Dawson cleared his throat and took my hand in his. Walking us over there. "We're here for the party."

"This is a wildlife park. No party going on here."

"You don't understand. We've been invited." The man's blank expression stayed. "By the owner of this land. The guy who lives in the massive mansion."

The guard looked between us. "I don't know what you've been smoking or how much you've had to drink. There is no mansion on these grounds. If you could move along I would greatly appreciate it."

Dawson stepped towards the gate. "Look, you don't seem to understand."

"No I don't. But if you don't move along I'll call the police."

"Let's do it a different way." Dawson's hand shot out and grabbed the uniform. Pulling him against the gate. The man looked so frightened. Not a reaction from someone who works for vampires. He even fumbled with his gun so bad it dropped to the floor. Dawson looked into his eyes and spoke with a steady voice. "Calm down and tell me what's going on here."

The guard stopped trying to wriggle free. Standing calmly enough the detective let go of him. "This is a wildlife park. I'm stationed at the back gate just in case we get any deliveries."

The vampire turned to me. "He's been glamoured to forget. He really does think this is only a wildlife park."

"Get him to let us through then wipe his memory."

"Yes, Miss." Grinning at the wink Dawson threw my way. Then he got to work on the guard. We were allowed through and then our presence was wiped clean. Taking the massive dirt track that worked up into the forest.

Hearing the birds chirping. Rustling around in the branches. The flaps of wings as they flew high above. It was very peaceful and such a lovely walk until we came to a second gate. A small hut sat there with another guard sitting inside. Dawson sniffed the air. "Human, like the last one. I think it's safe to say he'll know what's going on here."

He was right because as the track turned to gravel it lead up through the open area. Old fashioned street lights lined the way. The massive mansion loomed in the distance. Lamps and spot lights were all over the grounds. Lighting the building up. "So we go in hard."

"As you wish." Blinking and he was gone. Looking over and seeing him holding the guard by the back of his collar. The man's head swinging, out cold. I walked over with a slow clap. Out came Dawson after storing the guard out of sight. "You know, I'm doing all the work here. I think it's about time you do something."

"How about I smack you round the back of the head." Grinning and laughing as we made our way up the path. "We should probably keep our planning to a minimum here. Hard to chat privately when vampire ears are about."

"Agreed. If anyone asks we went for a walk for some alone time."

"I like the sound of that." Hooking my arm in his. Acting like I was a little drunk. "They'll just think I'm a human. Your own personal snack."

"Let's get this party started then." Moving up the concrete steps to the back of the mansion. The guards at this point where in black suits. Bulges on the inside of their jackets where they stored their weapons.

Each one gave us a look but it didn't go further than that. Moving inside the back door which was left open. Coming into a large room with a table running across a fancy looking rug. Massive chairs surrounding it.

Paintings on the wall. They looked ordinary until I took a closer look. Seeing the fangs on each person. Leaning in close and lowering my voice to barely anything. "Looks like the lineage of the vampire that lives here."

Dawson nodded and we made our way towards the music. About to push open a large wooden door when a voice came from behind us. "Where do you think you're going?" Turning to see an old man wearing an old-fashioned suit. Looking like a butler.

My partner pulled a massive smile. "Just about to enjoy the party."

"Not with her you're not. The rules stipulate that our leaders feed first. She's coming back to the kitchen with me." Fingers wrapped around my wrist and pulled me from my man. Feeling Dawson pass a little package over.

I peered down and saw the small bottle and a syringe. The poison with the drug already mixed in. Giving him a gentle nod and storing it into my cleavage whilst the butler wasn't looking. Shifting it around. The bulge uncomfortable but luckily the dress hid it well.

"Come on, lady."

"As you wish." Me and Dawson exchanged a quick look before he disappeared through the door. I let this man lead me. Concentrating enough to know he was human. Seemed they have a lot of them around here. Maybe the vampire numbers weren't as large as I first thought.

Getting taken to what he called the kitchen. But there weren't any cookers or counters. It was a simple room with bare walls. My eyes looking around at the women standing here. Many of them wearing dresses like me. Some of them more casual like they had been plucked right off the street.

The man left me there and vanished through another door. Swallowing as I walked to the middle. Checking out each woman until two of them came to introduce themselves. They pulled massive stupid smiles. "Hi, what's your name?"

"Megan. Yours?"

The one with the long blonde hair grinned wide. "What a lovely name. My name is Heather and this is Bernadette." Giving them both smiles. "Where did they find you?"

"Baldur City." Answering but letting my attention run across the others.

"So close. Bernadette is from Lockwood. And I'm not even from this country."

"You sound like you are."

"I've been having lessons from my master."

My head snapping back to her. "Master?" Taking a quick sniff of the air. Feeling a headache pulsing behind my eyes. There was no scent coming from her. Or anywhere in this room. They were all human.

"Yes. I met him years ago. He looks after me and in return." She screwed up her face as she thought for a moment. "Do you have a master?"

"I'm sorry. What do you give your master in return?"

"Enough of this talk. We should be making sure we're ready."

Following her as she walked around the room. She checked on the other women like it was her job. "I was wondering if you could help me."

"That's why I'm here." She spun, hair flicking out. Smile shining before she spun back around.

"So I see." Watching as she straightened one of the dresses. "I was wondering where they kept the food."

"I don't understand what you mean."

Leaning in close, "Something your master likes to drink. Possibly red."

She quickly turned around to me. "Um." Her face screwed up again. "We don't talk about that."

"You can tell me."

Her eyes darted around the room before she leant in slowly. "They'll come in and get a couple of us and take us to the leaders. And they drink."

"Right, where are the drinks?"

"We're the drinks." Another cautious look around before she pulled down the collar of her dress. Showing me the pin pricks in her skin.

The realisation that this room was filled with

the blood bags the vampires would be drinking. Cursing in my mind. Our plan was ruined. "Thank you for filling me in. I'm just going to go for a little walk before the fun starts."

"Oh, you can't leave the room unless someone comes and gets you."

"And what happens if I walk out of here?"

The blonde looked unsure whether she should tell me. "The last person who left, was never seen again."

"I can handle myself. Thanks for being so concerned. Have a great night." Rolling my eyes as I turned away. Biting my lip as I thought about our plan going down the toilet. The drugs now completely useless.

Running my hand over my chest where the package sat. Thinking about dumping it into a plant pot or something as I stepped towards the door. Jumping back as it came swinging towards me. A man came sauntering into the room. A sudden whiff of ash came to my nose as he stood so close. Looking down at me.

I arched an eyebrow back up at him. "And you are?"

A hand came out towards me. Picking off a stray hair from my dress. Flicking it to the floor. "What is your name?"

"Megan. How about yours?"

The vampire looked over my head at the rest of the ladies. Ignoring my question. "Heather. If you'd like to bring your close friend." He nodded over to

Bernadette who was checking her hair in the large mirror. "The lady in the white dress over by the window." His eyes came back to me. A long sigh pushed through his lips. "This one needs to come along as well. Apparently, Master Lennox has taken a fancy to her." Getting a stare before he turned and left the room.

Heather called after him. "Right away." Feeling the blonde hooking an arm in mine. "Aren't we the lucky ones?"

"Depends on your point of view."

"Especially you. Master Lennox is the leader. To catch his eye is a very rare thing."

"Lucky me." Pulling a massive grin but all I could think about is the worry twisting my stomach. "What about the other guests. When do they drink?"

"The rest of the girls will be taken out to the hall once we've been offered. They'll go around the room and be shared."

"This party just gets better and better." Heather let out a roar of a laugh. Her arm tugging me along as we walked through the door followed by the other two. Carrying on past the table and chairs and towards the music.

Passing through the door Dawson had used earlier. Coming out at the back of a massive hall. Filled with men and women. Some wearing hooded cloaks. Others holding up masquerade masks over their faces. Most in outfits you would find royalty wearing in castles.

Heather led me up the middle. Everyone

parting. Leaving a clear line up to the end where three men and a woman stood. Up above everyone else on a little stage. Red velvet carpet a sharp change from the black flooring I walked on. Our heels tapping loudly on the tiles.

My eyes landed on the vampire at the very back. His foot-length jacket was adorned with golden thread in wild patterns. He leant against a gold covered chair. Red cushions to comfort his body. Seeing his eyes on me the whole way up. Heather left my side to go before her master.

Lennox stepped down to the very bottom unlike the others. Taking up my hand. Seeing his long hair was pulled back into a plait that ran down to the small of his back. His cheeks were full of colour unlike the paleness that disappeared under his collar. Trying to look younger than he actually was. Which didn't bode well for me. The older the vampire, the more dangerous they were.

Breathing in sharply as he lifted my hand to his lips. Those pale grey eyes on me as he gave my skin a little kiss. Exactly how Dawson did but this time I felt my stomach churning. Wanting to snatch my hand away but I had to keep up this charade. Pretending I was a blood groupie just like the others.

His lips moved. A voice slithering out like a snake had been turned human. His speech accenting certain letters. "So pleased to make your acquaintance." Lips pressed to my hand a little higher.

"Master Lennox. The pleasure is all mine."

His touch moving higher. Fingers curling

around my forearm. The vampire's mouth kissing higher. "I don't see any undisturbed skin so far." Grey eyes moving to my cleavage. "May I assume this is your first time? Or will I need to hunt for my feeding spot." The vampire smiled and I saw his pin-pricked canines sitting close to the others. Making me wonder if he had fed before the party started.

"If you go searching. You might find more than you can handle."

He grinned. A laugh slipping out like he didn't know how to mimic one. "I could tell you had spirit when I spotted you on the camera."

"I have plenty of spirit." Digging my nails in my other hand to distract me from the impulse to run.

"Good. Maybe you will give me a run for my money later when we hunt." My heart racing at the thought of being tracked down by this thing. "Or, would you prefer to retire to my chambers whilst the rest are busy running around playing."

Biting my lip, wanting to argue that it wasn't playing for the humans. "That all depends. Do we get glamoured before the hunt?"

"Oh my dear." Feeling his pursed touch hitting on my shoulder as he stepped closer. The vampire standing barely an inch from me. His breath smelling metallic. "The only time I will glamour you. Is to make you mine. But you will still make your own choices."

"That sounds perfect." Swallowing past the lump forming in my throat. I couldn't be glamoured by any ordinary vampire. Only this one was clearly older than your average blood sucker. I didn't want to test my resistance. "I do have a question."

"Later. You can ask me as many questions as you like." His grip moving to my wrist. I was gently tugged with him as he backed up to his chair. Once he was seated I was pulled onto his lap.

Looking out at the crowd. Seeing Dawson over by the wall. Happy that he was keeping a close eye on me. Giving him a soft smile to tell him it was okay. Hopefully hiding the fact I could feel my hands trembling. This wasn't going to plan at all.

As the four heads of the nest sat on their thrones the other ladies were brought in. Some gravitating to vampires straight away like they did this all the time. Others hung around the walls. Clearly their first time to a party.

Lennox called out. Surprised his soft voice could fill the room so easily. "My family. We are brought here today to celebrate our new venture. Baldur City has been successful in the distribution of V-Dux. It took years to perfect it and a lot of money but the return already has been very fruitful."

The crowd cheered. A random vampire calling out, "When do we get to enjoy some?"

"Don't worry, you will all have the chance to have a taste. But first you have your ladies to enjoy." A hand softly cupped under my arm. Turning to see the vampire's fangs extend a little. His eyes moving over my soft skin.

Turning back I noticed the others doing the same. "You're shaking like a leaf. No need to be scared. This will be over very quickly." Taking a deep breath and holding it there. Fingers gripping my dress tightly. A gentle little prick that made me jump and that was it. Turning back surprised as he kissed where my blood leaked.

Noticing that the rest were following his lead. It wasn't a frenzied blood bath. It was all very elegant. Lennox pulled back. Licking his lips with a big smile. Returning my arm to me. "Thank you, my dear."

"My pleasure, master." Giving him a doe eyed look before turning to see Dawson. He was following suit. Being tender with the lady he was tasting. Hiding my arm under my hand since those little pin pricks would be gone within seconds.

Taking this moment to scour the crowd. Ignoring the faces behind masks. Looking at each one in turn. Looking for the Trevor that was responsible for Melanie's death. Moving across until I was pushed off balance as Lennox stood.

His hand caught me and held me to his side. Those pale eyes staring down at me. "Go enjoy the crowd my dear. We shall join each other again later. I promise you."

"I look forward to it." Not sure why but I curtsied which he seemed to enjoy greatly. Taking the steps down to the floor. Heading forward then making a gentle arc so I came to stand in front of Dawson. Striking up a conversation about nothing as we looked into each others eyes.

The detective gave me a gentle nod. Giving him one back to let each other know we were okay. Taking a deep breath as I turned to watch the leader. Noticing that snobby vampire who had brought us in was by his side. Whispering something in his ear. But he was walking off before I could eavesdrop.

The leader stood tall, chin up with pride. Hands cupped behind his back. Making his jacket tug tighter over his chest. The vampire wasn't muscular but I bet he could rip my head off with one swipe. "I have some very pleasant news. Our benefactor who made this all a reality. The one who has helped our nest for a long time has arrived. Please welcome her with a huge applause."

A lady came walking in. Wearing a suit that snugly fit her slim body. Standing tall. Long, thick blonde hair pulled back into multiple thick plaits. Looking more like art as it hung down her back.

My eyes going wide as I saw her face. Feeling my blood running cold. Watching her walking up the steps and giving Lennox a kiss to the cheek. Dawson's arm twisting me around. Pulling my body so close to his.

Feeling his lips touching to my ear as he spoke as quietly as he could. "What's wrong?"

"That woman." My hands grabbing hold of his jacket to try and stop them from shaking.

"I see her."

"She's the reason I have my scars. My mum's husband. That's the vampire that kidnapped him and starved him. That's his ex-wife. A centuries old vampire that promised to destroy my mum's life."

CHAPTER 10

Looking over my shoulder at the vampire who was soaking up the applause the crowd was giving her. Seeing that smile. Looking so damn smug with herself. Turning back to Dawson. Hoping a look in his eyes would control the anger that was threatening to blow our cover. "She must be the reason Baldur City was chosen. My mum heads the supernatural unit there."

"Not to mention your business. If she's so hell bent on hurting your mother. You'll be the best way to do that." His hand gripping my side tightly. "We should get out of here."

"The case needs to be finished." Gritting my teeth, trying to keep my voice down. "We need to finish this."

"And how do you suggest we do that? There aren't any blood bags to poison. The drug is out of the question."

"I don't know." My fingers tugged on his jacket. Hearing the slight tear of the fabric. "But we need to come up with something quick. Something I can focus on."

His hands cupped my cheeks. Barely able to feel

them as my anger filled every thought. "Your cheeks are burning up."

"It's just the anger. Do something to take my mind of it. Please." Blinking as he pulled me into a devilish kiss. Feeling his tongue snaking against mine. Tip-toeing up as he pulled me in hard. Letting out a soft whimper.

Dawson pulled back. Seeing the flare of lust in his eyes as we stared at each other. Then his look went past me. Coming back I heard my name being called. "Megan. Where have you run off to?"

Dipping my head down. Swallowing and turning. Trying to keep my face hidden behind the strands of curly hair. "Here, Master."

"Please. Come back to my side. Share your taste with our guest." As I stepped forward I heard him talking to her. "She has the most exquisite blood I've ever had."

"I look forward to finding out myself." Hearing her voice I stopped my feet. Standing just at the foot of the steps. Digging my nails into my palms but it was no good. Her voice coming again. "Looks like your guest is a little shy." A step brought her closer. "Lift your head, sweet child."

I felt her fingertip touching my chin and that's when I lost all control. Claws growing instantly. Lashing out across her arm. Digging through fabric and skin. Blood shooting across the velvet carpet. She coiled back in pain.

Rushing forward but there was a sudden blur and my arms were being held. I growled deep. Teeth growing into dangerous weapons. Biting at the air. Feeling their feet slipping as I took a step forward. My anger pushing my strength beyond their control. A forth and fifth vampire came to help them.

Growling at that woman. The sign of recognition coming over her face. "Is that little Meg?" She stepped closer. Fingers ripping apart my dress over my right side. Her fingers tracing those thick scars. "Oh yes, that is you. How pleasant to see you again."

I lunged forwards and just missed her neck with my jaws. "Come a little closer and I'll show you how pleasant it'll be."

"Come now. Have you not looked around. I'm completely protected by the nest. You're insane to come after me here."

"I wasn't here for you. But I'll gladly change that." My arms tensing. Bringing them forwards as my rage grew harder. "How about you and I go outside. That way you don't have to have your nest see me rip out your throat."

"So feisty. Is what I did really that terrible?"

The leader stepped forward. "How about we take this to a more private room." Hands grabbed my ankles and I was hoisted up over their heads. Carried as I squirmed for them to release me. Growling out.

On our way out I saw Dawson being grabbed as well. Getting brought along for our private chat. Passing through a long hallway before being carried into a small room. The ceiling was dark red. The walls the same colour.

They placed me down onto the plush carpet. Not seeing anything else as she came walking in. My stare locked on hers. "You really hold a grudge after all these years?"

The leader cleared his throat. He seemed annoyed at the interruption to his party. "What is this?"

"About a decade ago. I may have kidnapped her vampire step-father. Starved him then sent him back home to his family. You can guess what happened after that."

"And why would you do this?" A little surprised the leader was treating her like she was in the wrong.

"He killed me many many years ago. My anger kept me alive in limbo. Not able to move on because I'm a stubborn woman like that. But when the ley lines were damaged. There was a crack and I slipped free. Why shouldn't I have my revenge after obsessing about it for so long?"

"I understand that. However, this has brought attention to my home. What if there are others coming?"

"If there were, they would be here already. She's nothing more than a private investigator. I've kept tabs." She pulled a smirk at me.

"What about this man?" The leader waved at my vampire.

"I'm her partner." Dawson's chin was held high. Looking up at them from his knees beside me.

"And what was your plan here? To take us all out one by one?" My partner went quiet. "Check his pockets, her dress." The leader turned his back on us as his vampire minions did what they were told.

I growled as a hand went to my chest. A sharp slap knocked my senses wild for a moment. Feeling the package being slipped free. Seeing the drug we had brought to dispatch them along with the liquid Ivy had given me. The syringe sitting between them. The lady picked them up. "Looks like they were planning on drugging you all." She popped the lid and sniffed it. Pulling a screwed up face. "I don't know what it is but it doesn't smell very nice."

The leader snatched it and pocketed them both. "You'll come with me. My vampires will get rid of these two. I'll talk to my people in the force. See if they heard anything about my place. If it's just these two our plans can go unchanged."

"Yes, of course." She hooked her arm in his. Looking over her shoulder as they moved to the door. "It was a pleasure to see you again. For the last time. I'll make sure to stop by and give your mother the good news."

"You stay away from her!" About to move when a thud whacked the back of my head. Making my vision go blurry. Trying to shake it back. Blinking the view to normality. Looking over my shoulder at the vampire holding some statue from the shelf behind him.

With the door shut the action started. Feeling punches and kicks. Getting whacked with various items from around the room. Feeling like I was chucked into the middle of a prison fight. The beating not stopping until suddenly there was a whoosh of speed.

Uncovering my head and looking up as one of the cloaked vamps shoved another through the wall. They turned and sped to my side. Snatching the one hitting me with that statue by his ear. Chucking him through the shelves.

A punch and a kick and another two were on the floor. Dawson broke free of the arms holding him and elbowed the vamp between the legs. His body doubling over and dropping hard.

The saviour of the moment came walking over to me. Pulling me to my feet. Letting heavy breaths help me through the pain as it mixed with my anger. Holding me up for now. "Who the hell are you?"

"I thought you would recognise me." The hood was dropped and I laughed.

Feeling all my feelings pop like a balloon. Staring at this woman in disbelief. "Cassie?" Her blonde hair used to be long. Now it was a pixie cut and annoyingly it suited her just like everything. "My mum sent you to protect me?"

"Heavens no. I'm not here for you. I'm here for that woman."

"What do you mean?"

She walked to the door and cracked it open. Hearing music playing from down the hallway. No footsteps coming to investigate the noises. "For the last three years I've been off the grid. Me and Kat. Trying to find any shred of evidence she was still alive after what she did. Last couple of months we've been catching money transfers. This isn't the only nest she's been aiding. She's either building an empire or a good amount of friends who will protect her."

"It doesn't matter. She needs to die tonight."

"Based on what I know about her. She'll already be off the grounds. She's been too cautious for so long to stick around after your appearance. Not to mention the kind of shit your mother would throw her way if you were to be killed."

"So she's gone in the wind again. I lost her."

"You didn't lose her." Cassie came walking over. Slipping off her robe which dropped to the floor. Her hands rose to my cheeks. Thumbs rubbing gently. "I forgot how grown up you've gotten. So strong. Now tell me, what are you doing here?"

"We're following a case. Drug overdose in humans led us here to this nest. They're producing a vampire drug."

"That humans can't control."

"Exactly."

Her eyes moved to Dawson who was busy popping his arm and fingers back into place. "Who's this?"

"Dawson. He's my partner."

"Pleasure." She shook his hand. Seeing the look she was giving him.

Butting in quickly. "Where's Kat?"

"Keeping an eye on things. Hopefully she would have the sense to follow that woman. Which means I need to catch up with her. Are you okay here?"

"You're not going to send me home? Tell me to

behave myself?"

"Have I ever?" I got a nice tight hug before she flashed a grin and chose the window to exit the building. Looking after her as she shot off in a blur.

Feeling Dawson's hand on my shoulder. "Any more interesting revelations for tonight?"

"That's just my aunt."

"I've heard plenty of stories about Cassie."

"What kind of stories?" Turning around to face him.

"Just stories. Vampires hear things in their own circles."

"Uh-huh." He leant in but I pressed my palm to his chest. "Not yet. The next time we kiss I want us to be free of all responsibility. Because right now if you kiss me I'll just throw you down on the floor."

"I don't know if that's a good thing or a bad thing."

"Adrenaline to a werewolf is much like a little blue pill for a human."

"Gotcha. Looks like roller coasters will be in our future then."

"Shut it." Giving him a playful shove. "How are we going to stop them now?"

"They think we're dead. Gives us an advantage."

I saw the cloak Cassie had left behind. "Which means we can hide in plain site."

"Very nice." He leant down to pick it up. Swinging it around my shoulders and doing it up across my neck. "You're job is to find the leader and get out vamp poison."

"What good is that if we don't have blood to poison."

"We have something better. That dick that was drinking your blood mentioned having the drugs for everyone to enjoy. This really is a party. If we can get the poison and find where they're stashing their fun. We can pour the stuff on it and that's our delivery system."

"Perfect. Alright, I'll grab the poison. You find the drugs."

"Deal. Make sure you keep yourself safe."

"You too." Cupping his cheek. Giving him a soft smile and so badly wanting to kiss him. "See you soon."

"You got it." I headed out of the room first. Using the hood to cover most of my face. Making my way down the hall. Heading towards the music I saw all the vamps dancing. Many of them with their walking blood bags. Seeing some drinking a lot more viciously than before but the women seemed to be enjoying it. I never understood blood groupies.

Moving around the edge I noticed the leader and the other three weren't present. Seeing the snobby one standing by a door. Figuring he would know more about what was happening. But I stopped my feet.

My eyes locking onto a vampire who was carrying a small case in his hands. The same kind of case I saw at In The Ruff. The one with the little white pills inside. Watching Trevor move across and through another door.

Knowing I should be getting the poison but I

needed to punish him. If I couldn't get revenge on the woman who took my step-father away. I could at least get someone else's. Pushing through the crowd. Entering the door that had just closed.

Slipping through quietly. Moving down the hallway, following the footsteps. Seeing him move through another door. Stopping it before it shut and sliding through. It was a small study. Just like the rest of the house it felt like stepping back in time.

Ink and quill sitting on the desk. Dated décor from the small lamp on the desk to the much larger ones hanging from the ceiling. Fake candles but it still gave off that flickering light.

Trevor was leaning over the desk. The box open in front of him. Watching as he popped open a little bag and tipped out a pill into his palm. He chucked his head back and swallowed it. Grinning as I knew it would lower his natural ability to heal. Meaning I could exact revenge much easier.

The vampire put everything back in the box and shut it. When he turned he was startled by my presence. I kept the hood pulled down. My eyes watched his feet as he came closer. "Are you following me?"

The hood was flicked free. Shooting my forearms into his chest knocking him to the floor. The box dropped to the carpet. I used my foot to slide it behind me whilst I locked the door.

"Who are you?"

"We have a mutual friend."

"You're not a vampire."

"No I'm not but I wouldn't recommend messing with me. Not after you've taken your drug. Can you feel it taking affect on your system?" Enjoying that worried look on his face as he nodded. "My reason for being here, is you."

"Look, you can have money. I have plenty of it. Take the drugs I don't care."

Moving to a crouch at his feet. "What is your role within this group?"

"I'm a delivery boy. I work in distribution. I don't make this stuff."

I reached down and grabbed his ankle. Squeezing tight. "You made a bad decision giving that drug to a human."

"I don't know what you're talking about."

Squeezing tighter making him cry out. "I saw you. Compelling a young lady to take it. She overdosed and it's all your fault."

"Humans die all the time." I flexed my fingers and grew my claws. Slicing them through his ankle slowly. Using my fist to shut off his scream with a hit to his throat. A gurgling noise coming out of his mouth. "What do you want?"

"For you to suffer but I'm not the only one who wants to watch." Releasing his leg I flicked my fingers so blood splattered over his white shirt. Calling to the ghost as I stood. Feeling the chill running down my spine. Then fingers curled into mine.

The vampire seeing her appear before him. Squirming back so he sat up against the desk. "How is this possible?"

"I have certain gifts. Honestly I always thought they were a curse. But seeing your face right now. I'd say they're worth having."

The ghost beside me stepped forward. Her hand still in mine. His wide eyes frozen to her face. "You took my life. I was out having fun. Had my whole life ahead of me. And you made me take that drug knowing what it would do."

"I didn't know. I had no clue."

"You're lying!" Feeling the air getting colder. She swung her arm and the lamp shot across the room. Shattering against the wall. "You lie to me again and I'll make you scream."

"Alright. I knew it would happen."

"Why did you do it?"

"I just wanted to see it for myself. Others had admitted doing it. I was curious."

"You killed me because you were curious?" Seeing a tear shift over her cheek. The drop turning to ice. "That's your excuse?"

"What else do you want me to say? I'm sorry?"

"You're not sorry. You're a monster." She lunged forward and smashed her fist into his jaw. Surprised that it actually worked. Sending him down to the floor. Blood spilling over the carpet.

"Wow, I didn't think you could do that."

The ghost grinned. Looking at her fist. "Neither did I. I was so angry and wanted to hit him."

"Don't stop there."

"No. I don't want to become like him. This was enough. To see him like this."

"You sure you don't want to see him punished more?"

"No. I already feel, lighter." Her hands touched her chest.

I gripped her shoulders and turned her towards me. "If that's how you feel maybe you're ready to move on. There will be a voice. It's nothing to be scared of."

"An angel?"

"I don't think so. He'll guide you though."

"Thank you." She hugged me. Her touch cold at first but quickly warming up. When she pulled back I saw her cheeks filled with colour. A smile appearing on her face. "Will I see you again?"

"I doubt it but I'm happy you can finally move on."

"All because of you." Her hand lifted to cup my cheek. "It is a gift. You help people who can't help themselves."

"I'm starting to realise that." She hugged me again. That grip tight but it quickly faded. My arms no longer wrapped around her. Feeling a soft warmth in the air before it slipped away.

Looking down at the injured vampire who was still spitting blood. "Does that mean you're going to let me go? I'll run and never return to Baldur City. I promise."

"Your promises mean nothing to me." I grabbed his trouser leg and pulled him under me. A knee going to one arm. My foot pinning the other.

"But, she said she didn't want revenge."

"But I do." Swinging my fist down into his face.

Feeling his skull caving with one punch. Lifting it up and whacking it back down. Again and again. Crying out tears with each hit. The vampire's face turning into a pulpy mess. Nothing anyone could recognise.

That sickening noise drowning out my sobs. My arm starting to feel heavy. Slowing my hits until I stopped completely. Looking at the red mess. Pieces of bone strewn over the carpet. Like a bowling ball had been dropped from a great height onto his face.

I blew out a long sigh and dropped back on my arse. Using my arm to rub droplets of blood from my face. My breathing heavy like a pant. Feeling better after letting some of my anger out. It was aimed at the wrong person but he deserved what he got.

I climbed to my feet. Using his white shirt to clean my hands as much as I could. Flicking off pieces that used to be inside his head. Pulling his body behind the desk. I donned my hood again and grabbed the drugs box before heading out.

Back in the large room my eyes scanned the hall for Dawson. My hands tightly gripping the drug box. Pushing through until someone spun me around. "Is that the drug I've been hearing about?"

"Sure is but it's not coming out just yet."

Another joining in. "Sneak us a pill or two."

"Not yet, I'm afraid." Trying to turn away but they yanked me back. A grip on my arm that kept me in place. "Hey, let go of me."

"Give us the drugs."

Tilting my head and looking into their eyes. "Let it go."

"You let it go." Gasping as they both went for the box. Knocking it out of my hands. The container hitting the floor and splitting open. Baggies of drugs sliding across the floor. The vampires dropped and scrambled for it like animals.

Backing away as the crowd was drawn in. Hearing them mumbling about getting a hit. Vampires getting shoved out the way. I moved away from the mayhem until my back hit into someone. Spinning with a balled up fist but I stopped when I saw it was Dawson.

His eyes moved past to the idiots. "There goes that plan."

"Yep. Plan C?"

"You've got one of those?"

Looking past him as the leader came walking in. Master Lennox spotted what was going on. Shouting over the noise. "Cease your insolence at once." The vampires listened to him like he was their god. Standing up to reveal what they had been fighting over. "And where the hell did you lot get that from?"

Fingers were pointed to me. Dipping my head but Dawson wasn't that lucky. "Bring him to me, now."

Before the others could correct him I wrapped my fingers around his neck and bowed him down. Pulling an arm around his back. Whispering, "trust me."

He groaned in reply. Keeping he bent over as I pushed he forwards. Kicking the back of his leg to drop him down. Keeping my head lowered. A plan popping into my brain but it was insane. No idea if it would work but at this point we had no choice.

Lennox came forth. Kneeling in front of us. "If you're still alive that means your little friend will be as well."

"She's long gone. Ran after that evil woman."

"I doubt that very much. Being as old as I am. You get a keen sense of smell. Once I've met someone it's very hard to forget them."

Swallowing because I knew what was coming. My fingers loosening around Dawson's arm and neck. The hood being grabbed then ripped away completely revealing my ruined, blood splattered dress.

My eyes darted to his. "We have to stop meeting like this." Chucking myself at him. Wrapping my arms around his body and taking him down to the floor. Only he twisted us over, the momentum bringing us to our feet again. Backed up until he lifted and slammed me into the wall. Feeling it crack and crumble behind me.

One hand going to his arm. Feeling his palm pressing down on my wind pipe. Giving him a kick to the ribs but he dismissed it with a smile. So I reached for what my goal was in the first place. That pocket that held the drug. Fingers grabbing it but there was nothing there.

Looking down in confusion. "If you're looking for your poison. It's long gone." Rolling my eyes as another plan went awry. "Looks like you're out of lives." His fingers squeezed. My eyes rolled back as I tried to suck in air.

Head flopping forwards. Blinking to see Dawson rushing forwards on the attack. Lennox's vampires stopped him. Two of them holding him back. The leader turning with a smirk. "Let her watch him suffer."

"As you wish." The lady of the trio pulled her fist back then shoved it straight through Dawson's chest. Right down the middle. The snap of his rib cage so loud it made me wince. Seeing his face go vacant as the pain was too much.

The detective was let go. His body wavering for a moment before he dropped back. Thumping down the steps to the tiled floor. Watching as his hands moved to that hole. Blood pouring out, seeing his insides shifting.

Lennox dropped me to the floor. Coughing as I crawled towards my man. Not caring if they grabbed me or hit me. Wanting to be close to that vampire. Shifting his body to mine. Feeling so weak myself as my heart felt like it would split into two. Grabbing my dress and ripping a large shred off the bottom. Stuffing that hole like it would make a difference.

Pressing his hands to it. "You can't die. It's not fair." His chin quivered but he couldn't manage the words. His hand touched mine. Drawing it across his chest and into his jacket. Our eyes meeting as I felt the bottles. One big, one small with that syringe. Realising we had managed to complete each others' missions.

Hearing Lennox roaring with laughter. Everyone joining in with him. Anger rolling through me like a storm. I pulled out the contents of his inside pocket. Holding onto the syringe and Ivy's potion in one hand. The other gripping the poison.

So tight the bottle cracked a little. With one fluid movement I was up on my feet and running. Feeling the air rushing against my body. Catching Lennox by surprise. His mouth wide open I shoved that bottle down his throat. Knocking him back against the window which cracked.

Pulling my arm back and slamming it into his bulging neck. The glass shattering. Sending that concoction down his throat. Seeing the fear in his eyes as it started to burn. The vampire putting his hands up to stop it.

The fear in his eyes made me smile. Brining up my foot and kicking him through the window. Seeing him hit the ground where he writhed in pain. Blood being spat out of his mouth when he screamed. Turning to find all the vampires looking at me in shock.

Blowing out a sigh, feeling a weight lifting from my shoulders. "Your leader is dead now. Disperse before the government arrives and you find yourselves living in jail for the rest of your lives." Barely able to keep standing so I leant against the tallest chair.

Watching as a few from the crowd moved through the doorways around the room. Annoyingly there was still a fair amount of them left. "Run! This is your last chance."

One of the strongest vampires here smiled.

"That's not how we run things here. Lennox was in charge. With his death. Now I am." A pause in her words had my gut twisting. "Kill her!"

The crowd cheered before they rushed me. Getting knocked flying across the floor. Fists hitting me. Getting kicked and chucked around. My head slamming against the tiles. Curling up into a ball. Tucking my head in as they reigned punishment down upon me. Sick of being the one always getting beaten.

My hands shook as I gripped the bottle. Knowing what Ivy had said. Just a little bit but this wasn't the time to be measuring. I unscrewed the lid and chucked it down my throat.

Rolling onto my knees. Curling over as the liquid hit my stomach. Growling out low. The hits started to feel like nothing. Just bumps against my back and side. Claws growing. Teeth filling my mouth. My adrenaline shooting off the charts as I launched up into the air.

Hands grabbing one of the vampires. Throwing him to the ground. Then dropping my foot on his face. Crumbling it into a mushed up mess. Speeding to the next. Punching a hole straight through their face.

Barely even registering what I was doing. Pushing my body as I attacked and killed. Snapping necks. Ripping off arms. Feeling blood spraying over me. Making the beast roar inside my mind. Growling in honour of the kill.

When I did get hit my body barely registered it. It didn't even slow me down. Working my way through the crowd of vampires. Some of them deciding against the fight and fleeing out the hall. Feeling the numbers dwindling quickly until I felt a punch strike across my jaw.

Getting knocked sideways. Feet stumbling. Growling at the vampire. One of the three left to lead this nest. He punched again and the pain flared up the side of my face. A third time but I swung my claws across his arm as I dodged.

Shoulder barging him to the ground before a second vampire came for me. Then all three of them were swinging. Taking more hits than I was landing. Starting to feel the pain aching through my body.

Letting out a gasp as my throat was grabbed. Arms getting pinned as I was pushed to the wall. No matter how hard I tired I couldn't budge. Looking down. Teeth bared. Chomping at the bit for their blood.

The vampire tightened his grip around my throat. "You've become a nuisance." He looked around at the many dead bodies on the floor. "Knocked our numbers down by quite a bit."

"Not enough." Pushing my neck against his hand. Trying to reach him with my teeth. Arms wriggling, trying to pull them free.

"Needless to say, we'll be killing you now."

"No!" My voice coming out full of anger. Gritting my teeth. Feeling the spike in adrenaline again. That liquid still working it's magic on my system. Feeling my body heating up. Growing stronger. Getting bigger but not in the way I thought.

My eyes going wide as something in my brain snapped. Releasing all the anger I ever felt. That rage running through every nerve like electricity. My brain feeling like it was chucked into a vat of acid. But the pain was welcoming. Like I could sink into it and it would keep me safe.

My eyes focusing on the three vampires. Feeling so much power as I kept growing. Feeling something pushing out through my skin. The hands wrapped around my throat couldn't hold on. The vampires backed away allowing me to drop to my hands and knees.

Looking up at them as a low growl rolled out of my mouth. Teeth becoming huge. Looking down and seeing my hands morphing. Getting covered in fur. Claws curling against the tiles beneath them. Feeling my tail swinging behind me.

Baring my teeth at my three enemies. Standing up to their shoulders. Feeling amazing. Nothing like the horror stories I have heard about bones breaking and deforming. I haven't felt this amazing my whole life.

Stepping towards them. The woman blurred but it was slower than before. Seeing her lunging for my neck. Swinging my head and smacking her so hard into the wall she left a hole. Falling through into the next room.

A growl popped from my mouth as I pounced for my next enemy. Jaws clamped around his arm. Blood flooding into my mouth. The vampire screamed as I lifted him up and swung him down into the floor.

Shaking my head furiously until that arm ripped free. Dropping the limb and going for the last vamp.

The guy running for his life. Knocking into him. Making his body swing through a door. Trying to push through myself but I was too big. Taking a step back and slamming my body into the door frame. Snapping it to pieces. Hitting again, sending the brick to the floor.

Finally swiping massive claws through the obstacle. Splintering it to shreds. The vampire on his feet now. Seeing a shine of metal as a knife came slicing through the air. Feeling it dig into my side. Knowing it pierced my flesh. Feeling blood starting to dampen my fur.

Only I didn't care about the pain. Stomping forwards as he picked up another weapon. Swiping it across my face. Blood spurting out down my snout. Growling deep. Opening my jaw wide and snapping off his head.

The body stood for a moment before dropping into a lump. Dropping the head on top before throwing my head back and letting out a long howl. My strength and power shaking my body. Releasing the anger and the rage. My body shifting again. Growing smaller. Fur slipping back through my skin.

Letting out heavy breaths as I sat there on my hands and knees naked. Panting as I got used to my human form again. Pushing myself up but losing balance. Hitting into the wall. Holding myself there.

Letting my head hang for a moment before tilting it up. My eyes moving and seeing Dawson laying on the floor. Quickly stumbling over to him. Pulling on his collar to yank his head up. Giving his cheek a gentle slap. "You better not have died on me. That would be bloody selfish."

A soft whisper coming from his lips. "You're naked."

"That's the first thing you notice right now? You're ridiculous. You need blood." Sitting his head under an arm and offering him my wrist.

He shook his head slowly. "No, I won't drink from you again."

"Stop being a baby. You do it or you die and I'm not ready to let you go out like that. I want you in my life."

"No."

"So stubborn." Pressing my wrist against his mouth but he didn't open. "If you don't drink you'll die, do you understand that?"

Those eyes lifted to mine. Lips curled into a gentle smile. "I won't take from you like that again."

"You're not going to do anything again." Blowing out a frustrated sigh. "Dawson, you win the bet."

"Huh?"

"The bet we made on the first day of working together. You told me that I would admit that I needed you. And I need you. You can't just come into my life like this. Make me happy then sod off just because you're too stubborn. I need you here, with me. Now drink otherwise you're going to piss me off." Shaking my arm in front of him.

There was a gentle nod before his mouth open. Feeling his normal teeth pressing to my skin before those canines extended slowly. Pushing through my arm. Ripping a mess of my skin and flesh.

His sucking coming next as he drank. Feeling the blood draining through my body. Watching as there was a little more colour coming to his cheeks. The whole time he drank my blood his eyes didn't leave mine. And when a tear trickled down I caught it before it turned to ash. Wiping it away.

Sitting there with him with all those body parts and blood around us. Feeling peaceful amongst the chaos. His teeth slowly retracting into his gums. "You got enough?"

He nodded, "That should sustain me until I get a blood drip. I need to get to the city blood bank."

"Alright. Can you stand?"

"Sure." I helped him up. Once on his feet he pulled back the material I had pushed into that hole. Revealing it to us both. The bleeding had been stopped but the sight of it had me feeling nauseous. Dawson grinned and put the cloth back in. "I can't believe they ruined my suit. Do you know how long I've had this thing?"

"Glad to see your humour is back."

"Like that was going anywhere." Feeling his stare moving down my body. "I think we need to find you some clothes."

"Maybe get you another jacket. Don't forget we got a taxi here."

"I'm sure one of these gents won't mind us

taking their car." Watching him look around the floor at the mess I had created. "What the hell happened exactly?"

"I got angry."

"Alright, Hulk." I laughed as he did the same. Then we found him a new jacket to cover up that horrible hole. Managing to find a dress that hadn't been too badly damage during my onslaught. On our way out I pulled a cloak from a hook by the front entrance.

I cracked the door and saw the guards still standing there. Holding their positions like they hadn't heard the pain or saw the vampires fleeing the party. "They must be glamoured to stay out here. Seems a bit pointless of having them around."

"Maybe they're just here to keep people out. The amount of weird stuff happening here would be hard to ignore." As soon as we stepped out their heads turned to us. Freezing there as they stared from behind those sunglasses.

Looking the other way and seeing the others doing the same. "This isn't good, is it?" In unison they turned and pulled out pistols. Shouting words at us to get down on the floor. "After surviving all that inside. If we go out like this I want a refund on life."

"I second that." Feeling his arms coming around me. Kissing my forehead. "I'm really happy I got to meet you."

"And be together." My hand touching to his cheek. Lifting up to kiss those lips. If I was going to be taken out then it would be in a moment of bliss. A loud noise riding the air which made my body jump.

Looking into his eyes. Trying to see if he had been hit. But he was smiling. "What?"

"There'll be another." Creasing my brow as I looked over my shoulder. Seeing one of the guards on the floor. The others looking around. Another bang ringing out. A second guard receiving a bullet hole through the head. The body dropping to the floor.

Hearing the rumble of engines as three jeeps came driving down the track. Spreading out in front of us. Bodies flooding the area. Some of them holding guns. Others speeding with impressive speed. The guards being taken down violently.

All of them dealt with within seconds. The tide of the fight changed drastically. Looking over as a woman came out. Blowing out a breath as I realised it was my mother. Wearing a long black coat. Her fingers coming up and pulled shades from her face.

Seeing her eyes on me. The look of worry so clear in her expression. I took a step from Dawson. Standing like my drill sergeant was about to inspect my performance. Opening my mouth to speak when she pulled me into a tight hug.

Wincing as she squeezed so hard. Feeling her lips kissing my cheek and the touch of wet as she let out a tear. "Mum."

She pulled back quickly. Hands on my arms. A soft smile on her lips. "Mum?"

"I said it, don't make a big deal of it."

"I'll try." She stood there in silence. Hands rubbing my arms. "Are you okay?"

Letting out a big breath. "My body aches a little and my dress got completely ruined." Smiling a little. "But I think I am. I'm starting to realise things about myself."

"Such as?"

"I shifted." Unable to stop the grin bursting across my face. "I actually shifted."

"That's amazing. Your father will be ecstatic to hear that. I am as well."

"Thanks. Look. This week has been pretty mental. But things have happened that may have changed my view on things."

"And?" Her voice filled with hope.

"And I think I've been a little critical of certain things."

"That is a big change."

"Yeah." Giving her a smile. "It'll take time but."

"But it's a start and something I'll really enjoy. It's been a long time coming."

"Yeah, I guess it has." Feeling my eyes starting to well up. Not able to keep the control on my emotions anymore. "I'm really sorry."

"You don't have to apologise, sweetie. You never have to say sorry to me. We'll just have to make up for lost time and that will be that."

"Sounds good to me."

Dawson cleared his throat, "If it's not too much trouble. Could I get a lift to a blood bank?" My mum's eyes going wide as he showed her his injury. "I really could do with some rest and a little blood."

"Of course. Let's get you in the car. Maybe you

should lay down in the back."

"If you think it's best." We both helped him to the nearest jeep. Piling him into the back seat.

As I made my way around the passenger side my mum shouted orders to the people under her command. "Clean this place up. Any survivors need to be in chains before the sun goes down. I want this place empty and any information you can find on anyone linked needs to be on my desk when I get back. Get moving!"

Seeing in her in action for the first time in a long time was nice. She was in charge of all these people. The head of the supernatural unit. Smiling as she came back to the jeep. Her face back to being soft and open. Her voice gentle. "What?"

"Nothing." Smiling as I climbed in. My mother revved the engine and sent us out of the wildlife park. Heading to the blood bank to get Dawson a private room. Giving him somewhere to relax and drink up until he was back to full health.

The journey to drop me off back at my apartment was done in silence but it wasn't awkward. I was enjoying the company of my mother without the need to rip her a new one. I could look over to her and feel calm, peaceful. Almost like the wolf had been dealt with in my head for the time being. Knowing that it would come back and I wasn't sure if I would be able to shift again.

Had it been a one time thing because of the situation or was my ability now unlocked for me to access. It would take training to hone my skills and my mother offered that help. Not only with my werewolf side but she also said I could get better with my leeching abilities. Having had a little chat about the bad headaches I had been getting. The future a bright promise.

She pulled up outside my apartment building. Grabbing the door handle to get out but I paused. Turning back to my mother. "Mum."

"I'm liking the sound of that more and more."

Smiling but it quickly faded. "That vampire. The one who..."

"I'm familiar with her." Seeing the serious look on her face. "I know what you're going to ask."

"I think I already know your answer." Biting my lip as I watched her.

"Megan. I could give you a speech about not wanting to lose you. I've only just got you back and sending you after someone so dangerous is not what I want to do. I could go on and on. Reeling off a million reasons why I should say no"

"Should?" Feeling hope warming my heart.

My mother reached over and stroked my cheek. Tucking one of my curly strands behind my ear. "Under my conditions. After you've trained."

"I'll take it." Reaching over and giving her a tight hug. Feeling her lips pursing to my forehead, "I'd love to get lunch with you some time."

"That would be great. I was also thinking. We could ask Drew to help with your werewolf training. And, we could perhaps, go see him together. Not for training but to talk. Chat. As a family."

Pulling back with a huge smile. "Really? I think that would be really nice."

"We can chat about setting a date."

"Sure." I opened the door and slipped out. Stopping there I turned. "Thanks for being my mum. I know it couldn't have been easy with your job and raising me with Drew and Kellen."

"I'll never regret the extra love you had in your life." I quickly made my way around the car. Pulling open the door and grabbing her for another tight hug. Enjoying the embrace. "I'll chat to you soon, mum."

"Sounds perfect." She kissed my cheek and I went upstairs. Making sure to let my room mates know I was okay before I passed out on my bed. Thinking about my future and how much things had changed in the last week. Such a turn around for the better.

CHAPTER 11

"You need to get your rest, mister." Putting my phone to my shoulder to thank Sally as she slid my coffee in a take-out cup onto my table. Using my spare hand to pour in some sugar as I spoke to Dawson again. "You need to stay at the bank for a little longer. Then as soon as you're better. We can test out your stamina."

"I'll hold you to that, Megan."

"I look forward to it." Looking up as the door opened with a bing. Seeing my client come walking in. "I have to run. Chat soon, alright."

"Sure. See ya, babe."

Grinning as I hung up. Quickly pushing that smile away as my client came over to my usual table. Standing up to greet her. "Good morning, Mrs Clark."

"Megan." We shook hands and sat back down. Sally came over to ask the client if she needed anything. "Thank you. A coffee, black. To go, please."

The owner gave her a small smile before heading back to the counter. Mrs Clark grabbed some of the sugar packets and slipped them into her handbag with a stirrer. "I'm glad you could come today."

"I have to be honest, I was hoping to get a response a lot earlier than this."

"This case did take a lot longer than I first thought. I'm sure you don't want to know all the details." Looking up from my coffee. Seeing the expression she was giving me. "Alright. Let's just say it had to do with a drug ring that was trying to get a foot hold in the city. Plenty of blood and guts later."

"Okay, I don't need to know the details. All I want to know is if the man responsible for my daughter's death got what he deserved. I hope you managed to get the police involved."

"Detective Dawson was very helpful with the case. Together we managed to find the person who was responsible."

"So he'll be behind bars for the rest of his life."

Smiling before sipping my coffee. "He definitely got what he deserved. If it's not too bold of me to say. Your daughter has moved on peacefully."

A tear falling from her eyes. "How could you possibly know that?"

"Trust me. I know." Reaching over and rubbing her hand gently. Pulling back when her coffee was delivered. Watching as she poured the sugar packets inside and stirred it all together. She took a few sips. "Could I ask a little, small favour?"

"What's that?"

"Would it be okay if I came to the funeral? To see her off."

The lady smiled. "Of course, dear. You've given me something I never thought I would get."

"What's that?"

"Peace of mind that another parent won't go through the same thing I have."

"I'm glad." She dug a hand into her bag and pulled out an envelope. It was the other half of my payment but something felt wrong in my heart to be taking it. I placed my hand on her forearm. "Don't worry about it."

"No, of course I will pay."

"I insist. Really. I've learnt quite a lot about myself over the last week. This has helped me just as much as it has you. So, don't worry about the payment."

"That's very sweet of you." She still slid the envelope across the table. "The fact you just said that makes it even easier to part with this. You earned it. I have no qualm paying you."

"Let's hope you never have to ask for help again."

"Let's hope." She stood with her takeaway cup. "Thank you again. I'll send over the details for the funeral."

"Thank you." She turned and left the cafe. I waited for a little bit. Sipping my coffee before it was my time to leave. Moving through traffic on my motorbike. Arriving outside the mental hospital. Seeing the large black jeep parked near the entrance. My mum leaning against it.

This time she wasn't dressed for work. She wore a nice white dress with red roses dotted all over it. A white cardigan giving her whole demeanour a lighter touch. I climbed off and walked over in my jeans and a long sleeve top. Looking very much the casual one out of us two.

She smiled wide and I couldn't help but do the same when she spotted me. I got a nice tight hug and a kiss to my cheek. Pulling back and seeing the way her lips quivered. "Are you okay?"

"Sure, of course I am." Her eyes shifted from mine quickly.

"You're nervous."

She paused then let out a sigh. "Is it that obvious? Do you think Drew will notice?"

"He's not blind, Mum."

"I can't help it. I haven't seen him in years and once upon a time we were very close."

"Please tell me stories of how close you two were are not going to crop up in conversation."

My mother giggled. She stroked fingers through my hair. "You have no idea how long I've waited for this."

"I may have not wanted to admit it at the time. Or even knew it at the time. But I have as well. Deep down. At least neither of us have to wait any longer."

"No." I got another hug. This one tighter than before. When she pulled back I noticed the tears gathering at the bottom of her eyes. "Do you think he'll remember me?"

Feeling a twang on my heart strings as I watched her getting so worried. "He talks about you when I come visit. He remembers you."

"Send me into a coven of witches and I'm fine.

This and my hands won't stop shaking."

I took up her hands in mine. "Let's get things started then. The sooner we head in, the sooner you'll realise there's nothing for you to worry about."

"First, before we head in. I have something to ask you."

"Yes." Feeling a little nervous as I saw the expression on her face.

"I didn't want to say yes to anything without asking you first."

"I might be open to training with you but definitely not working for you."

"Oh no. I understand that completely. The supernatural unit isn't the place for you and I mean that as a compliment to your talents. You're better off helping people like you did this last week."

"So what are you asking me?"

"You've steered away from supernatural stuff. But my friend has a problem."

"Can't you help her out? You are the director of the biggest supernatural police force, you know."

"I had noticed that." She laughed. "I have to worry about species making war. Nests or covens trying to seize power from us. And of course every day I have to worry about the general public finding out about them. Can you imagine how chaotic the world would be?"

"Humans would never be able to accept it. There would be death everywhere."

"Exactly. So this problem is a little on the small side for me. But perfect for someone like you."

I bit my lip as I thought about it. My mother was right. I had steered away from supernatural life choices. But I wasn't the same person I was back then. This was the new me. Someone who was being trained by my mother to accept my other sides. My talents and what came with them. "What exactly is the problem?"

"Her name is, Lara. She was a witch. With the ley lines getting damaged she could no longer access her power and lost touch with it. Along with her shop. So she started dealing in ancient artefacts that still held that old magic. Something was stolen from her and she would love to get it back."

"My first guess would be witches but that's not necessarily true. Could have been a snatch and grab. Wrong person to steal from."

"You always had a smart mind."

"Thanks. Why don't you give Lara my number and I'll set up a meet. Hope she knows how expensive I am to hire."

"I told her she was getting a bargain since you're very under-priced for how talented you are."

"That's sweet of you." Feeling my cheeks blush. That sense of pride coming through her words like a warm hug. "Shall we get inside. I bet he's waiting for us."

"After you." I led the way. Greeting the nurse like I always did. When her eyes landed on my mother she grinned.

The nurse led us through the normal hallway. Out into the gardens where I saw my father frantically sorting his flower bed out. Pressing down the soil.

Perking up droopy heads as best as he could.

The nurse left us to walk the rest of the way ourselves. Stopping a few metres back my mother turned to me. "Is everything okay?"

"Yeah. Go on. He's waiting for you."

"What?"

"You two need to meet each other again. Without me. Just you two. I'll be right here but you both need it."

This time she did cry. Wiping it away with her fingers. "Thank you, sweetie."

"Go on." Watching as she turned and walked the rest of the way. A clearing of her throat announced her presence. My father turned and jumped up to his feet. Wiping his hands on his jeans so quick dirt flicked off.

Seeing the light in his eyes. The way they sparkled when he grinned. Seeing how my mother looked just as happy to see him. Watching as they said hello to each other. Holding hands for a moment before they hugged.

Tears falling down both of their faces. Feeling my heart welling up and I couldn't stop my own tears from falling. Rubbing my eyes quickly so I could enjoy this moment fully. Watching them embrace each other and open up their hearts to forgiveness and the future.

BOOKS BY THIS AUTHOR

Leecher Chronicles

Moonlit Blood
Sunlit Blood
Burning Blood
Drowning Blood
Dead Blood

Clearwater Legacy

Shadows in the Light

Everfae And Titans

Crystal Darke

An Erotic Tale From Marie's

Steamy Research

Printed in Great Britain
by Amazon